PURSUIT

CHRIS CROWTHER

TALEWEAVER

Other books by Chris Crowther

The *Jack Fellows* series of murder-mysteries:
WATERPROOF
STILL WATERS
THE WATER FROLIC
WATER UNDER THE BRIDGE
MURKY WATERS
DEAD IN THE WATER
WATERSHED

Younger Reading:
TIMECRUISER

Aviation Thriller:
BLADESTRIKE

First published 2022
Taleweaver
Hoveton – Norfolk – England – NR12 8UJ

www.chriscrowther.co.uk

ISBN 978-1-9998111-3-6

Cover artwork by David Rowlands – www.davidrowlands-art.co.uk
Cover design by Jane Dixon-Smith – www.jdsmith-design.co.uk

CHAPTER ONE

Cloud. A complete blanket below me covering trenches, battlegrounds and all the waste and tragedy of what was already being called The Great War. Normally, such weather would be more than a concern to any pilot returning to base, but not this cold 1916 winter morn, because right now that cloud was the only hope I'd got.

On my tail were two Hun Albatros fighters whose green tail feathers showed they were from Jasta 5. We'd met this gang a few times before and they'd quickly shown they weren't fresh out of flight school, and certainly not the two now hell-bent on my destruction. Those sleek, but mean-looking two-wingers had pursued me down from eight thousand feet to one, with me throwing my Nieuport around until it was a toss-up whether structural failure or those spitting Spandaus behind would get me first. From the holes appearing in my upper mainplane, it seemed like the latter. The Nieuport 17 was a great machine, but it did have a reputation for shedding its wings in a dive and if ever I was going to prove that for myself, now was the time.

We'd been out on a long patrol before the black cross boys jumped us, already frozen to the core by hours at high altitude and perhaps with our thoughts too much on hot coffee and warm quarters ahead than those menacing skies behind. Now, with 7.92 millimetre lead joining the slipstream screaming its icy blast through the rigging, cold was the least of my worries. That cloud deck below was my only salvation and I dived towards it like a rat down a drainpipe.

I'd thought that cloud-cover was total, but now, through ominous gaps, I caught glimpses of our front-line trenches surrounded by the usual sea of mud, but strangely pristine in a first dusting of snow. Life down there must be as horrendous as it could get, but at least it was life, which was more than Mark Kingsley would be experiencing much longer if I didn't soon lose myself and those well-flown Albatrosses.

They were even closer now, the leader seemingly almost set to chew my empennage with his prop. I resisted the temptation to give another jink, choosing instead to keep up my speed to the cloud now just a hundred feet below. Another burst of sparkling flame reflecting in my mirror from his muzzles told me that might just be a hundred feet too much. It was a fear soon accentuated by the disintegration of one of my interplane struts as his three second burst turned it to flying matchwood.

And then I was in the cloud, its clammy but blessed interior enveloping me in a vapour so dense that even the Hun behind was now lost to sight. Reprieve. I eased out of my dive like my aircraft was made of glass, at the same time throttling back the Le Rhone. The stress of anything more violent would have been critical to even an intact Nieuport, but to mine, with a good chunk of its rigging now flapping in the vortices of the wing's trailing edge, it was a tightrope walk between delicate control and total disintegration.

I flew on, airspeed slowing faster than my heartbeat and with no conception now of position, attitude or direction, but content to be alive and still flying... just. But for how much longer? I eased up the revs to a low cruise and tried to keep on an even keel. Not easy with my world reduced to a goldfish bowl of freezing milk and my senses scrambled to jelly by the tumbling confusion of that mad free-fall around the heavens.

The Huns were gone from sight now. In fact, everything was gone from sight leaving me bewildered as to whether I was even right side up. It didn't feel I was, because strange sensations and even stranger sounds were affecting what little I had left of my natural senses. I held the stick in a white-knuckle grip that said more about my state of mind than any sort of technique, but the sound of wind in the wires was rapidly building to a scream accompanied by a protesting vibration from the ever-speeding two-blade prop in front.

A quick glance at the instruments told me why: height was peeling off like a falling rock while the airspeed had pegged at a number way above that which the Nieuport usually started shredding itself. But, this wasn't a straight dive, because the compass too was turning faster than a demented carousel. We were spiralling down and I needed to stop it before this cloud gave way to solid earth. I hauled back on the stick and all that happened was the spiral tightened while my cheeks and mouth seemed set to sag through the bottom of my face.

Perhaps everyone experiences a sudden clarity in the last seconds of their lives. In mine, I knew my first priority was to stop this turn. Against every instinct, I eased the back-pressure on the stick and instead moved it sideways to roll into what I hoped was level flight. Straightway, I felt my body-weight decreasing, while a glance at the compass showed the turn slowing and then stopping. We were still diving though and, disregarding my shot-up rigging, I hauled back on the stick.

Too much, because, as the altitude started once more climbing, so the airspeed dropped away at a rate that told me the nose must be near damn vertical. I gunned the throttle and pushed the stick forward but, even as I lifted out of my seat to the limit of my harness, so another sensation over-whelmed all others: a violent flick as one wing dropped away and the other rolled over me.

Those wings were still attached to the fuselage, but that was little comfort as the whole contraption now rolled and dropped at a rate gut-wrenchingly more violent than that previous spiral. For the first time since I'd entered that cloud, I knew exactly what the aircraft was doing: it was spinning to oblivion.

Round and round we dropped as one wing stayed stalled and the other followed it. I'd spun before, sometimes as a way of escaping pursuing Huns, but this time, cloaked in the all-enveloping cloud-mass, I experienced complete disorientation. Which way was I even spinning? In what might well be the last few seconds of my short flying career, I pulled back the throttle and gained at least some consolation in the immediate cessation of that throaty roar. Oblivion was now doubtless only seconds away, but at least it would be more peaceful.

The Nieuport was still spinning, the cloud still enveloped, probably right to the ground, but I felt a moment of strange peace broken only by a disembodied voice telling me something about New York being in sight. That couldn't be right. My old home city was a good three thousand miles from these death-ridden skies above Flanders. But there it was again ... "New York in sight, Boss."

*   *   *

"New York in sight, Boss."

The voice through my headset awoke me with a start as I realized it was 1986, I really was flying, but seventy years on from those war-torn skies over the Western Front. As happened so often in this, my ninety-first year, the vibration of the S76 helicopter had sent me dosing within minutes of lifting off from our summer home on Nantucket Island.

"Thanks, Chuck." I looked ahead to where the familiar skyline of Manhattan was indeed just emerging through the thin morning mist. "Any chance of a quick pass over the Bronx for old time's sake?"

I couldn't see, but could sense him smiling at this recurring request. "Shouldn't be a problem, Boss, but I'll need to clear it with LaGuardia Tracon."

"Okay, but don't push it if traffic's too heavy."

Chuck Arnold had been my corporate skipper for six years now and, although our flying days were at either end of the aviation spectrum, his time flying Hueys in Nam meant we did share memories of combat aloft in far-off lands and ensured an element of mutual respect in our relationship.

As he called for clearance, I sat back in my comfortable seat and compared this latest in rotary wing technology to the contraptions of wood and wire in which we'd taken on the Hun *Jagdgeschwaders*. Crude and quaint our trusty old Nieuports and Spads might now seem to modern eyes, but our dog-fighting back then had often been at eight times the two-thousand feet we were now flying, not much slower and, unless a 7.92 round had clipped my prop, with probably less vibration. Even so, I preferred helicopter flight to the high-tech pseudo-spaceships that now passed as aeroplanes. Helios at least were good old stick-and-pedal machines and something I still understood.

Not that I got my hands on controls these sedentary days, but I had the memories, and flying remained one of the true joys of my life, despite the nightmares it still produced in my sleeping moments.

"Tracon have cleared us over the Bronx at eight hundred, Boss."

No time now for nightmares or sweet-dreams as an increase in slipstream told me we were swapping height for airspeed. "Good. The usual location, Chuck."

Those extra knots soon had us winging over the outskirts of the Bronx, and low enough now for me to start searching for landmarks. Soon, I'd picked out again the four storey redbrick office tenement where the leading New York law firm of *Kingsley Legal* had first taken root. Now, as we went scooting overhead, I thought back sixty years to that night long ago in 1926 when I'd dragged myself from yet another of those Western Front nightmares, rolled off the office couch and staggered to my desk to answer the incessant ringing of my office phone.

*   *   *

"Mark Kingsley Legal."

"Hmm. Glad to hear I'm not the only dumb ass working, because I need you over here right now."

"Not working, Pat. Trying to sleep for Christ's sake." I tried to brush the remnants of it from my eyes and didn't even need to ask who was calling me in the early hours. Apart from saving ever-scarce bucks, sleeping in my rented Bronx office did mean I was a convenient first choice when the 48th Precinct had a suspect demanding a lawyer, and Inspector Pat Nolan, their Chief of Detectives, never cared too much about unsociable hours. "So, what you got for me this time? Some dyspeptic caught swigging bootleg hootch or just a vagrant pissing in public?"

"Neither." The slightly lilting remnants of Nolan's Irish roots had long ago taken on the weariness of a working life spent dealing with the ungodly. "How about a homicide?"

"Homicide!" The shock that someone was actually requesting my professional services above the misdemeanour level had certainly shed my doziness, though my thoughts were still tempered by a good dose of skepticism. "What's the catch, Pat? For that you'd usually be calling one of those high-flying legal brains who actually have a bed to sleep in."

"Unless the suspect asks for you personally, which this one has."

"He asked for *me*... by *name*?"

"Yep. Seems he's a veteran who knew you out in France and heard you'd set yourself up as lawyer in our fair city."

"What's his name?"

"Vennington."

"*Lee* Vennington?" It hadn't taken a second to match that name to the face I'd known all those years ago. "He was my best friend out there."

"Yeah, well right now you're probably the only one *he's* still got." It had obviously been another long night for Nolan and one he wasn't anxious to prolong. "How soon can you get here?"

"If I can find a cab... about twenty minutes."

"Too long. I'll send a squad car to pick you up in five, but make sure you're awake because your old buddy's going to need all the help he can get."

One advantage of sleeping in your clothes is that you only have to splash some water on your face to be up and, if not running, then at least moving. Two minutes, and I was heading out into the cold, damp night. If *I* was Lee's only hope, I guessed he must be desperate indeed.

*   *   *

The patrol car was already waiting when I exited the block, the ice-cold early-morning air managing to wipe away any last vestiges of drowsiness. We drove straight off with thumping wipers through the East Bronx's sullen innards, me in the back and a young detective next to the driver in the front. His breath straightway misted the windshield as he probed my connection with Lee.

"I hear you knew this guy in France."

"Yeah, we were in it together right from the start."

"What, in the trenches in seventeen?"

"No, years before that."

"How come?"

It was too early in the morning for a third-degree. With the sleet doing its damnest to turn to snow and memories of long-ago dawn patrols, I could have done with one of those rum-laced French coffees that used to revive us when we landed back at base. Not here and now though, because six years earlier puritanical forces had pushed through the Eighteenth Ammendment and for Prohibition to lay its uncompromising hand across the nation. In those years, the Bronx had gained a fearsome reputation for bootlegging and all the violence that went with it, and only God knew what deals and vengeance were being enacted in some of those bleak, dark tenements now sliding past. I gave up trying to even imagine and let my own thoughts wander back again, three-thousand miles from here and a dozen years, to a far different world and sunnier climes where I'd first met Lee Vennington.

*   *   *

It was September 1914 and the place was Toulouse in South-West France, where the *Legion Etrangere* had sent us for initiation into the harsh realities of military life. In just the three months since a student called Gavrilo Princip had shot the Archduke Franz Ferdinand and his wife Sophie in

Sarevjavo, a tangle of alliances and imperial ambitions had seen Austro-Hungary turn against Serbia who then called in her old friend Russia for help. Thereafter, old treaties were dragged out of drawers and dusted off, allowing Germany to side with Austro-Hungary while Russia turned to her old alliance with France who in turn called in the support of the British. Within a few short weeks, the charming old Europe in which I'd been languishing as a washed-out student from Harvard, managed to immerse itself in a cataclysmic spiral of death and destruction.

I was in Paris at the time and could easily have taken the next boat home, but the wrath of my father at dumping a career on which he'd set his sights for me was more formidable than all the Kaiser's armies and, when they decided to enact their long-held Schlieffen Plan to retake Alsace and Lorraine and march through neutral Belgium, I was as incensed as the next man, and determined to do my bit to stop them short of Paris.

The British forces across the channel might have seemed the logical choice for someone with English as a first language, but one gem of knowledge I'd picked up at Law School was that my US citizenship would be automatically forfeited the day I swore an oath of allegiance to another country. But I'd picked up some working German and French during my European motor-cycle wanderings, and the *Legion Etrangere* required only an oath to the legion itself. After taking a whole five minutes to think it over, I'd stashed my Rover 3-speed in a Paris friend's garage and headed for the *Bureau de Recruitment* in the Rue St. Dominique where, after a perfunctory physical, a bored military surgeon had begrudgingly admitted I was fit enough to die for them. From there I'd joined twelve hundred other *Engage Volontaires* languishing in the *Ecole Profession pour Jeunes Filles*, while the military machine got into gear.

For someone all set to practice the profession of arms, it had been a frustrating time of menial work and endless drilling, but we did at least get our uniforms; not the green epaulettes and white *kepi* of my romantic dreams, but disappointingly standard horizon-blue serge like the rest of the French army. Accordingly apparelled, in a few weeks we were sent by train down to Toulouse where mild breezes from the Mediterranean Sea just ninety-three miles away, did little to appease my impatience at being far from the scene of imminent battle. I gathered there had been several dozen fellow Americans join at the same time as me, but only one other had found his way into our *escouade*. Luckily, I formed an immediate liking for him. It was Lee Vennington.

*   *   *

A sudden lashing of sleet on the patrol-car windshield as we turned down rain-washed East Tremont Avenue, en route to Barkley and the Precinct HQ, brought me back to the present. Lee, it seemed, had now got himself into a tighter fix and I focussed my thoughts on how I might help.

It was hard to imagine that clean-cut football half-back I'd shared so many adventures with, now facing indictment for homicide. There again, perhaps it wasn't that unreasonable when I thought of how the military had transformed us both into the killing machines we eventually became in and above those mud-slicked trenches. Perhaps the two incarnations were connected. I'd soon know, because we were just pulling up beside the grim walls of the 48th Precinct.

*   *   *

"I tell you, getting toe-to-toe with Richthofen will seem like kid's play compared to what you'll face getting this guy off." Inspector Nolan was leading me through the detective department's main office where, even at this graveyard hour, the 48ths finest were handling their usual night's haul of low-life pulled off the borough streets.

"Except I never did make the acquaintance of the Red Baron," I corrected, following him into his glass-partitioned office with *Chief of Detectives* emblazoned on the door, "or else I probably wouldn't be here right now enjoying your company."

"We'll see how enjoyable it is. Take a seat." Sinking into his own chair the other side of a desk piled high with case-files doing battle for space with at least two overflowing ashtrays, he pulled out a pack of *Lucky Strike*s and tossed one across.

"Thanks." I leant over and lit up both from my old cartridge case lighter. Through the smoke of our first drags, I asked, "So, what's the story?"

"Not a nice one, actually." He sat back and took another deep inhale. In spite of the near-zero temps outside, he was in his shirtsleeves, tie pulled loose and an expression as weary as thirty-two years exposure to the worst in human nature can produce. "Vennington reckons he hails from south of here in Queens."

"That's right. Comes from a good family, went to Harvard and studied architecture."

"Did he now?" Nolan tapped some ash off his gasper while making an effort to appear unimpressed. "Did you know him there?"

"No, he was ahead of me by a couple of years."

"But reckons he flew with the Air Service in France."

"That's right, but before that he was with me in the LFC."

"The Lafayette Flying Corps. How come a guy with his education went and threw in his lot with someone else's army?"

I shrugged. "He'd already decided he preferred art to architecture, dropped out of Harvard and headed to Europe to live the bohemian life painting in the Latin quarter of Paris. When Kaiser Bill decided to invade Belgium and France, like me, he got angry and signed up for the Legion. At least there we got three meals a day ... if we were lucky."

"Yeah, well he's not so lucky now. Pretty down-and-out by the look of him, but I guess even Ivy-Leaguers can go off the rails sometimes, given the right circumstances."

"And what particular 'circumstances' got him arrested for an *alleged* homicide?"

"No 'alleged' about it." Nolan stubbed his smoke and leaned a little closer across his desk. "Caught with the knife in his hand while his victim pumped the last of his lifeblood."

"Where, exactly?"

"Saint Winifred's."

"The Catholic Church down Castle Hill Avenue? What was he doing there?"

"Reckons he'd arranged to meet the victim, but won't say why. Probably went to beg for alms from the poor box. Like I said, the guy's right down on his heels."

"But caught red-handed, you say. Who by?"

"The assistant priest there, Father Peter Huber, who heard a cry, went to investigate and found your friend bending over the body of Father Richard Magee."

"Another priest?"

"*The* Priest in charge. The good Father had been stabbed and your buddy was holding the knife. Then one of our patrolmen arrived, alerted by some passer-by who'd heard a commotion in the church."

I shook my head. "All very neat and convenient, Pat, but from what you tell me it's even more unlikely that it was Lee who did it. The Vennington I knew was a dedicated Catholic. No way he'd even raise his voice to a man of the cloth, let alone kill one."

"Well, he did this one." Nolan leaned even closer. "Listen Kingsley, you know as well as I do, that men who've been through a war can do things way out of character when they get home. And this guy seems to have had a harder war than most, judging by the scars the police surgeon found on his body."

"*Honourable* scars, Pat. He picked those up in Flanders along with so many medals it deflected his compass."

I could sense Nolan taking that on board, but for all the wrong reasons. "Plenty of experience at killing then. Perhaps one more didn't make much difference."

It wasn't the time to argue that point. I stubbed my *Lucky* and nodded towards Pat's ever-steaming pot of coffee. "May I?"

"Go ahead."

With a good mugful, I sat down again and took a welcome swig. "So, what motive are you theorising?"

"Who knows? He looks pretty down on his luck. Perhaps he went to ask for help, the priest turned him down and he got angry. Or maybe he went to rob the poor box or even get his hands on the Sacramental Wine. In spite of the Eighteenth, the churches are still allowed that, you know. Whatever, the good Father could have caught him in the act and got murdered for his trouble."

"What does Lee say?"

"The usual for guys in his situation. That he didn't do it, had found the priest like that and was only trying to help him."

"Perhaps he was."

"And pigs might fly."

"Not as well as Lee used to. But this knife you say he was holding ... have you got it?"

He nodded. "Yep, and before you ask, the prints on it were just your client's."

"I'd still like to see it."

Nolan went to a metal filing cabinet, unlocked the top drawer and took out a long object wrapped in a towel. Like some jeweller presenting a priceless necklace, he laid it on his desk and pulled back the folds. The viciousness of the weapon revealed was certainly heightened by the blood and human gore still clinging to its fourteen inch serrated blade. "Look, but don't touch."

I had no inclination to, but could still make a technical correction. "That's not a knife, Pat. That's a bayonet, and German army issue at that."

"But the kind of thing a veteran like Vennington would bring home as a souvenir, right?"

"We all did, Pat, but if Lee was as impoverished as you say, he'd have sold his long ago for some eating bucks."

"Unless he intended using it as a means to get bucks some other way. And he wouldn't have got much for it anyway, would he? Stickers like this must be two a penny amongst you vets."

"Not that sort. It's got a sawback blade."

"Yeah, and a gory mess it made of the good Father when it got pulled out. Brought half his guts out with it." Even Pat gave a little shudder. "Trust our Germanic brethren to think up something that bloody."

"Except they didn't ... not for killing, anyway. Far be it for me to defend my old adversaries, but on that one they can plead innocence. That *Seitengewehr ninety-eight*, the so-called 'butcher bayonet', was designed like that simply to give it a dual purpose for sawing wood. But with the disembowelling job it did on the human body, the allies spread the word that they'd shoot on sight any prisoner captured with one. That was pure fright-talk on our part, but the Kaiser's generals didn't want anything to hold back their footsloggers' resolve, and so they withdrew the sawbacks and from then on only issued them to NCOs."

"Thoughtful of them, but how come an ex-flyboy like you knows so much about infantry tooling?"

"Because I was a foot-slogger for starters. Remember?"

"And Vennington?"

"The same. We trained together."

Ah, that training. We lit second *Lucky*s and, through the fug, I let my thoughts drift from that smoke-bound office to memories of those early months in Toulouse and the rigors of Legion life, made bearable by new-found friendship with a guy I learned I could trust with my very life.

*   *   *

As fellow New Yorkers, Lee and I had formed a close bond from the start, and an even deeper one when we discovered we were both Harvard drop-outs.

Not that there was much time for casual chat in those first gruelling weeks of Legion indoctrination. Divided up into 30-strong *escouades*, each under the charge of a *caporal*, morning *reveille* was at five o'clock, when the *garde-chambre* would rouse us from our beds with a large jug of strong black coffee which he poured into our out-held mugs. That coffee was about the only good thing I remembered about my time in Toulouse. After gulping it down, we then had fifteen minutes to sort our kit into a neat *paquetage* from which not a single item could be one milimetre out of place. Then a quick sweep under our beds before inspection by the *caporal*. Ours was Prazerie, a short, moustachioed little weasel of a man who made up for stature by lean toughness and a viper's tongue which he exercised freely from morning to night. It started with that first inspection which had to be over by five-thirty, when it was then out onto the parade ground to start our daily training.

This usually began with drilling followed by either long route-marches or physical training on the large open field beyond the main barracks. Here we did basic gymnastics and boxing, but more often simple double-marched running for hours on end. With college football not long behind me, this shouldn't have been a hardship, but I found it no kid's play carrying 120 pounds of pack and equipment, almost ten of which was the Lebel rifle.

Like the rest, I'd been glad to get my hands on this piece of hardware, making me feel that I truly had entered the profession of arms. Fifty-one inches long and bolt-actioned, it wasn't a bad weapon except for its magazine. This was tubular, below the barrel, and in which the eight 8mm cartridges were loaded nose to tail. A neat arrangement in some ways, but the snag was that any attempt to indulge in a bit of quick reloading and firing could result in a round striking the primer of the one in front with explosive results. Steady and sure was the name of the game when firing the Lebel and its shortcomings would be brought home to us very soon in cruel and dramatic fashion.

For now, though, we just concentrated on turning them into our personal instruments of war and there was healthy competition between Lee and myself to get the best scores on the range. I'd always had a good eye for a shot and usually came out on top, though many was the time I'd have given a year's pay for a five-round, standard mag Springfield.

But training progressed and gradually our polyglot of derelicts, comprising twelve different nationalities, were transformed into a reasonably competent unit of the 11/1st *Regiment de Marche du 1er Etranger*. Now Second Class Legionnaires, we could march for hours on end with heavy kit, obey simple commands to execute various military maneuvres and shoot, with reasonable accuracy, anything within a hundred yards. And, yes, use our bayonets.

*   *   *

Bayonets like the one now lying on Chief Nolan's desk. I picked it up and weighed its near-seven pounds in my hand. "Not the lightest of weapons to be carrying around on the off-chance, Pat."

"Unless you planned using it in the first place." The Chief took another drag of his smoke and shrugged. "Whatever, it certainly did the number on the good Father Magee."

"But not by my client, Pat. I'm sure he's not your man."

"Yeah, well that's something you can ask him yourself." Chief Nolan stood up and opened the door. "Let's go meet tonight's Public Enemy Number One."

*   *   *

Lee certainly didn't match that description when Nolan led me into the interrogation room. He was already sitting at a plain table, watched over by an armed officer, but jumped to his feet, smiling with recognition and relief, as I walked in.

It had to be nine years since I'd last seen him and the man I remembered as a straight-backed athlete, clear eyed and with the air of constant watchfulness common to all those who relied on their own wits to survive, was obviously long-gone. In his place stooped a shadow of that recollection, his knee-holed pants and threadbare shirt hanging baggily on a frame now gaunt and round-shouldered. Beneath the tangle of thinning, greying hair that had once been a shock of blondness, his features were drawn and tired, but he still came straight over and gave me a hug of old comradeship before being ordered down by the guard. He was left with just words, spoken with high emotion, but still a model of

17

educated modulation. "Thanks so much for coming, Mark. And, boy, do I need you."

"You've got me. We always promised to watch each other's backs. Remember?"

"In the *First Regiment Etranger* and then the glorious old N66? Ah yes, good days, Mark."

"Were they? A good way to get yourself killed, if I remember right."

"Better than the one I might still get though." He sat down again. "Right now, it seems you're the only thing between me and the Death House."

"There'll be a jury too, but I don't intend it ever coming to that." I took my own seat. "We got ourselves out of plenty bad fixes before, Lee, and we'll do the same with this one." I raised questioning eyes to Nolan who took the hint and went to the door.

"You got fifteen minutes. No longer and no physical contact."

"Yeah, I know the rules."

He nodded the guard out as well and we were left alone, facing each other across a table, bare except for an ashtray. I pulled out my pack of *Camels* and he eagerly took one, his eyes on mine as I lit us up from the same flame. "Glad there isn't a third to take the light, Mark. Remember the old superstition?"

"That the Boche saw you on the first light-up, took aim on the second and fired on the third." We didn't really have the time for reminiscing, but it did at least serve to put him at ease. "A pity we didn't keep in closer touch, Lee. So, how did you know I was even around here?"

"I saw your name as attorney in old newspaper court reports."

"At least you're still getting to read the papers then?"

"Only after I've got to sleep in them first." He gave a little chuckle, a bit forced and something he didn't seem to have practiced much for a long time. "But it was good to know you'd carved a notch for yourself by finishing that law degree, and forging a successful career."

It was my turn to laugh. "Depends what you mean by 'successful', and I'm not sure it'll ever be a career. I get to defend some of the unfortunates the 48th choose to throw my way, manage to get some off, and just a few even pay me."

"Which I won't be able to do." He shrugged. "At least you've made something of your life, Mark. Mine's been pretty well downhill all the way since the army."

"How come?"

"Just never seemed to readjust again to peacetime life out of uniform. When I arrived home from France, it was to find both my parents dead from Spanish flu and the family business gone to hell. Trying to find work only proved there weren't too many vacancies for shell-shocked veterans whose only skill is to paint pretty pictures and kill fellow-humans in twenty different ways. I ended up hitting the bottle and even that turned to worms after 1920 with Prohibition."

"Yeah, the puritans probably thought they were curing the country's ills, but I'm still not sure."

"You would be if you'd drunk some of the devil's brews I have."

"Don't tell me you ended up on meths."

He shook his head. "No, not that low, but some of the bootleg stuff is pretty rough stuff and had me on a downward spiral until Richard took me in hand."

"Richard ... Father Richard Magee, the priest you're supposed to have murdered?" I glanced at my watch: half our precious time gone, so I was glad to get on to the present dilemma. "You knew him?"

"Yes, and from way back in France. He came over in seventeen as a padre with the forty-second division. I met him soon after I'd transferred myself to the U.S. Air Service. I liked his approach to the faith and he liked my paintings and we became good friends. I even had him take my confession, which helped ease my conscience over what I'd done."

"What had you done?"

"Oh, you know ..." He paused for a second to take a long drag before watching the smoke climb ceilingwards, "... all that killing ... how did that old doggerel go? *'Every bullet finds a billet – Some bullets more than one – Perhaps, dear God, I killed a mother – When I killed a mother's son.'*"

I lit another *Camel* off the stub of my first. "We all did our share of that, Lee. Not something to dwell on,"

"No, but not as bad as mine."

"How do you mean?"

He shook his head as if that could erase the memories. "Oh ... nothing."

"But Father Richard gave you some solace?"

"He did that. And then, when I found myself on the streets here, I remembered him saying that he'd be returning to his old church in the Bronx when he was demobilized. So I looked him up, reckoning a return to the faith might be the only way I'd get my life turned around."

"And did it?"

"It was getting that way. Richard had seen enough shell-shock to recognise its effects, straightway saw my problem, talked a lot of sense without pushing the religious angle and arranged for me to sleep at the Saint Winifred's shelter on the coldest of nights."

"You mean you don't even have a home, Lee?"

"Not unless that's what you call subway tunnels or park benches."

"Jesus!" I glanced again at my watch. "Time's going, Lee, and I need to ask some questions."

"Go ahead."

"Well, for starters ... did you do it?"

I couldn't tell whether his expression was one of shock or hurt. Probably both, but either way, his answer was clear enough. "Absolutely not."

"Good. Now, tell me what happened the night of the murder."

He blinked. "I only came to the church because Richard had said he needed to see me urgently."

"*He* needed to see *you*. How come?"

"I don't know, but he left a message with his sister, Tara, at *Winifred's Welfare* for me to call him urgently."

"*Winifred's Welfare*?"

"Yeah, the shelter Richard set up after returning to this parish. It was his way of supporting ex-GIs down on their luck and with much the same problems as me. Tara ran the place and I spent a lot of time there. Anyway, when I called he sounded pretty disturbed and said he needed to talk about something that was happening and which wasn't right."

"Did he say what?"

"No, but he promised to explain as soon as he saw me, so I headed straight there."

"What time was this?"

"Late in the day by the time I got there. It was already dark, sleet coming down, but a big full moon shining between the scudding storm-clouds and beaming through the church's stained windows."

"You went straight in?"

"Yes, and that's when I found him, close by the altar, still alive, but writhing in pain from the bayonet still in his guts."

"And he didn't say who'd done it?"

"He was in agony, Mark, and struggling to breathe, let alone talk. He knew his time had come and all I could do was comfort him in his dying seconds."

"So he said nothing?"

"Just one word. 'Traditor'."

"Traditor. What does that mean?"

"I think it's latin for 'traitor'."

"What did he mean by it?"

"I thought at first it must have some connection to his own time in the military."

"What made you think that?"

"It was the only thing we had in common in our other life."

"How long did you know him out there?"

"Less than a year until he was taken prisoner at Cantigny. When the Germans counter-attacked, he stayed behind to care for some of our wounded, was taken prisoner with them and ended up a POW."

"He doesn't sound the sort to be easily spooked. When was the last time you saw him before the murder?"

"About a week before."

"And he seemed otherwise okay then?"

"Absolutely. We shared a coffee in the vestry and chatted about old times in France."

"So whatever it was he needed to see you about had been triggered in the week since."

"Must have."

"Right, well somehow I need to talk to someone else who *might* know what was bothering him. You say he had this sister ... Tara?"

"Yep, nice girl too. And there's an assistant priest at Saint Winifred's, Father Huber, who I've never liked too much, but he might know something."

"We'll see, but isn't he the one who came in and found you leaning over the victim?"

"That's right. He lives in the rectory next door to the church. Reckoned he was busy on the parish accounts, but suddenly needed to come check the candle store or something and stumbled right onto the scene."

"Of you with Father Magee dying in your arms?"

"Correct."

"And, presumably, getting you pretty bloodied in the process?"

"Very much so, and even more when I pulled out the bayonet."

"A German issue sawtooth. Inspector Nolan showed me."

"Right. Nasty piece of hardware."

"Did you bring one back from France, Lee?"

"Yeah, along with other mementos, but all long since gone to pay for booze."

"You got any proof of that?"

"Only the hangover I can still feel if I close my eyes."

"Okay, so let's get back to Saint Winifred's church on the night of the murder. You find the good father murdered and dying and then a patrol cop arrives on the scene and arrests you. Who or what do you think brought him there so quick?"

"Probably the figure I saw hurrying away through the church's back door as I came in. He has to have been the murderer, Mark, and me arriving almost caught him in the act."

"And probably explains why he didn't even stop to pull out his bayonet. Can you describe this guy?"

"I sure can, and you'd be able to too if he's the guy I think."

"You ... *we* ... know this character?"

"We did. From way back, but there were only a few lights on in the church, so I still can't be sure it was who I thought it was and, anyway, it *can't* have been him. But it would explain what Richard was referring to with his last thoughts of 'traitor'."

"But who do you *think* it was?" I glanced impatiently again at my watch. "We've got just a minute, Lee, so spit it out."

"You won't believe me."

"I'll try."

"Okay. I think it was Meunier."

*   *   *

'Meunier!' Straightway, my thoughts went back to training in Toulouse and the first time we'd met a man we both soon came to hate with a passion.

We were about half-way through our training when we were joined by yet more trainees from Sidi-bel-Abbés, the Algerian depot of the Legion's First Regiment. The Legion, ever a multi-national force, had stopped short of discharging any men from the axis powers, but had wisely kept them in Algeria, well away from the European conflict. Now the remainder of those recruits, all of nationalities supposedly loyal to the allied cause, had been sent to join us for the remainder of their training. Amongst them was a hulk of a man and, to us, a bastard of the first order. The name he used, or at least the one given by the Legion, was Meunier.

It was certainly a tradition, if not a requirement, for the majority of recruits to adopt a name other than their own for the duration of their service. Reasons were many, though evasion from the law was probably the abiding one and a practice certainly encouraged by the Legion. If any authority came knocking at their door looking for a man, they could simply say no-one of that name was in their ranks. It wasn't surprising then that many were reticent to talk about their lives, though Meunier seemed more secretive than most, not even giving a hint as to his nationality. Both Lee and myself suspected he might have actually been a fellow Yank, but that was something he wanted to hide, going by the way he stuck to basic French and avoided *our* company in particular.

Whatever his lineage though, his few extra months of soldiering in Sidi-bel-Abbés had clearly made him feel superior to us humble recruits. Added to that, he seemed strangely flush with cash, way above the meager pay of a humble *engage volontaire*, but something he used unashamedly to avoid the worst of our fatigues.

For, in a unit where all had to take their turn in cleaning latrines and digging ditches, Meunier was always conspicuously absent on 'other duties'. There were murmurings of his paying off Prazerie to gain these privileges, though some of our fellow-recruits seemed more than happy themselves to maintain Meunier's kit for the few extra *sous* he tossed their way. Consequently, in the late evenings, while the rest of us polished brass and leather by the light of a dim barrack-room lamp, he lay on his *paliaise*, hands behind his head, contemplating the rest of us with ill-disguised contempt. *Caporal* Prazerie, who had his own bed in the corner of our *caserne*, seemed blissfully content with this arrangement and made no attempt to curtail it, only deepening our suspicions of corruption.

And so we slogged on through that interminable training, endlessly drilling and spending whatever little spare time remained at the end of each day cleaning our weapons and kit. However, in the last third, one small privilege we did gain was being able to enjoy an hour or so each evening at the regimental canteen. Here, for half a *sou* a bottle, rough Algerian wine helped us forget the hardships of Legion life and brought us at least close to what we used to call 'relaxation'.

It was on one such evening, the smoke of a hundred pipes and cigarettes drifting across the rowdy canteen and the wine already working its magic, that Lee and I fell into a particularly contemplative mood. I lit another *Gauloises* and loosened the collar of my rough serge tunic. "Well, Lee, I guess it'll be the front line for us pretty soon."

He smiled. "Don't be too impatient. From what I hear, things up there have already reached a kind of stalemate, with both sides digging in either side of a line from Lorraine to the Belgium coast." On the table before us lay our soft peaked caps, a poor alternative to the *kepi*s of legend, but a symbol of our calling none-the-less. Lee picked his off the table, dusted the crown and placed it back. "No, Mark, it'll be a long time yet before all this ends, and who knows if either you or I will be here to see it."

Lee was right about the military situation slowing to near standstill. The Germans had managed to stop a Russian invasion at the Battle of Tannenberg, but only at the expense of needed reserves and their own drive towards Paris. And so a French offensive into southern Alsace had been rewarded by limited success, the Boche being pushed back fifty kilometres to the Marne where they had then dug in, leaving both sides glaring at each other across a half-mile wide band of open ground. The trench war had begun, but right here and now we had enough troubles to contend with, and one had just entered the canteen.

I nodded across the rest of our fellow *poilus*, gradually subsiding into mild intoxication, to the bulky figure of Meunier just entering. This surly fellow-recruit made no effort to join our table or any other, but found one of his own in a dark corner of the canteen. "Solitary cuss, 'aint he?"

But in the Legion, any man with spare cash in his pocket didn't lack friends for long. No sooner had Meunier got himself a bottle than he was joined by Pavlovic, a little ferret of a Serbian, one of those sent to join our *escouade* from Si-di-bel-Abbés and clearly a past acquaintance of Meunier. We couldn't hear exactly what was being said by either man, but it was easy to surmise that the Serb was asking Meunier to stand him a drink and being just as quickly refused. Pavlovic had never struck me as being in any way tough, but perhaps the wine had gingered his ire because he responded to the rebuff with a burst of invective in a mixture of basic French and bastard English and loud enough now to make clear he was throwing out a threat.

"You think you can treat me like dirt. I'll show you. I know things about you ... what you are doing here."

Amazingly, Meunier gave no reaction. He was a bear of a man and could probably have crushed the Serb with one hand, but he just sat there with a humorless smile playing over his hard features while some of Pavlovic's compatriots came and pulled him away.

"I'm surprised Meunier managed to control himself like he did," remarked Lee, begrudgingly.

"But for how long?" I didn't share Lee's benevolence. There was something in the smile playing around that bully's features that told me he wasn't finished with the little Serb yet. Perhaps I was wrong. We'd see.

"Anyway, time to hit the sack." Lee got up and put on his cap. "Enough excitement for one night and we're on the ranges again tomorrow, so I need my eyes sharp to beat you." He nodded towards the door. "You coming?"

"Not just yet." After the talk and action of the night, I needed just a short while yet to finish my bottle and think some thoughts. Lee left, and I lit my third *Gaulois*, poured the last of my wine and, by the time I'd finished both, Meunier also was leaving the canteen.

I was only minutes behind him, but noticed he didn't head direct for our *caserne*, but deviated off behind the armory. Still not ready for sleep and curious as to his movements, I lingered just long enough to stay surreptitiously on his tail.

It didn't take long for me to discover his mission, for waiting just by the armory door was a figure, glancing about him to check they were unobserved. Determined to keep it that way, I slipped into the shadows to watch and listen. Soon, by the light of the armory lamp, I could identify Meunier's secret contact, and when I did, it was a revelation beyond belief.

Considering the awe in which we humble recruits held even the forbidding likes of *sous-officers*, it was beyond understanding that Meunier's assignation tonight was with Colonel Lepayre himself, Commanding Officer of our 11/1st *Regiment de Marche du 1er Etranger*.

Just why someone we regarded as a god incarnate should meet with a mere *légionnaires de 2e classe* was something their hushed tones and my distance prevented me finding out before they quickly parted and disappeared wraith-like back into the darkness. Trying to make sense of it all, I crept back to our *caserne*, concluding only that it held no good omens for the rest of us.

The truth and reality of that came on the five-thirty parade next morning. We knew something was amiss when we saw that Meunier wasn't with us in the ranks, but standing beside our *caporal*. Prazerie didn't beat about the bush. "As of this morning, in accordance with unit orders, Legionaire Meunier has been appointed *Soldat de 1re class*. You will, of course, show appropriate respect and obey his orders as though they were my own."

What that meant for us all was soon apparent when Prazerie instructed the new lance corporal to march us to the rifle butts.

"*Mon caporal*," acknowledged Meunier, saluting, as was the custom between NCOs in the French military. "Squad, attention. Right turn. By the left, double march."

Even Prazerie usually spared us doubling the three kilometres to the ranges, but Meunier was obviously keen to flex his new muscles. The summer was already fading, but in our thick, grey, double-breasted *capotes* with the great pack on our backs and the heavy Lebel slung from the shoulder, it wasn't long before we were all sweating freely. Thankfully, just above the treeline, a fluttering red flag told us the ranges were near and soon we were doubling onto them, straightway ordered into firing positions and immediately letting loose with our Lebels.

This was our tenth session on the ranges, with most of us now reasonably proficient, but our new NCO was far from impressed. Ordered to fire off one full magazine of eight rounds, he seemed to take great delight in pacing behind our line cursing our every effort.

One recruit coming in for special attention was the little Serb, Pavlovic. "What the hell do you think you're doing ... trying to win a furry toy at the fairground?" bellowed Meunier in guttural French. "Speed up that rate of fire or you'll feel the end of my bayonet up your ass."

Pavlovic fired and reloaded at a faster rate, but with each crack of his Lebel, Meunier demanded more and more speed. Even with the complete magazine expended, a reload was ordered, followed by yet another session of firing and inevitable cursing. We watched, standing now behind the firing line, feeling for our victimized comrade while just as quickly realising there was going to be only one end to this drill.

'Crack!' went the little Serb's rifle ... "Faster!" ... 'Crack!' ... "Faster!" ... 'Crack!' ... "Faster" ... 'Crack!'

As he yelled his orders, we noticed Meunier moving slowly back from the prone figure of the little Serb working the Lebel's bolt action like a man demented. And then, instead of another 'crack!', there came a dull thump, and Pavlovic jerked back and lay still. The Lebel lay beside the Serb's inert form, its magazine and breech a contorted mess of fractured metal. We all knew why. That enforced rate of fire had caused one round to strike the primer of the cartridge in front, causing an explosion within the tube magazine and with Pavlovic's face on the receiving end.

It was Prazerie who went to the lifeless body, made a quick examination and then called for two men to carry it clear of the butts and cover it with his *capote*. Two fellow Serbs answered the summons while the rest of us stood deep in thought. We all knew this was no accident and that those words of the night before had been paid back a thousand-fold.

It was a sombre group which then doubled back to barracks under Meunier's continually withering tongue. Not that we had much time to muse on the subject.

Back on the parade square Colonel Lepayre was waiting to give us some news. Ever increasing casualties in Flanders demanded replacements. Our training was over and we were finally off to the front.

*　　*　　*

A plethora of memories from years back, but ones that took only seconds to recall before reality bought me back to the precinct interview room and my old comrade needing practical help.

"Are you sure it was Meunier, Lee?"

His eyes narrowed. "It was only a fleeting glimpse, but that was one man I'd never forget."

"You and I both." Even as I tried to assimilate this revelation, there came the footsteps of the others returning. "Time's up, old friend, but I'll do everything I can for you."

"I know you will."

We both stood up and before the police guard could stop us, I gave him a reassuring hug. Then I was back outside in the corridor and taking the chance for a last few words with Pat Nolan.

"The patrolman ... the one who did the arrest ..."

"Officer Burroughs."

"I'd like to talk to him."

Pat shook his head. "Sorry, but not something I can allow at this stage."

"Then I'll have to call him as a witness at the preliminary hearing."

"There won't be one, Mark. The DA has already indicated

this will be by Grand Jury. Being so open-and-shut, it means we'll get him for trial all the quicker."

"Which seems to me what this whole set-up is about." I could see the way this was going, felt the anger already rising in my throat and, just as quickly, swallowed it down to a more moderate tone. "Okay, Pat, but at least let me have a description of the man the cop says reported the disturbance in the first place?"

"I should check with the DA ..." He paused, scanning my creased and worn suit, my down-at-heel shoes. I'm not saying there was pity in his eyes, but perhaps just a little empathy. "Okay, as a one-time favour, I'll check his report and have a personal word."

"Thanks, Pat. I knew you were a fair guy."

He gave a cheerless laugh. "Only when the other side has a lost cause, but I'll call you when I have what you want."

That was as much as I could do for Lee Vennington right now and I headed out into the emerging dawn in search of an early breakfast and somewhere to collect my thoughts.

*　　*　　*

I found both in *Harry's Diner*. Just four blocks from the precinct headquarters, it was something of a grease-pit, but with the invaluable asset of being both cheap and warm.

My eating habits these lean days were dependant on New York City Law Department checks, and Lee had at least provided the means for some to come. On that basis I took a table by the window and ordered double scrambled eggs. Waiting for them to arrive, I sat watching the wind-blown sleet outside while recalling an equally bitter winter scene in 1915 as we marched those final fifty miles into Champagne.

*　　*　　*

CHAPTER TWO

Ah, Champagne. I recalled its chalk plains and hills lying between Lorraine in the east and Picardy in the west and scene of the failed first French offensive in the early months of the war.

Slogging our way through that fought-over territory with the rumble of heavy siege guns getting ever closer, the mark-of-the-beast was already apparent in the burned out villages, ruined crops and historic destruction. Watching our *marche* to the front through anguished eyes were the pitiful inhabitants of this scene of carnage, now without homes, living or, it seemed to me, much hope. Having wanted this moment since we joined up, we were now experiencing the cruel reality of war and I could sense that Lee, marching beside me, was equally shocked by the senselessness of it all. During our training we'd probably both asked ourselves why we'd volunteered. Now that question was being answered, and all too clearly.

Not that the Huns hadn't already paid a price for their barbaric acts. Along the roads and lanes we were marching, there was strewn the debris of recent battle: abandoned guns and limbers, carts and wagons, the rotting carcases of the horses that had pulled them and the bodies of the men who had manned them. Lurking in the surrounding woods and fields were enemy still on the run, loathe to surrender, we were told, because their officers had assured them the French would shoot them out of hand. Seeing the looks of bitterness on the faces of our French comrades as they surveyed the desecration of their homeland, that warning might not have been totally misplaced. Before nightfall, we finally arrived at the outer line of trenches at Navarin Farm, the area of ravaged land that the *11/1st Regiment Etrange* had now been assigned to hold.

Nestling in what had been the region's wine-growing center, this seemingly innocuous name had given itself to a line of high ground bitterly contested in the ill-fated offensive. By the time we arrived to relieve the battle-weary regiment that had been holding it, ferocious fighting had already reduced the farm itself to a mere name, but one that had already gained a grim reputation within the ranks of the French forces. Now, as we came within earshot of crackling rifle-fire, the stutter of machine-guns and the crump of shells, we knew we were about to find out just how grim.

Our greenness in the profession of arms might have had us quaking with nervous anticipation at that prospect, but youthful naivety meant we were still as keen as mustard to sample the adventure before an inevitable and imminent cease-fire. Perhaps the gaunt lifeless expressions on the faces of the army unit whose trench we were taking over should have warned us, but we put that down to pure exhaustion and something our tough Legion training had equipped us to handle. On a personal level, just the fact that Lee and I had managed to stick together was an added uplift as we settled into the routine of trench warfare.

For already, our opposing armies had dug-in to what was to become a jagged system of deep, mud-caked trenches stretching from Switzerland to the North Sea. Between us and the Boche's own outer line lay a mere eight-hundred yards of gutted houses and shattered trees. We seemed to spend much time simply mounting guard and, between, burning the lice out of our uniforms with a lighted candle or forlornly attempting to keep our kit and weapons clean from the ever-encroaching mud.

At other times though there would come a fusillade of fire from somewhere down the trench line and the cry of "Aux arms, aux trenches" as a probing Boche patrol tried the weaknesses in our front-line. Even at that stage, I was surprised at how often they were found, and put it down to good reconnaissance from the enemy biplanes we sometimes saw flying overhead.

I viewed these early aerial contraptions with a mixture of envy and awe. They certainly appealed to my love of all things mechanical, and floating up there, way above all this mud-bound hell, certainly seemed an infinitely better way to fight a war. On the other hand, it was an awfully long way to fall when things went bad, though many of us would fall before this war was over and the distance in the end wouldn't make that much difference. At least those fly-boys up there would have slept in a bed and had a good meal before their inevitable appointment with the Grim Reaper.

In those early days though, the evenings were something of a respite. Then, after sunset, there seemed to be a form of truce when each side went out into No Man's Land to recover wounded, re-dig trenches or just attempt, for a short while at least, a mental escape from the dismal existence we were enduring for four cents a day. Sometimes from the Boche trenches would come the lilt of singing voices or the notes of a mouth-organ, which took me back to those innocent pre-war days in Paris and a life now seemingly eons away.

This stalemate, however, was destined not to last. Soon there came the order for our own night-patrolling in No Mans Land and the task of gaining intelligence of enemy positions. Clearly our High Command was planning a major assault which, to Lee and me, held the chance at least for a bit of real action. That promise, though, was quickly counteracted by the identity of the newly-promoted *sergent* sent by battalion headquarters further down the line to lead some of these recces. It was Meunier.

*   *   *

Back in Harry's Diner, an attractive waitress delivering my breakfast, broke through jaundiced thoughts. The eggs tasted good, but I barely noticed as memories of past dangers and conflicts shared with Lee came back to haunt me. I knew that bonds of comradeship and my own personal part in all that had gone before meant I was more intimately involved in this new case than any lawyer should be. But the mystery of how and why this specter from our past had now returned was something that was going to dominate my every thought and action until solved.

And solved it must be. To me it presented a challenge, work and even dollars. To Lee, though, it was going to be the difference between continued life or its degrading end in Sing Sing's electric chair. That thought alone spurred me to wolf down the eggs and head straight out for Saint Winifred's Church and the scene of the crime.

*   *   *

It was about a mile from here to the church and I could have taken a streetcar, but I felt the need for exercise, some cold fresh air, and time again to think of the way ahead. And so, huddled in my old *British Warm*, hands in pockets and head bent against the icy wind off Long Island Sound, I bashed on to Saint Winifred's where I hoped to find at least some answers to the questions already invading my thought process.

Like, why had this Father Magee suddenly found the need to call a man in such dire straights as Lee? It must have been more than just the need to talk. He surely could have confided in his own assistant priest for that. Perhaps it was knowing Lee, a man imbued with the singular skills of war, was a fighter he knew he could trust. If so, why did an ex-padre need someone to watch his back? Who would want to harm an apparently popular priest? I was still musing on that one by the time I reached his church.

Saint Winifred's was surrounded by ornate iron railings and neat gardens that, together with its twin turrets, gave it an almost cathedral-like appearance in something approaching Byzantine Revival, though the Connecticut Brownstone used in its construction hinted at the late eighteen-hundreds when the Bronx borough was in one of its more affluent incarnations. Normally it would have stood out as an oasis of peace and sanctity, but the police guard still standing before the large oak main doors was evidence enough that these were now more violent times.

Clearly though, everyday church life was already returning to normal, me receiving only the most cursory of nods from the officer on duty as I entered. He probably assumed I'd come to join the well-attended service already taking place.

Beneath the vaulted ceiling, in an atmosphere of incense and latent distress, a thin and sombre cleric I presumed to be the assistant priest, stood officiating. I paused at the back, not wishing to disturb the proceedings, and realising from the tears of the worshippers that this had to be a service of remembrance for the late Father Magee. By now Huber had completed his words of commemoration, and, pew by pew, the parishioners were filing up to take communion. I was not of their faith, but I was a communicant and joined the line.

It was slow-moving, but it gave me the chance to study the figure in black cassock up there giving the wine and wafers, his thin, pointed features displaying neither humor nor compassion and the first hints of grey in his hair, giving some idea as to his age. When my turn came to take the sacrament, he eyed me suspiciously as someone outside his normal flock. With the service over, I confirmed the fact by buttonholing him before he could retire to the vestry.

"Father Huber?"

He turned around abruptly, clearly not pleased at the intrusion. "Who are you?"

I ignored the brusqueness and introduced myself as Lee Vennington's defense attorney.

He gave a slight snort down his long pointed nose. "You're representing the man who murdered poor Father Magee."

"*Alleged* to have murdered. I understand it was you who was first at the crime-scene?"

His cadaverous chest puffed out just a little. "That's correct. I was next door in the rectory catching up with church accounts, but then needed to check our candle stock. On the way I heard a groan and when I came into the church itself, it was to see your client bending over the body of our dear Father."

"But you didn't see the actual act of murder?"

"No."

"Then how come you're so sure as to the identity of the perpetrator?"

"The police seem to be."

"Based on the evidence of persons such as yourself, however accurate or inaccurate that may be. Until a jury decides its own verdict, the law says a man is innocent until proven guilty." I gave Huber a look of mock surprise. "You, as a man of the cloth, should know that."

He stiffened slightly. "I know the difference between good and evil."

"Good. Then you might be able to tell me if you've seen any other suspicious characters hanging around the church in the weeks preceding Father Magee's demise?"

"I've seen many." That was one answer I wasn't ready for, but Huber was quick to explain. "On wet days we have a constant invasion of lost souls seeking food and shelter at *Winifred's Welfare*."

"The soup kitchen that Father Magee set up?"

"Indeed, and an establishment very dear to his heart."

"But not to yours?"

I'd detected a distinct lack of enthusiasm in Huber on the subject and his next words told me why. "Like I told you, I keep the church accounts, and so I see how much it costs to help those who seem to have no desire to help themselves."

"Many of them were men who fought in France, Huber. Instead of helping themselves, they helped their country, which has done precious little to help them since."

"There was no conscription here," argued Huber. "Those that went, did so of their own accord."

"Like your own Father Magee. I'm sure he related to you just how much suffering our troops endured out there."

"Yes, but without any sympathy for those left behind to run things in their absence."

"You're talking about yourself here?"

"I am indeed. Someone had to keep Saint Winifred's operating while he went out and played soldiers."

"But not a game you fancied 'playing' yourself by volunteering as a padre?"

He seemed almost insulted at the mere suggestion. "Very noble, I'm sure, but I find it difficult to reconcile Christian principles with the profession of arms."

"How long have you been here as assistant priest?"

"Ten years. I came straight from the seminary and ordination."

"Then surely a Jesuit such as yourself can only applaud military calling. Didn't your founder, Ignatius Loyola, have a military background, and doesn't your Order always refer to themselves as 'God's soldiers'?"

"How do you know I'm a Jesuit?"

"Because I'm judging your age to be nudging forty, Father. Assuming you went to your seminary straight from school, you must have been training for twelve years. The training period for Catholic priests is normally only four and a half. Only Jesuits study for twelve."

His eyes fixed me with a mixture of reluctant admiration and wariness. "Very perceptive." He glanced about him with contrived impatience. "I have much to do. Have you any more questions?"

"Yes. Was Father Magee also a Jesuit?"

"No, he was a simple Diocesan Priest."

"But not simple enough to stop some person-unknown deciding to murder him." It was time to get this conversation back on track. "You were saying there were several veterans in and out of here from *Winifred's Welfare*?"

"Yes, but the one here most often before the murder was your client."

"Ignoring that aspect, can you think of anyone else who would have reason to kill Father Magee?"

"No, he was a priest popular with those who liked his more familiar approach."

"But I understand there was something bothering him in the days before his murder?"

Huber shrugged. "We who care for the spiritual needs of others have much to concern us."

"Like the candle stock I understand you'd come here to check when you stumbled across the crime scene." Sarcasm wasn't a medium I usually liked or chose to exercise, but I felt it was time to drive a stake through this sanctimonious martinet's ecclesiastical smugness. "With such weighty responsibilities, I can understand you being oblivious to normal human frailties, Huber, but think again if you noticed anything different in Father Magee's manner."

"Perhaps I did get the impression that he was shouldering some mental burden."

"Did he say what?"

"No, we tend to confide in God when something disturbs our own souls."

"So, nothing else you can tell me?"

"I don't think so, other than the note."

"The note?"

"Yes, the slip of paper I found in his hand when I knelt to give him the Last Rites."

I was getting a little tired of Father Huber's secretive exposés. "And could you possibly tell me what this note said?"

"Yes, it was simply a quotation from Shakespeare's *Julius Caesar.*"

"Which said ...?"

" '*Ingratitude, more strong than traitors' arms.*'"

"Have you any idea to what treachery this quote was aimed?"

"No, but perhaps he sensed that this Vennington was about to betray all the help he'd given him."

"Did you pass this note on to the police?"

"No, I didn't think it important."

"But you still have it?"

"Not any more. I threw it in the fire as soon as I was back in the rectory."

"Very far-sighted of you." I swallowed my anger and instead asked, "Father Magee's sister ... does she still work at *Winifred's Welfare?*"

"She runs it."

"Good. Then perhaps I'll get a bit more sense out of her. Before I go though, one more question. Did you ever see a hulk of a man – six feet one, over two hundred pounds, probably now in his early forties and with an evil-looking scar running down the left side of his face – in this church?"

He thought for a moment, stroking his chin. "Yes I did, just once, talking earnestly to Father Richard, though he never told me what about." Father Huber frowned. "I don't know who this man was. Do you think he was connected to the murder?"

"Possibly. Good day Father Huber. May your parishioners' spiritual welfare prosper in spite of you."

I left him standing there fuming, but a little less arrogant than when I found him. Had he known it, though, the con-clusion of our conversation had been a painful reminder for me of memories I'd spent the last few years trying to erase. Now they'd returned with a vengeance and I couldn't decide whether I was relieved or disappointed that Father Huber had recognised that description. However, just the fact that Father Magee seemed to have had more than one meeting with Meunier was good reason to pursue this line of enquiry.

Whatever, as I walked away from Saint Winifred's I was mentally far from this Bronx sidewalk and once again back in the hell-hole of 1915 Flanders where Meunier had now returned to once more blight our lives. That is, if living was something we would be enjoying for much longer, now we were back in that man's clutches.

*   *   *

He came back to our unit, courtesy of Headquarters Company further down the line, to organize our intelligence gathering missions. Newly promoted *Sergent*, he wasted no time in establishing patrols into the wastes of No Man's Land, even to the extent of choosing the men to take on these almost-nightly sorties. Certainly there were no volunteers, seeing as Meunier consistently returned with fewer men than he left with, only adding to the ingrained suspicions both Lee and myself harbored for the man.

I considered sharing them with our company commander, but *Capitaine* Icardo, though a brave soldier and a fair man, had a weakened constitution and strength of character from years of opium smoking in Indo-China. It was going to take a strong officer to handle his new NCO and, knowing how adept our new *sergent* was at fixing things to his own advantage, our *capitaine* was not going to be the one to do it. Meunier had probably landed our company for that very reason, so I kept my silence, but not my determination to find out just what was going on out there.

That opportunity though was slow in coming, seeing as *Sergent* Meunier was strangely loathe to choose either Lee or myself for his missions. In fact, he seemed to make a point of avoiding any contact with us at all. Perhaps we should have been thankful for that sidelining, but it only served to deepen our suspicion that Meunier was in fact a fellow American.

In the end, that mystery was resolved one particularly miserable morning in the last winter months of the New Year. After a night of incessant rain, the muddy trench bottom had turned into a veritable sea of filth and squalor that spilled over the duckboards and the tops of our boots so that even the pain of incipient trench-foot was numbed by its icy touch. Lee and I were at one of the sharp S-bends in the system, designed to prevent any invading Boche patrol getting a clear line of fire straight down the company.

In the grey light of dawn, we were leaning miserably against the trench sides, our sodden greatcoats failing to combat the insidious cold and the only spark of comfort being the sound of the coffee-orderly ladling that blessed beverage from his dixie as he made his way along the line. We gratefully pulled tin mugs from our packs but, just as he arrived, someone else turned the corner from the opposite direction.

It was *Sergent* Meunier, doubtless fresh from handing *Capitaine* Icardo his report of another night's intelligence-gathering, stressing his own personal bravery and glossing over why none of the three men he had taken with him had managed to survive the foray. Whatever, he was ready for his *café* as much as the rest of us and, as behove the man, pushed straight in, grabbed the mug off the first legionnaire in line and ordered it filled. The orderly complied, but at the same time we heard the drumming feet of someone pounding down the trench, but hidden from sight by the zig-zag of the corner. It turned out to be a runner *en rou*te to headquarters, probably with Meunier's own report. Such was his haste that, rounding the corner, he ran full-tilt into the man himself just as he was raising the mug to his lips. The result was steaming black coffee spilling over his reddening square face, and scalding fists already clenching into bunches of violent retribution.

Amusing as all this was to us surrounding *poilus*, it was sheer horror to the young runner as Meunier's anger spilled forth with a blistering tongue-lashing.

"You goddam son of a stupid bitch. You'll pay for that."

Even as the runner squirmed his useless apologies, Lee and I were swapping our grins for the realization that our *Sergent*'s invective had been spat with all the nasal drawl of home-grown American.

Meunier fixed both Lee and myself with glaring eyes, only too aware now of his mistake and thinking fast of how to neutralize it. Another second, and he ordered its solution.

"You two … tonight … patrolling."

So, we were finally going to discover just what was going on out there in that dark forbidding waste of No Man's Land, though something in the way we'd been detailed made me think it was a knowledge never destined to find its way back to our lines.

*   *   *

Right now, though, finding my own way to *Winifred's Welfare* was first priority. It turned out to be in a disused office block close to the mother church with its entrance in a side-street discreetly shielded from public scrutiny. From that doorway, a shuffling queue of men trailed out like the tail of some reptile one step from extinction, a ragged group in which every last vestige of self-respect seemed to have gone the way of their hopes and dreams. That some of them had previously had a more worthy life was evidenced by dangling campaign medals pinned to threadbare coats or even the remnants of an old uniform once proudly worn. But it was difficult now to imagine those rounded world-weary shoulders ever being broad and straight, the stubble-dark chins ever raised until necks touched collars or those long mops of unkempt hair ever short beneath a cap or helmet. They'd certainly queued for food before, but that had been to refuel bodies honed to fitness by exercise and worthwhile endeavor. Now it was for the simple act of surviving in a society happy to forget all they'd gone through on their behalf. Those care-worn eyes had seen sights difficult to describe, but now they watched me bypass them devoid of any resolve to challenge someone seemingly trying to cut in line.

Inside, that queue led to a long counter where, in an

atmosphere of equal despair and unwashed bodies, several females were ladling something from large steaming cauldrons. These women, presumably volunteers, were all dressed in similar light blue housecoats and small peakless caps. It wasn't a uniform that did anything to enhance their figures, but to the men eagerly offering them their metal soup-bowls, it was probably the nearest they would ever come again to female companionship. To one side, a rather more mature, sterner-looking woman stood checking the numbers. I went up to her and asked for Tara Magee.

After a quick head-to-toe appraisal of my leather-patched elbows and scuffed down-at-heel shoes, she said, "Wait here," and headed for the counter.

Relieved this woman wasn't the late priest's sister, I watched her whisper something to a younger volunteer dishing soup, who gave me a sharp glance before impatiently handing over her ladle and striding my way with a less-than tolerant expression.

"I'm Tara Magee, and this isn't a good time." She was in her twenties, upright and slim and with a hint of huskiness in her voice that I immediately found attractive. It suited her business-like brusqueness, probably honed by daily exposure to life at its most desperate. Only a few wisps of dark auburn hair escaped her small uniform cap, but the face beneath was fine-boned with a straight nose, down which her striking blue eyes were now examining my lack of sartorial elegance. But those same eyes betrayed an underlying compassion for those whose life has dealt a rotten hand. "How can I help you, Mr ..."

"... Kingsley ... Mark Kingsley." I pulled a card from my pocket and handed it across.

"Counselor at Law." She read my hard-earned title dismissively and handed back the card. "I don't need an attorney, Mr Kingsley."

"Perhaps not," I didn't take it back, "but my client does, and would appreciate your help."

"Your client?"

"Lee Vennington."

"The man who murdered my brother?" Those blue eyes had quickly hardened. "You're actually defending that scum."

I nodded towards the slowly diminishing food-line. "That 'scum' went through the same war horrors as some of your other clients, Miss Magee, as did your own brother. And as regards defending him, well, someone has to." Perhaps that wasn't the most robust of arguments and I hadn't expected it to be met with particular enthusiasm, but having tried to justify the justice process once this morning, I decided Tara Magee wasn't the best person to try a repeat. Lawyers should never give a personal viewpoint, but now seemed a good time to break that rule. "Lee Vennington was a friend of your brother's and, I'm convinced, totally innocent of his murder." I lowered my voice to a tone I hoped sounded more compassionate. "My sincere condolences for your loss, Miss Magee, and I know how bitter you must feel, but you, more than anyone, must want to see the right man pay the price for killing your brother. For that reason alone, surely you'll help me."

She stood for a few seconds, thinking over what I'd just said. Then she glanced at the address on my card that she was turning over in her soup-stained fingers. "Your office is near to here?"

"Yep, and it's also where I live."

She took another second to scan my threadbare appearance and matched it with what I'd just disclosed. I was hoping compassion for the less-than-blessed might make her more receptive and I was right. "Like I said, Mr Kingsley, now's not a good time to talk, but ...."

Further discussion was cut short by a wreck of a man,

ten times scruffier than me, shuffling to her side, a battered army forage cap held between fingers that were trembling in unison to his lips.

"Excuse me, Miss Magee, but will there be a bed here for me tonight?"

"Of course, Joe." She laid a caring hand on his skeleton-thin wrist and nodded towards the food counter. "Go get yourself something to eat and see me later."

"Thanks, Miss Magee. I'm really grateful."

He shuffled away, with me trying to avoid the eye-watering stench of his breath. "What in God's name has he been drinking?"

She shook her head. "Who knows, Mr Kingsley, but I don't think God had any part in it, and can only hope our work here helps men like him remember the true faith."

It was my turn to be dismissive. "I think it's more a need to *forget* that probably drove him to drink in the first place. By trying to obliterate the memory of the horrors he witnessed in France."

"Were you over there?" She asked it, not as a challenge, but more a sense of discernment.

"Yes."

"Right, but this talk you want to have with me ... how about here tonight?" She gave a sideways glance at my somewhat drawn features. "In fact, you look like you could do with a good meal yourself, Mr Kingsley. Come at seven-thirty after I've finished serving and there'll be food as well as words."

"Seven-thirty it is, but please call me Mark."

"That depends on how you ask your questions." She said it with just the ghost of a smile over her shoulder as she hurried back to her food-station. No 'goodbye' or 'nice to meet you', but leaving me with a feeling I was still struggling to analyze as I made my way back outside.

It was still arctic cold out there, but a welcome relief from the inside odor of unwashed bodies and stale vegetables. Clearly, I hadn't made that good an impression on the feisty Miss Magee and I paused to take a deep breath of air and stand aside as a late contender for the midday soup issue lurched towards me. He was a bedraggled figure with two crutches and just one leg, nodding towards the still-open door. "Am I too late?"

"I'm sure you're not." I indicated his missing limb. "Where did you lose that?"

"Saint Mihiel. Cut off by a shard of flying shrapnel from a fifteen-centimetre howitzer."

"Bad luck."

He managed a smile. "Yeah, but at least I came back. Thousands of our boys didn't."

"True, but you still paid a pretty hefty price of your own." I felt myself reaching into my jacket pocket and pulling out some loose change. I handed over the few cents and dimes. "Here, at least get yourself a proper coffee some time."

He pocketed the coins and balanced on one crutch to throw me a salute. "Thank you sir, I will. God bless."

And then he too was gone, swinging his way into *Winifred's Welfare* for his meagre fayre.

I turned up the collar of my coat and made my way along the sidewalk, surprised at my own miserly, but uncharacteristic, open-handedness. How come my hard old heart was suddenly softening? Whatever, that encounter with the disabled vet had stirred other far deeper thoughts. His wounding had left him a shadow of his former self, whereas mine should have been the death of me. Instead, it became the passport to new and challenging experiences.

I leaned against the ever-fresher wind blowing off the Sound and remembered the icy coldness of the night we followed Meunier out of our trench and into the eerie blackness of No Mans' Land.

*   *   *

It was nearing midnight when Meunier ushered us up the short trench ladder and out into the jaw-aching cold of that inhospitable bit of wasteland. Up there, with moon and stars alike hidden by low scudding cloud, the blackness of it all had the effect of making even the squalor of our trench below almost cosy by comparison.

The companionship of fellow-legionnaires might have given us some reassurance, but Meunier had detailed just Lee and myself for this sortie. It was a situation that didn't auger well and which I raised with *Capitaine* Icardo. Our company commander listened, but explained that Meunier alone would be venturing right up to the enemy lines and that he only needed us to 'watch his back'. As we heaved ourselves up onto the trench top that night, it seemed to me that it was *our* backs that were the more vulnerable, and I went with the firm intention of never exposing mine.

One thing we did acknowledge though as we followed our *sergent* forward in a stooping crouch, was his undoubted intimate knowledge of this God-forsaken expanse of bat-tered broken ground between us and the enemy. Not that it made the going any easier, weighed down as we were with our packs, rifle and ammo as we clawed our way through knee-deep mud and strands of clinging barb wire from one rain-filled shell crater to the next. Pausing in one of these, we listened to the far-off boom of artillery and the rattle of machine guns that, eighty miles to the east, marked the start of the oncoming bloodbath of Verdun. With the flash of those guns reflecting off the low cloud-base, it only added to the demonic impression of that sector being the ante-room to Hell itself.

Not that our own situation was much less precarious. Very

close to the German lines now and reduced to crawling, we sheltered in a foxhole near enough to hear the heavy breathing of enemy out on some night fatigue, the faint click of their spades working away and the curse of an NCOs urging them on to harder labour. In a barely-audible whisper, Meunier ordered us to stay put while he went for a closer recon of what was going on.

As he crawled away, pistol in hand, my natural inclination was to obey that instruction, but there was something in his assured manner, the way he'd seemed to accept the peril of adjacent enemy as almost routine, that hardened yet more my suspicion of this man. I leaned close to Lee and whispered, "I'm going to follow him."

He nodded, but said, "Let's both go?"

I shook my head. "Not a good idea. One of us disobeying orders is bad enough. But if I don't come back and Meunier does, get away from him as soon as you can and report to Icardo."

"Okay, but watch yourself."

"It's *him* I want to watch more right now." I shrugged off my pack and rifle. "Look after these for me."

The low stratus was beginning to clear now and, in the emerging moonlight, I could see Lee frown. "What if you run into the Boche?"

I managed a smile. "Then, I'll be running like hell anyway and all the faster without these." I pulled my long bayonet from its steel black scabbard. I'd never had a great love of the Lebel rifle, but this bit of kit was something I'd come to take a personal pride in, mainly for its handle now glinting in the spasmodic but piercing moonlight. With the war in its third year, austerity meant bayonets now being issued with handles made of brass and no quillion, but mine was of the old design with a beautifully curved quillion and a handle fashioned from nickel-silver. Apart from marking me out as a comparatively 'old hand', that twenty-inch blade had always seemed a suitable sticking point to have between me and the enemy. This night could well prove whether or not that theory was a valid one.

We'd soon see. With no need for further words within hearing distance of the Boche, I gave my comrade a slap on the back, crawled my way out of the foxhole and slunk off as silently as I could in the direction Meunier had taken.

Up and down the Western Front, three million men were now engaged in desperate conflict, but here in this little corner of man-made purgatory I felt more alone than ever before in my life. Not that there weren't other men close by. I could still hear the working party, their grunts and occasional curses ever closer now as I inched my way forward. In spite of my perilous situation, I still had time to wonder at this crazy business in which we tried to kill men pumping the same blood, worshipping the same God and part of the very same humanity that loved life and feared death.

Perhaps now wasn't the time or place for such philosophy, especially as another ten yards of crawling brought me my first sight of them, four field-grey soldiers of the Fatherland shovelling away and their *stahlhelm* steel helmets and rifles stashed close by. Watching over them was the cursing NCO and, further away, standing aloof, straight-backed and seemingly arrogant even in this wretched hell-hole was their officer. Even more disconcerting was the man standing talking to him. It was *Sergent* Meunier.

The two were speaking in German, their actual words inaudible, but the content only too clear as Meunier pointed back to where our foxhole and Lee lay. A sharp order from the officer to the NCO had him barking instructions to his men who immediately dropped shovels, grabbed their rifles and helmets and prepared for action.

Clearly, Meunier had no intention of us ever returning to

our own lines and reporting his treachery. I needed to do just that, and the sooner the better, but first I had to collect Lee. Abandoning caution, I straightway hot-footed it back to him.

Perhaps some caution might still have been the wiser course. Not only was the working party close enough to hear my stomping feet galloping away, but sentries in the near-by trench system seemed only too glad to have something to occupy their tedious night-watch. There were some sharp utterances in German followed almost immediately by the zip of bullets winging their way through the moonlit night in my direction. I put an extra spurt into my wild dash.

But whereas clinging mud and pot-holed ground will slow even the fittest of men, it has little effect on flying bullets, especially as those Mauser 7.9mms had now been joined by an MG08 machine gun speaking with its characteristic metallic 'clack-clack'. As I stumbled past the discarded remains of some ammunition boxes I heard the clear-cut twang of a round striking home followed almost immediately by a searing pain in my left arm as the next corrected one found its mark. It spun me around and as I dropped, the ground beneath me seemed to open up as though Hell itself was admitting me to its unwanted bosom.

I hit bottom to find that instead of the fiery furnace, I'd landed, jarred, dazed and bleeding in the waterlogged bottom of an abandoned slit trench. I lay for a second, pulling myself together, catching my breath and thankful that I'd at least escaped the immediate attention of the *Deutsches Heer*.

This salvation though was bound to be very short-lived. That machine gun opening up had doubtless kept down the heads of pursuing Boche, but now they'd be fanning out to locate which little rat-hole I'd managed to disappear down.

And it didn't take long for one to find it. I heard pounding feet close by and had only a second to pull my bayonet from its scabbard with my one good arm. Then a figure appeared at the trench edge, going so fast that he slithered down to land within a foot of where I still lay. If finding me there was a surprise, he soon recovered. It was Meunier, fixing me with an icy grin and his 8mm *revolveur* aimed right at my heart.

For some reason, he hesitated to fire and I took advantage of the only hope I'd got, lunging forward with my bayonet and feeling it contacting with the side of his head. Whether his pistol fired with deliberation or simply due the shock of that bayonet strike, I didn't even try to analyze. My immediate concern being whether the flash and crack of that pistol meant it was game over anyway for Mark Kingsley. A second told me I was still breathing and with the pleasing sight of Meunier holding his hand to a very bloodied face, redness streaming through his fingers and his *revolveur* now dropped into the miasma of the trench bottom.

Time now to recover it and my wits quicker than him. That pistol was within reach, and I straightway dived for it, grasping its mud-slicked grip with my one good hand and aiming straight for our *sergent*'s heaving guts.

Perhaps I shouldn't have allowed myself a half-second to enjoy at least some semblance of fear in his treacherous eyes, because it turned out to be just a half-second too long. Even as my finger tightened on the trigger and he held up one hand, there came a furious burst of rifle-fire nearby, the crack of more than one Mauser and the returning fire of a familiar Lebel. The Boche had found Lee's position.

All the firing at my fleeing figure had surely alerted him and now he was giving some back, albeit against overwhelming odds. This new engagement was also distraction enough for Meunier, his face still a mask of blood, to take his chance to escape up the trench-side. Before I could even get a bead on his retreating backside he was gone, and then another furious ripple of firing close by told me where my priorities now lay. With my bloodied arm hanging useless at my side and the other still clutching the pistol, I used a pile of ammo boxes as my steps back to ground-level where I found that here, even in those furious last minutes, things had surprisingly changed.

Bright moonlight still bathed this battlefield with not even a hint of the approaching dawn. Above in that lunar light, the sky was now a myriad of stars, the cloud completely gone and the coldness of this graveyard hour intense enough to bring the ever-saturated air below its dew-point. The result was a heavy fog now rolling in to cloak any sight of friend or enemy alike and muffle even the sound of the continuing rifle-fire. Lee was still blazing off for all he was worth, well more than the eight rounds in his own Lebel and not time enough for a reload. I guessed he must have swapped to mine, but there couldn't be many more rounds left in that either and I quickened my pace in the direction of their cracks and, in so doing, ran straight into one of the enemy.

It was the NCO, still bellowing orders into the precipitating ether so loudly that he didn't hear my hurried footfall. Neither would he hear anything else again as a quick shot to his head had him dropping like a slaughtered bull. I hastened on and almost tripped over the body of yet another of the Germans, the blood still oozing from his chest where one of Lee's shots had obviously found its mark. There was no chance now, in the thickening fog, of either side getting a bead on the other, but it provided the blessed cover we needed for our own escape.

Another shot from a Lebel as Lee let the Boche know they still couldn't take him unscathed. By the same token, he could well use that last round on me as I emerged from the murk. I decided to take my chances on that and plunged on, rolling into the filth of that foxhole sooner than expected and with just enough consciousness remaining to see the startled figure on its other side raise his rifle and pull the trigger.

Instead of that familiar crack, there was just the click of the firing pin striking an empty chamber.

"Lee! ... for Christ's sake ... it's me."

"Mark ..." His relief seemed to mirror mine, "... I thought you were a gonner."

"I nearly was." Another shot rang out from a Mauser. The Boche were still out there probing. "And we both might still be if we don't get our asses out of here." I nodded in the direction of our lines. "Come on."

At that moment a starshell exploded overhead, its sparkling glow all the more eerie through the fog layer, but giving enough light for him to see my uniform was black with ebbing blood. "You're wounded?"

"In the arm, but my legs are still good, so hand me my rifle and be ready to give a helping hand when we're clear." Without further discussion we set off, stumbling as ever through the detritus of war, but knowing every yard we took was one away from the enemy and nearer our own lines.

We staggered on, but with me becoming increasingly aware that my blood loss might well exceed my remaining endurance. After clawing our way out of yet another tangle of barbed wire, I finally sank to the ground. "It's no good, Lee, I'm bushed. I can't go any further."

"You can if I help you. Let's get a tourniquet on that wound and then you can lean on me."

I shook my head. "I'll only slow you, and then neither of us will make it." My seeming self-sacrifice was actually an excuse for diminishing resolve. In spite of the icy cold, I just felt like lying down right there and going to sleep. For ever.

But Lee was having none of it. "No way. If nothing else, we need to get you back to report on what happened out there." He pulled off his scarf, tied it as a loop around my upper arm and used his own bayonet to wind it blood-stoppingly tight. "That should hold things until we get you to the medic. Now come on." He pulled me to my feet and then onwards, step by stumbling step with my rifle trailing beside me. "Use that as a support on your other side. It can't be far now. Remember the Legion never leave their weapons."

Or their wounded either, and Lee was intent on fulfilling both traditions. We lurched on before finally coming up to a particularly dense tangle of wire. To me it seemed insurmountable, but Lee recognised it for what it was. "It's our own front line, Mark. We're nearly there. I reckon it's worth the risk of identifying ourselves." Before I could protest he raised his hands to his mouth and called, "Bon jour, mes legionaires. Can you hear me? We are one wounded."

Back came a blessed French voice. "*Vous identifiez.*"

"Kingsley and Vennington. Eleventh first regiment de marche etranger."

"*Vous allez rester là jusqu'à ce que j'en décide autrement .*"

Personally, I had little option or inclination to do other than 'stay there until we direct otherwise', but agonising minutes later figures in blue-grey greatcoats emerged from the vapor on the other side of the wire, directing us just a little further down the line to where others were waiting by a guarded gap.

By the time we reached them, my feeble body was finally giving up and I collapsed completely into an exhausted heap at their feet.

The next I knew, I was opening my eyes, back in our old trench system, being tended by an orderly and with Lee standing close by.

He straightway broke into a smile. "Heh, looks like I'm not going to get your rations after all." It was a weak attempt at hilarity, but preferable to any other emotion, and I managed an equally insincere one in return.

"Your own fault, Lee. If you'd left me out there you'd be supping them by now."

"Ah well, something I'll probably always regret." He nodded towards the orderly's disappearing back. "*Capitaine* Icardo told him to let him know as soon as you regained consciousness. He wants to know what happened to Meunier ... and so do I."

I glanced about to check no-one was within hearing distance. "Like we suspected, Lee, the man was playing a double game, but let's just keep that between you and me. I'm just going to report that we were surprised by an enemy working party and our *sergent* went missing in action."

"If the guy's a traitor, why cover for him?"

"Because *we* know he was a fellow Yank, and that's something I'd prefer to stay between you and me."

There was little time for further argument before our company commander arrived. I told him of how the Boche seemed to be strengthening their defenses, falsely explained Meunier's disappearance and was almost ashamed when Icardo accepted it. "A good man lost," he said, sadly shaking his head, and I didn't disillusion him as he cocked his head towards our reserve trenches, the *zone des étapes* and blessed safety. "And now it is the hospital for you, *mon brave* and where they will take you at first light." Pausing, he indicated my old *Lebel* lying close by. "That is something you will not need for a while now, Kingsley, but good that you brought it back." He smiled. "You will make good legionnaires ..." he nodded towards Lee still standing close by, "... both of you."

As commendations went, this was as good as it got, but what none of us then realized was that fate was already bringing our time in the Legion to an end and that even greater adventures, and perils, in this 'war to end wars' still lay ahead.

*   *   *

CHAPTER THREE

A good walk back to my office to clear my head of old memories would have seemed the best plan right then, but I had an evening date back at *Winifred's* and things to do, so I took a cab and made up for the lost exercise by running up the three floors to my live-in chambers.

A phone call to the Precinct took some precedence and, between click and buzzes as the operator put me through, I sat back in my squeaky desk-chair and scanned what represented both my place of work and humble abode.

I'm not sure what Tara Magee had imagined my law office to look like, but doubtless her thoughts were a whole lot better than the reality. Across from me was a battered wooden filing cabinet surmounted by a model of a Nieuport fighter. To the side of that, my clients' couch sat as unused as was normal these lean legal days, but still with the blanket thrown aside from when I'd got Inspector Nolan's call, God knows how many hours before.

Was this really still the same day? So much had happened in the intervening hours and that thought alone made me realise how little sleep I'd had in the last twenty-four. No time now, though, for a catch-up with things to do before returning to that welfare centre for a sickly meal with the tetchy Miss Magee.

To keep my mind off that and sleep, I scanned the desk in front of me, barely visible beneath a scattered jumble of working case files and unpaid bills. The latter outnumbered the former ten-fold and enough to probably paper the peeling office walls where hung what amounted to a summary of my life so far.

There were some framed but faded photos of *Escadrille* days, comprising a line-up of Nieuports, their engines running as they warmed up for a sortie, one of me posing in front of my Spad and another standing beside Lee, us both looking appropriately war-like in our shabby kepis, tunics, breeches and leather knee-boots. Although only corporals, we flyers had been kitted out more as officers, giving us an air of dignity enhanced all the more by the metal pilot *brevet militaire* pinned above our breasts.

Dangerous days, but honorable ones compared to the fate Lee might now be facing. Between the photos was my framed lawyer's diploma, a fading scrap of professional proof that seemed woefully inadequate as the only thing standing between him and two-thousand volts in Sing Sing.

I was shaken out of that morbid thought by a formal voice in my earpiece telling me I was through to the 48th Precinct. A few more clicks and Inspector Nolan was on the other end.

"I guess you're calling for that witness description, for what it's worth." I could hear paperwork being turned over. "Right ... big man ... well over six feet ... well built ... bit of a bullet head ... close cropped hair ... nasty scar running down the left side of his face. Have you written that down?"

"I don't need to, Pat, but thanks a million."

"You're welcome and don't even tell me what you plan to do with it."

"Not yet, anyway, but any word from the DA with the Grand Jury date?"

I could almost hear him sigh. "Come on, Mark, you know

as well as I do that Grand Juries are secret and not something either you or your client need to know."

They were indeed almost clandestine affairs where only the prosecuting DA, a reporter and the sworn jury had the right to be present. Not a judge, a clerk, or even the defense lawyer with his client unless the latter decided to give testimony. Ninety-nine percent of Grand Juries voted for indictment and, with a police witness and no legal need to offer any exculpatory evidence, Lee's would, almost certainly be one of them.

No point in even arguing the point further with Pat either and so I hung up, consoling myself that perhaps a preliminary hearing in front of a judge, with not a gram of evidence so far to offer in Lee's defense, might have had an even more adverse influence on a later trial. What I *did* know, though, was that my main, and perhaps only, route to getting Lee an acquittal was by bringing the real perpetrator to book. I still didn't have a clue as to what motive Meunier might have for this crime, but I was convinced he was the man I needed to be after.

With that sliver of promise, I got preparing for my evening with Tara Magee. A handout meal in a church shelter wasn't the most attractive of prospects, but something I could put up with it if it gleaned some further information on how this girl's spiritual brother might have got himself murdered.

*   *   *

A few more scarce cents spent on another cab got me back to *Winifred's Welfare* and ringing the shelter doorbell at the appointed seven-thirty. It was answered by Tara herself, glancing back to the clock on the wall behind her.

"Right on the number, Mr Kingsley."

"That's an aviation background for you."

It was the best response I could make, distracted as I was by the girl herself. My recent memory of her as a slightly officious do-gooder in housecoat and ankle socks, had now been pleasantly obliterated by this transformed image in knee-length dress, shapely silk-stockinged legs and high heels that brought her face almost level with mine. A face that seemed so much softer, framed as it was by ringlets of auburn hair previously hidden beneath that ridiculous little cap. And I could even detect a whiff of perfume that almost neutralized the institutional odor already creeping out from the shelter behind. Sensing what I was thinking, she beckoned me in. "Don't worry, we'll be eating upstairs in my apartment."

Relieved, I followed her through the main canteen, still with a few lingering vagrants mopping up their evening fayre, and then up two flights of stairs to what was obviously a staff-only floor. Unlocking a door marked PRIVATE, she led me into a different world of homely domesticity and tasteful furnishings.

Taking off my coat, I extracted something concealed in the inner pocket and handed it across. "Here, just to make the evening a bit more special." It was my turn to read thoughts as she eyed the bottle like it was a live shell. "And don't worry, it's not hooch, but an old Bordeaux bottled well before the madness of this century's first quarter."

"But illegal, nonetheless, Mr Kingsley."

"Only if I'd bought it off some backstreet bootlegger. As it is, I earned it honorably fighting for world freedom."

"During your service in France?"

"Yep, and faithfully stored away for a time like this." Actually, I'd really brought it to mollify Tara Magee's pre-judgement of my client, but now my last statement seemed nearer the mark.

"Well it'll be a treat to taste something with a bit more zing than iced water again. Thanks." She placed the bottle on a small round table laid for two and ushered me into a nearby armchair before returning behind the counter of her open kitchen to finish whisking something. "Nothing 'special' about tonight's meal though, Mr Kingsley. Just plain ol'e American pancakes if that will do you."

"Certainly will, and kick that 'Mr Kingsley' will you ...Tara."

"Okay." She smiled again, but this time it was reflected in her eyes and wide enough to show white and even teeth, "Mark it is. At least for this evening."

A limited concession, but just the fact that she'd remembered my first name was enough for now.

As she went about the pancakes I took the chance to scan her pad. It was quite small but, with its velvet drapes, warm rugs and subdued light from silk-shaded lamps, clearly a haven of comfort from the harsh reality of life below. Reading appeared to be a major interest, going by the bookcase well-stocked with works on social welfare and modern art. In confirmation of the latter, I noticed two small French impressionist paintings adorning the wood-panelled walls, and was about to ask how she'd acquired them when I noticed the framed photo on her sideboard. I went over and picked it up, a studio portrait of a young man, fresh-faced, well-groomed, smiling and wearing army officer's uniform with the small cross of a chaplain pinned above his left breast. "This must be your brother?"

She nodded, sadly. "Richard ... yes ... he had that taken for me just before shipping out for France."

I indicated the paintings. "Did he bring you those two Durrennes?"

"Eugene Antoine." She seemed surprised that some dry as dust lawyer would even look at a painting, let alone recognise the artist. "You're obviously a lover of artwork yourself, Mark?"

I shook my head. "Not really, but Lee Vennington knew his masters and I picked up a bit from him during our leaves in Paris."

"Ahh. Well, yes, Richard found these in a backstreet gallery during one of his own Paris leaves." She rolled dark blue eyes. "They must have been an awful burden to haul back all the way here, but better than the usual gifts most doughboys brought home."

With or without that fancy lace and perfume, she didn't seem to be doing too badly, but I cast my eyes back to her brother's photo, taking in the firm chin and expression of complete loyalty that I could imagine being directed to his God, country, service or any other cause he felt would benefit from his strength of character. "He must have been a good man, your brother?"

"The best." She swallowed down a lump in her throat. "I'll miss him dreadfully. He was my only remaining family and had so much more to give to the world. Now he's gone."

But not his memory, ever, in this girl's heart. This might have been a good excuse to bring up his murder, but there was a magic right now I didn't want to break. Instead I nodded toward the pan she was holding. "The pancakes smell good."

She blinked, nodded and the smile returned. "Right, so let's have them while they're still hot."

Dishing them onto two large plates, she brought them to the table and I took my place across from her, pausing only for a moment's silence while she said a short grace. Then I opened the wine, poured us a glass each and raised mine in toast. "Here's to honesty, truth and justice."

"And may all three be found in the same court," she completed, perhaps a little cynically, before taking a sip and sighing. "Ah, that's good, Mark." She nodded towards the pancakes. "Better than this plain food I'm giving you."

I smiled. "Don't worry, I love simple home-cooking." I dug in with enthusiasm and the pancakes were indeed very good. "A meal like this was something I dreamed about in the trenches."

"So you were in the army yourself?"

"Yes, but not ours." She raised inquisitive eyebrows, so I quickly explained, "I was in Paris when it all began, decided I needed to play my part, and signed up for the *Legion Etrangére.*"

"The French Foreign Legion." She was wide-eyed now. "My goodness, that was a pretty extreme move wasn't it?"

"No more extreme than some of the other things I've done in my life ... like getting myself booted out of Harvard Law School."

"Oh dear." She said it with a half-smile rather than admonishment. "How did that happen?"

"Pure boredom, probably. Pouring over the hundred and one sections of some dull-as-dishwater Act wasn't my idea of living, whereas tinkering with my 1911 Harley-Davidson 7D V-twin seemed so much more worthwhile. Unfortunately, getting caught testing my latest re-tune by racing around the Old Yard coincided with the results of the end-of-semester exams."

"Which weren't good?" she asked with a half-smile over the top of her glass.

"Worse than bad, actually. I think the only thing they actually liked about my motor-bike was that it got me away from their hallowed halls all the quicker. My dad wasn't that pleased either, cancelled my allowance, told me I was worthless and that was the end of college fees." I shrugged. "Suited me anyway as I'd already decided I needed to see something of the world, so I sold my Harley and used the dollars to get me a passage on a cattle-boat to Europe."

"But you went on and eventually qualified as a lawyer?"

I raised my eyes and nodded, well aware of the contrary direction my life had taken. "I'm afraid so. I guess 'fighting the good fight' in France, had made me more than ready then for a spot of boredom. When I came home I did a season of barnstorming and instructing as a way of paying myself through Law School. That and making use of my semester hours at Harvard finally got me appointed to the New York Bar."

"So, do you still fly?"

"Unfortunately not. I can't say I'm snowed under with legal work, but what little I have keeps me pretty well grounded."

"I hope it's worth it."

She'd clearly guessed I wasn't the most high-rolling legal hack in the state, and now didn't seem the time for disillusionment. "I just about pay my way some months." I glanced again at her endearing face, that coy smile, the wisp of perfume drifting across that small table. "It is right now."

She wrinkled her nose in a way I hope showed under-standing. "Well, at least you're now safe and living in some comfort, which must be better than a mud-filled trench."

I nodded between mouthfuls of her delicious pancakes. "Amen to that, though I managed an upgrade from can-non-fodder quite soon in my Legion life."

"How come?"

"By catching myself a seven-millimetre round in my arm and getting shipped back to a field dressing station behind the lines. They got it out, but I needed some expert sewing up and convalescence and so I then got sent to ..."

*   *   *

"... Paris."

Even as I recounted that turning point in my life, my mind was ranging back to the *Jean-Antoine Villemin*, the military hospital conveniently situated between the *Gare du Nord* and *Gare de l'Est* that had been a Franciscan friary before finding a more martial role in the Napoleonic era. Despite its antecedents, though, there was precious little spiritual feeling now amongst the thousands of wounded jammed within its ancient walls. Here, the fragrance of incense had long been replaced by the sickly stench of suppurating wounds, and its peace, by the cries and groans of wounded warriors in far worse shape than me.

It was now early 1916 with the blood-bath of Verdun in full swing and casualties being counted by the hundred thousand, so perhaps we should have been grateful for a solid building rather than the many temporary wooden infirmaries now springing up around the city.

I for one, though, couldn't have cared less as to my abode as long as I left it soon and got returned to duty. Thankfully, that Mauser round had just missed my humerus, leaving just torn flesh and sinew to heal as fast as twenty stitches and moderate care allowed. That care had mainly been in the hands of young French nurses, many of them pretty, though mainly unappreciated by us patients, surrounded as we were by shattered bodies, pain-wracked life and incessant death. Little wonder then that the male libido was ever at low ebb in the *Jean-Antoine Villemin.*

For me though, the fact that those nurses were starting to appear ever more attractive was an indication that I was on the mend and ready again for action. Granted, to many, swapping a warm hospital bed for the squalor of the trenches might not have seemed the best of moves, but to me it was infinitely better than a moment longer in this cauldron of broken bodies. That escape though came sooner and in better form than I could ever have hoped.

It was spring by now, the first rays of sun beginning to find their way into our twenty-bed wards and a day when other female volunteers from the *Société de secours aux blessés militaire* came in to cheer our wearisome lives. Much as I enjoyed some interaction with these good ladies, this morning I was more intrigued by the tall, dark-haired, moustachioed figure following them in and asking, in a refreshing American accent, for me by name. Directed to my bed, he introduced himself as Doctor Edmund Gros, Director of the American Ambulance Corps.

It was certainly good to converse in my mother tongue again as he questioned my family background in New York, how I'd volunteered for this war, the nature of my wounding and subsequent recovery. I told him I wanted to return to active service as soon as possible.

"But not as a humble soldier in the trenches, surely?"

He made the statement as though he could offer a better alternative and I imagined him possibly considering me for transfer to his Ambulance Corps, an offspring of the American Hospital established in 1914 by wealthy Americans living in Paris. Manned solely by volunteers, it had performed invaluable and sterling service throughout the conflict, but I quickly pointed out to my distinguished visitor that it was a passive role, a whole way of life away from my own need for action. "Sorry, Doc, but I'm one of those who reckon the quickest way to stop this slaughter is by giving as good as we get."

Doctor Gros nodded agreement. "Indeed, Mark, and there is a place where you can continue that, but in a role far more tailored to your own talents."

I didn't understand, told him so, and asked him how he even knew I was here.

"The authorities have been very good at letting me know of any American volunteers returning to Paris." He smiled.

"You'd be surprised how many of you Harvard men have signed up with the French for the duration."

"Not many people know *my* background, Doc, so how do you?"

He winked conspiratorially. "By mentioning your name to one of *my* volunteers ... another Harvard man... Norman Prince ... do you know of him?"

I thought back to my own academic days and the mention of that name. "Sort of, but he was years ahead of me and eventually took up a practice in Chicago."

"But only for a year or so. Like you, he found the legal world not to his taste and instead applied himself to his real love of flying."

"Flying!"

He could see he'd caught my interest. "Yes. I'm no pilot myself, but it's clearly a vocation that spurs men to great things. Have you ever flown, Mark?"

"Unfortunately, no."

"Would you like to?"

"Viewed from the trenches, it's always looked a better way to fight a war."

"And something I know you'd be good at." He leaned a little closer and smiled. "Prince told me the story of your departure from Harvard. No glory for you there, but that sort of nerve and mechanical aptitude is just what we're looking for in the *Escadrille Americaine*."

"The what? Who are they?"

"An all-American unit of flyers who've already started building a reputation in the *Service Aeronautique* ... and you could be one of them."

I nodded. "Nice thought, but I've already told you I can't fly."

"Don't worry, you'll receive full training after an honorable discharge from the Legion and transfer directly to the French air service. And still with no loss of U.S. citizenship."

"Hmm." I'd always made a point of never agreeing to anything without at least a few minutes consideration. "And what are my chances of coming out of this caper alive?"

Doctor Gros shrugged. "No worse than spending the next few years dodging bullets in the trenches."

At least he was being honest. I took his hand and gave it a firm shake. "Doc, you've just talked me into it." I glanced outside at the cloudless spring sky. "Now tell me just how soon I can get soaring into the wild blue yonder."

*   *   *

"And so you became a pilot?"

Back in Tara's cosy apartment and reality, I was ten years on and happy that I'd managed to relate at least one pleasing aspect of my old life.

"Eventually, after four months training."

"And what about this Lee Vennington?"

"Same route as me. I got word to him about the *Escadrille Americaine*, and he hot-footed it to Paris on his next leave, made contact with Doctor Gros and signed up."

"You must have got to know him very well indeed." She fixed me with questioning eyes. "Enough to be convinced he didn't murder my brother?"

"Absolutely, but someone murdered Richard, and we need to suss out who. Can you think of anyone with a grudge or who might have crossed him lately?"

She shook her head. "No, nothing and no-one. Richard was loved and admired by all who came in contact with him, either at his church or this shelter."

"Not everyone, Tara. There was one who must have had some reason to violently kill him." I cast my mind back to the account Lee had given me of the priest's war service. "Your brother was a POW, wasn't he?"

"Yes, but only for a few months, before his status as a padre got him released on a prisoner exchange."

"Okay, but I'm wondering if he experienced or witnessed anything in that time."

"Such as?"

"I don't know, but perhaps something someone didn't want him talking about."

I could see this exercise was a painful one for her, but she was keeping control by rummaging her memories, and soon the welling in her eyes was replaced by a glimmer of recollection. "Yes, I do recall something now. It was when Richard was telling me of his journey into captivity. It was by train to Cologne, I think. Anyway, when he arrived at the station, I know he saw something that concerned him."

"Did he say what, exactly?"

"No, because he wasn't completely sure and refused to explain further, saying he was probably mistaken anyway and didn't want to be the cause of unnecessary suspicion."

"Hmm. Obviously it was significant enough for him to have mentioned it to you. Lee told me Richard was anxious about something and needed to discuss it with an old comrade. It could well have been connected to whatever your brother saw in Germany. I wonder what though. Do you have any idea?"

"Not specifically, but something did come up a week ago that seemed to upset him."

"Go on."

"Once again, he didn't say, but I remember it started while he was reading the morning paper."

"The newspaper?"

"Yes, the *New York Herald Tribune*. I'd gone around to the rectory to have breakfast with Richard, as I did every Tuesday morning to catch up and generally relax. Anyway, we'd finished eating and, over coffee, he was scanning the *Tribune*. Suddenly he spotted something in there that made him start."

"What?"

"I don't know, because he obviously didn't want to discuss it with me. I just remember him saying 'That can't be right!' and then hurriedly turning the page and changing the subject."

"And you've no idea what it was that disturbed him?"

"Not specifically, though he did say something about treachery and what a terrible sin that was."

'Treachery', that word again. "Did he say in what context, Tara?"

"Oh, just that he knew someone guilty of it and how it was a difficult thing to forgive."

"Did he say who he was thinking of?" I knew who *I* was thinking of, but needed confirmation.

But she shook her head again. "No, he didn't. I just assumed it was a hangover from his own army days, but something he didn't want to discuss."

"But, perhaps, connected to what he saw that morning on Cologne station?"

"Possibly, but he didn't say and I didn't want to push the matter. He'd got lots of painful memories from those war days, and the last thing I wanted to do was make them all the more vivid." She shook her head sadly. "Now I wish I had. If it's connected to his murder, perhaps I might have been able to steer him along a safer path."

"I doubt it, Tara. I didn't know Richard myself, but I'm imagining a man who followed his own lights wherever they led." I leaned a little closer. "You sure you've no idea what it was he spotted in the *Tribune* that morning?"

"No, though it could well have been some political thing he didn't agree with." She smiled reflectively. "Unusually for a priest, and probably as a result of all he'd seen in the war,

Richard did take a keen interest in politics and government, both federal and local, and closely followed everything to do with it."

"And you think what he read that morning might, perhaps, have been something political?"

"I just don't know, Mark. I'm only guessing, but he seemed very reluctant to share it with me, whatever it was." She shook her head more in frustration than denial and gave me an apologetic smile. "Sorry I can't be of more help."

I was just pleased she was finally using my first name. "Don't worry, you're doing great, and you might just have put your finger on something."

"I can't see how it will help if I don't know what."

"But we can find out. Did you happen to notice which page he was reading?"

"No."

"But you say this was last Tuesday?"

"Yes."

"So I need to get hold of the paper for that day and try and find some contentious issue."

"Will that really help though?" She pushed away her plate, the pancake only half-eaten. "Just because he may have spotted something that upset him wouldn't be cause to get him murdered would it?"

"It depends what it was." I wasn't going to let my own chance of a good meal get away that easily and quickly cleaned my plate of the last bite. "Did Richard normally discuss political matters with you?"

"All the time." She rolled her eyes. "He'd go on for ages about what was right and what was wrong, and I pretended to be interested though, in reality, I have very little interest in politics myself."

"But this time he chose not to discuss it with you?"

"That's right."

"Which makes me think it was something more serious than mere local shenanigans." I supped back the last of my wine. "Anyway, something to work on for starters."

"It all seems such a very long shot though." She got up and began clearing the table. "From what you say, the police seem intent on convicting your friend."

"Only because they're being pushed by Gary Shreeve. He's the Bronx DA, but with sights set on being the state's next Attorney General."

"Even if it involves prosecuting someone who may not be guilty?"

"I'm afraid so." I was glad she was starting to share my own take on things. "I'm not saying he'd knowingly send an innocent man to the chair, but it's awfully easy to convince yourself of anything if it helps your own cause and, let's face it, the evidence doesn't look good for Lee."

"Which is all the more reason *we* need to be sure." She sat down again and poured us both another glass. "So, how can we do that?"

Professionally, the '*we*' bit should have concerned me, but on a personal level I was definitely liking the idea. Nevertheless, I needed to still show some discretion. "I understand you wanting to be involved, Tara, but leave all that side to me."

"With what assets?" Cradling her glass in both hands, she leaned forward challengingly. "Come on, Mark, you sleep in your office and you dress not much better than some of those poor guys shacking up here for the night." Before I even had a chance to protest, she'd lowered her tone to one of mild compassion. "You're going to need more than loyal idealism to get the real take on this whole affair. I'm not saying I'm that flush with bucks myself, but I have a few and using them to find out who really did murder Richard will be worth every darn cent."

"But you've no experience of crime investigation," I countered lamely.

"No, but I'm a pretty good judge of human nature and that might be a better aid to you than that useless diploma you probably have pinned to your little office wall." She raised her glass. "So, how about you quit the macho-sleuth angle and we become partners in the pursuit of justice?"

There are times when stupid pride has to take second place to what seems both logical and infinitely agreeable and this was one of them. I raised my own glass. "Once again, Tara Magee, you've talked me into it." I leaned even closer, hoping this new-found companionship could be cemented with even more than wine and words.

But she drew away with a coy smile. "Good, and a full night's sleep and a clear head will get us going on that path all the better in the morning." She stood up and, rather disappointingly, handed me my coat. "So, off you go, Mark Kingsley ..." she paused while I begrudgingly put it on, but then took hold of both lapels and pulled me closer, "... but know that I'll be with you in more ways than one."

Her kiss had a wonderfully sensual warmth of sincerity, be it only a brief moment before she pulled away again and spun me around towards the door.

I accepted this cold dose of reality mixed with promise, and left with only the assurance I'd be in touch again as soon as I found something out.

Walking back to the office along those jaw-achingly cold Bronx streets, I knew, with warmth in my heart, that I'd already found something. Whether it would help or hinder justice was yet to be seen.

*   *   *

I awoke the next morning, not sure if my recollection of the evening before was enhanced by wine or my own wishful thinking. I chose to decide it was neither and felt glad I had at least one positive angle to work on. Ten minutes and a quick splash of cold water had me out on the main-street and another five approaching the small store of my local newsagent.

"Great to see you again, Signor Mark. You look good. How's business?"

With their good looks and natural charm, you can forgive the Italians for all their insincerity, though Mario's last enquiry might have been inspired by genuine concern. Anyway, I tried to sound convincing when I cheerfully answered, "Fine, thanks, Mario, and I should be able to clear my bill any day now, for ..."

"... twenty-one newspapers and three copies of *Aero Digest*," he completed. "And that was back when you were still reading, Signor Mark."

"Ah, yes. Too many case-files for that now, Mario," I hedged, "but I'm here to ask another favor. I need a copy of last Tuesday's *Tribune*. You do still keep back-numbers, don't you?"

He nodded enthusiastically. "Indeed yes. Some of my customers are very keen on backing the horse, and some like to check old results for ... how do you say...?"

"Form ... but that's not what I want it for, Mario. Let's say you'd be helping an innocent man clear his name."

"Then for him, and you, Signor Mark, I am happy to provide."

He disappeared down behind his counter and, after much thumping and rummaging, resurfaced proudly brandishing the requested edition. "Brilliant work, Mario. How can I ever thank you?"

"By winning the freedom for whoever this is going to help, and by settling your bill when you can."

"I promise, Mario, just as soon as I get my next Justice Department check."

And I meant that, but right now I was more intent on scanning that week-old edition of the NYHT. I headed to the nearest diner for a needed coffee and a table to spread the pages.

*   *   *

Like the scene of yesterday's breakfast, *Fat Harry's* wasn't the most salubrious eating place in the borough, but the atmosphere was always warm and cheerful, the coffee good and Fat Harry himself never minded over-stays of his hospitality just as long as you kept the orders coming. I ordered some eggs to go with my coffee, which I reckoned made me good for at least thirty minutes, and got scanning the print.

Rather than read every word on every page, I flicked through to see if anything caught my immediate attention and it was on page five that I found it. It was the photo of a well-built, smartly-dressed man posing to shake hands with an obvious down-and-out.

SENATORIAL CANDIDATE MILLER PLEDGES TO IMPROVE THE LOT OF BRAVE VETERANS

Reading through the accompanying article, I could see why this had caught Father Richard's attention. It explained how this Wilson Miller, 'a New York financier and industrialist' had gained sufficient backing at the primaries to offer himself as an independent candidate for the forthcoming election for Senator to the U.S. House of Representatives, and that one of his first campaigns would be to better the lot of 'all the brave boys who went out there and fought in the name of democracy.' Even more eye-catching was that the veteran in the photo was none other than my own client, Lee Vennington.

The piece went on to explain how Candidate Miller was determined to work with veterans such as Lee to get them the support they'd earned and needed. Just what Father Richard had found in this that 'wasn't right' didn't stand out, though there was something in that posed photo that left even me slightly uncomfortable. My eggs arrived, but I left them untouched while I studied that photograph in even greater detail to determine just what it was.

Then I saw it and those eggs remained uneaten as I pushed them away, paid my tab and set off for the 48th Precinct. It was going to be a long walk, but a good one to clear my head and concentrate on the whole new direction this case was taking.

*   *   *

CHAPTER FOUR

Arriving at the 48th, I was told that Pat Nolan was busy on some other case but, after hearing from the desk sergeant that Lee's Grand Jury hearing in the Bronx County Court was scheduled for next day, I got clearance for a quick interview with my client.

"How's it going, Lee?" Down in the cells, I asked the question even though I could see his spirit had hit rock bottom.

"Not so good." He took my offer of a *Camel* and we both lit up. "So, my indictment hearing comes up tomorrow." He leaned closer with an almost pleading look. "You will be there to defend me, won't you?"

I'd been fearing this question and the answer I had to give. "No, Lee, I won't be there, because you won't be either."

"You're not serious." He sat back again like a man who's just taken a blow in his solar plexus. "Why not?"

I glanced down at his spare haggard frame and tattered clothing. "For starters, your appearance. That jury would only take one glance at you to have you down as guilty as hell."

"You mean it's an offence now to be destitute? Surely that could be put right by you fixing me up with a suit or something?"

I shook my head. "No time for that now, Lee. I could try and file for an adjournment, but with Shreeve flat out for a trial it wouldn't get past the first hearing and even if it did, it would only delay the inevitable."

"That I'm going to be convicted?"

"No, that you're going to be indicted. The only purpose of the Grand Jury will be to decide if there's a case to answer and whether you should go for trial." I took a drag on my cigarette. "Unfortunately, with a glory-hunting DA like Shreeve pushing his case, we've a snowball's chance in hell of avoiding it, and you giving testimony could only make it worse."

"How come?"

"Because, right now, there's nothing you could say that DA Shreeve wouldn't blow into the next county. Believe me, our best bet is for me to get some real evidence to present at trial."

He took a deep breath and shook his head. "So only you can save me from the chair."

"Me and the truth, Lee," I forced a smile of encouragement, "but a long time yet before it comes to that and, in the meantime, I'm going to pursue some leads and get that evidence. For starters, I need to know if you ever showed Father Magee a photo of Meunier?"

He thought deeply and then smiled with recollection. "Yeah, I did, come to think of it. A group picture they took of our *escouade* back in Toulouse. But why is that significant?"

I told him about the piece I'd found in that week-old *Tribune*. "You didn't tell me you'd chummed up with that prospective senator."

"What, Wilson Miller, you mean? Yep, nice guy. I hope he gets in, because he seems to genuinely want to improve the lot of us vets."

"In what way were you going to 'work' with him?"

Lee took a drag of his *Camel*. "Simply explaining how little the government wanted to know about shell-shock and other combat-related mental issues." He shrugged. "I'm just one example in thousands, but I guess I might have explained it a little more articulately."

"I'm sure you did." I took the newspaper clipping from my notebook and pushed it across. "In your meetings with the senator-elect, did you notice anything familiar about him?" He pulled it closer and frowned. Our time was short, and so I gave him a hint. "Look closer at that tall, broad figure and that bullet head. Knock thirty years off his appearance and tell me who he reminds you of."

He stared again at the posed camera smile that failed to hide an air of suppressed ruthlessness that bode ill for anyone opposing whatever ambition he was currently nursing. And then recognition dawned. "My God, it looks just like Meunier."

"Exactly. My guess is that he's our old Legion comrade's father, and that Father Richard saw that photo and recognised a threat you needed to be warned of."

But Lee still didn't seem convinced. "Warn me of what?"

"That Wilson Miller could be Meunier's father. Did you ever tell Richard about Meunier?"

"I might have."

"Well that right there could be motive enough. If Wilson Miller suspected that Richard knew of his son's treachery, it would be threat enough to his senatorial ambitions to have him disposed of."

"That would still leave me to spill the beans though."

"Not if *you* were fingered for the murder and then got speedily indicted and tried." It was time for brutal truths. "One two-thousand volt blast of Sing Sing's chair would ensure for good that the truth *never* came out."

He gulped, stubbed out his smoke and sat back to consider that very disagreeable option. He still had one objection to the theory though. "But the names don't tie up, Mark. It might be just a coincidence that Meunier and Wilson Miller have a resemblance."

I stood up to go. "Not the way I see it. Remember, the Legion always gave the option of having an alias. If you finished your service you even got a French passport in that name. But we're missing the most obvious clue here, Lee. Our senatorial candidate is called Miller. A miller ground corn. Tell me the French name for a miller."

He slapped his head. "Of course! *Meunier*."

*   *   *

"Wilson Miller! What do you want to know about him for?"

I'd been more than happy to have a reason to call Tara Magee again so soon, even though my sleuthing ability seemed to fill her with little confidence, and even less when I explained that I was pretty sure it was Miller's photo in the *Tribune* that had caught her brother's attention. "I've only got a vague suspicion of 'why', but a bit more family background might give me something more to go on."

I could hear the rattle of kitchen pans in the background preparing the day's handout. She was doubtless pretty busy, which probably accounted for her slightly clipped response. "I don't recall Richard ever mentioning him other than in general terms about the forthcoming election. I certainly don't think he knew him personally." She gave an impatient sigh. "Sorry I can't help further."

"I think you might though. I need to know more about this Wilson Miller and whether he has a son. I was hoping you could find this out for me."

"I thought you were the great investigator? I'm busy here. Why can't *you*?"

"Because I'm thinking that your brother might have polit-ical contacts who may be able to help."

"I *might* know someone. I'll make a call this afternoon. If I find anything, how can I reach you?"

"How about me standing you supper tonight and hearing what you've found out then?"

"It might be nothing."

"I'll take the risk on that. Whatever, I'll be glad anyway to repay your hospitality of last night, so how about meeting me at *Mancini's* on Arthur Street at seven?"

There was a slight pause before she sighed quietly and said, "Okay, but I'm not promising anything but an appetite."

* * *

I was hoping that wouldn't be too great as I approached the restaurant on the dot of nineteen- hundred, its illuminated sign swaying slightly in the drizzle-laden gusts blowing down this main street of the borough's 'Little Italy'.

Mancini's was a slightly upmarket joint where one of my more affluent clients had once treated me to lunch. It hadn't been cheap and this evening I'd raided my practice emergency fund for what I hoped was enough.

I found Tara already there, waiting inside wearing a small cloche hat and fur-collared coat, which I took from her as Mancini himself showed us to a conveniently discreet candlelit table in the far corner. As she scanned the menu I told her how good it was to see her again and she smiled and said it was nice for her too. Then Mancini was back to take our orders and, while we waited for the food to be served, she reached into her purse and pulled out a small notebook.

"Right, the information you wanted on Wilson Miller, which was pretty easy to find, seeing as he's been making the local news for the last few months."

"I'm not a great newspaper-reader," I confessed, while managing, just for a few seconds, to stop eyeballing the figure before me in light-blue dress and wearing little makeup. She seemed prettier than ever in the candlelight, pushing back her long wavy hair while those blue eyes scanned neat lines of notes.

"I gathered that. Anyway ..." she flipped some pages, "... it seems Wilson Miller is a second generation immigrant who inherited an engineering business from his father and then went on to expand it into other fields."

"Such as?"

"A variety of concerns, but all aligned with technical research and development. Naturally, they prospered in the Great War with government contracts, especially in their aviation division."

My water glass stopped halfway to my lips. "Aviation!".

"Yes, I thought that would get your attention." She glanced back at her notes, smiling. "They still have a research base somewhere, but the only aviation concern here is a flying school on Governors Island."

Mancini arrived with our meals, a bolognese for me and a risotto for her. I topped up our water glasses, as much to give myself time to remember what I knew of the small isle just off the southern tip of Manhattan.

"Governors does have quite an aviation history. That's where Wilbur Wright flew from in 1909 for a flight around the Statue of Liberty. Then Glen Curtiss landed there from Albany in1910 to win a $10,000 prize. I seem to recall the army had a flying training base on the island in the war, but I didn't know about the civilian outfit flying from there."

She shook her head. "No, there's not too much to be found about that except it's called Miller Air Services and that they operate six Curtiss ..."

"... Jennies?" I offered, before she found it in her notes.

She nodded. "Correct. But you would know that, wouldn't you?"

"Only because I flew one when I was barnstorming around the country. A nice old kite, if a bit underpowered with not the most reliable of engines, but it did the job." I paused to wind some spaghetti onto my fork. "I can't help thinking it would pay me to visit Miller Air Services."

She stopped eating and gave me a suspicious look. "To find out ... what?"

"I'm not sure until I've scoped out the place, but if they keep the operation a bit under wraps there might be some clue that connects to Richard's murder."

"I don't see how." Her skepticism came over as clearly as her snappy words. "Surely you'd be just wasting time on the strength of some news item that may or may not be the piece that disturbed my brother."

"Except there was something in that photo that disturbed me as well."

"Really? What?"

"Something that may be just a coincidence or a definite link to the whole mystery. I can't say more though until I've checked things out." I left it there, preferring not to stretch her incredulity even further by mentioning the likeness of Wilson Miller to Meunier.

"But, what motive could an established figure like Wilson Miller have for getting involved in such a despicable crime? Why would the head of a wealthy corporation and a senatorial candidate want to murder someone as popular as Richard?"

"Perhaps the answer to that lies in his very ambition. When you're running for high office, just a hint of scandal could scuttle your chances. I'm thinking Richard knew something no-one else does. If that newspaper piece triggered a memory, perhaps he went so far as to contact Wilson Miller direct, got a violent reaction and then contacted Lee as someone to 'watch his back'. We'll never know one way or the other if I don't check it out."

"Or give yourself the treat of some kickback to your flying days."

I'd have argued with that if I hadn't already admitted to myself that the thought of once again being close to fabric wings and roaring engines didn't have some personal allure. Instead I tried to soften the atmosphere with an attempt at nonchalance. "It won't take me long and I'll let you know what I find."

Her eyes narrowed slightly. "I've got a better idea."

"Which is?"

"That I come with you to Governors."

I smiled and shook my head. "Not a good idea, Tara. This is probably one investigation better done alone."

"You think so?" She put down her fork and leaned closer. "Well, Mark, this is my brother's murder we're investigating here, remember, so I'd like to be there. And, just in case you think I'd be some sort of drag on your 'investigation', tell me just how you plan to get out to the island."

"I guess I'll find some boatman to run me there."

"Paid for with what?" Those lovely eyes gave an impatient roll. "Admit it, Mark, you don't have two spare cents to rub together, let alone some bucks to go slipping your mythical boatman."

"Well ..." But that was as far as I got.

"'Well'... what?" Then her tone softened to something more like the compassion I'd seen during last night's supper. "Look, Mark, it might surprise you to know that I do have access to a boat."

"You do?" This girl was full of surprises and I liked this one. "How come?"

"An old friend of my late father. He used to take Richard and me for trips together out in the bay, but now he's getting past boating and hasn't used it in years. He's kept the boat though and said it was mine to use anytime I wanted."

"What, even in winter?"

"Why not? It's kept in a boatshed on Manhattan's Lower East Side, so it won't take us long to reach the island. I'll call him tonight and fix it up."

"Sounds good, but who's going to drive the thing?"

"Me of course." She dived back into her risotto with renewed enthusiasm. Clearly this was a girl who liked a bit of hands-on action. For my part, I had the feeling that in the last two short minutes, rather than controlling events, life was now controlling me. Strangely, it was something I didn't find that disagreeable but, just to bring the ball back a little bit into my court, I asked another question. "Did your research find out if Wilson Miller had any children?"

She nodded between mouthfuls and flicked a couple of pages in her notes. "Yes. In 1883 he married and a year later they had an only son, Carl."

"So, this Carl would now be forty-two?"

"Yes."

Which meant he would have been thirty in 1914, just the age Meunier seemed when I first encountered him in Tolouse. I dug back into my own bolognaise, more assured than ever that I was on the right track.

*   *   *

We arrived at the East River boathouse early next morning, but not by the streetcars I'd planned, thanks to yet more support by Tara.

She'd called me later that night, only an hour after our supper date, to confirm she'd not only got loan of the boat, but also the use of an automobile for the day. "One of my brother's worshippers who had a high regard for him," she explained. "He gave Richard the use of his auto for getting around the more far-flung outposts of the parish. Unfortunately, though, Richard couldn't drive, so I chauffeured him when the need arose."

"You drive yourself?"

"Of course. Why not?"

I realized I'd said the wrong thing, and bit my tongue even more next morning when she rolled up outside my office block, dead on the stroke of seven, in an open two-seat Dodge 30 Roadster. I pulled my old flight jacket closer around me and climbed on board.

"Nice wheels, Tara, if a bit drafty for a New York winter."

"Surely not something to bother an old fighter jock who spent the war in open cockpits."

I noticed she was swathed in thick overcoat, woollen neck scarf and tea-cosy hat, but didn't get the chance to offer a defense before she'd given the engine a bootful of revs, shoved the three-speed gear into first and shot us into a tight u-turn that had us straightway heading southwards towards Manhattan. "And, anyway, I figured if we're going to be speeding down-river in an open boat, a bit of preliminary acclimatization might be a good thing."

"Absolutely." I sat back to enjoy the ride as she skilfully double-declutched us the through the Bronx's lower district between horse-drawn wagons making their early morning deliveries, streetcars full of commuters en route to their downtown jobs and an ever-increasing number of automobiles. As we cleared the Willis Avenue swing bridge and on into an even busier Manhattan, she turned towards me with a half-smile, her scarf and wisps of escaping auburn hair flailing in the slipstream.

"Not far to go now to the boatyard. Then it'll be a quick

trip across the Buttermilk Channel, and you'll be back in the world of flying."

"Sounds good, though I doubt Miller Air Services will be doing a whole lot of flying just yet." For visibility was rapidly decreasing as we neared the waterfront, with the East River itself cloaked in a dense fog that shrouded the now-redundant shipyards and dry-docks along its banks. After several more miles, a dilapidated boatyard emerged from the clag and Tara announced we'd reached our destination.

First impressions weren't encouraging. With not a living soul to be seen, the whole yard had an almost haunted air, while the leaning, low-roofed clapboard main-shed suggested the boat inside would be anything but ocean-going.

"It'll be big enough," assured Tara, accurately diagnosing my thoughts while expertly backing the Dodge between the rotting skeletal hull of some abandoned workboat and a pile of rusting deck gear, "so don't worry." I saved my response until I'd seen the actual craft, though her faultless driving here suggested she was more than competent to skipper us out to the island.

In fact, Tara Magee seemed to be one of that growing band of females who, buoyed by the way they'd competently taken over men's jobs in the war, now felt the world was a place they could enjoy on equal terms. Already, some were learning to fly and, given half a chance, I could imagine her up there with the best. But I kept those thoughts to myself as we climbed out and I followed her to the boathouse's small entry door. It needed a whole lot of wrenching and pulling before finally admitting us to its interior where flotsam-filled river water lapped against the rotting dockside. I peered through the stygian gloom, anxious to see just what was going to bear us to the island.

But, already, Tara was hauling back one of the big outer doors to admit fog-filled light that revealed a sleek speedboat way above my expectations. "Gee whiz, Tara, a Chris-Craft 26."

She nodded. "Right first time, Mark, but I didn't know you knew about boats."

I almost made a joke about female patronization, thought better of it, and instead explained I had an interest in anything with lots of power under the lid.

And the source of this boat's power was all too familiar when we lifted the dust-covered hatches and peered into the midships machinery space. "Heh, it's a Curtiss OX-5, the same engine used in the Jenny."

"Is that good?"

"Eight cylinders giving ninety horsepower at fourteen hundred rpm. It's certainly enough power for a boat."

"But one you reckoned wasn't too reliable." Her eyebrows did a slightly cynical rise. "So, let's see if we can get it started."

"We will, but this V8 is liquid-cooled, so first job is to check the coolant level." I twisted off the cap on the header tank, saw there was some liquid in there and screwed it back. "That's fine. How about fuel?"

"The owner said he'd left her with full tanks."

"But, judging by all this dust, pretty old, so it'll have lost some of its guts, but let's give it a try." My only experience of this engine was swinging the prop on a Jenny, but this marine version had a crank handle. "Can you remember the settings for getting it burning and turning?"

"I think so." She pulled off the canvas cover of the for'ard cockpit, revealing a largish steering wheel and assorted levers and knobs, which she started arranging into some sort of workable order. "Let me think ...retard back ... throttle set an inch ... ignition on and ... give that a go."

I swung the handle a few turns and the only thing seeming set to go were my lungs. I straightened up for air and ideas. "It probably needs priming." I felt around the carb, located the small needle valve and gave it a generous few pumps. "Right, let's try again, and ease back that throttle just a smidge."

"Okay."

I cranked away again and, just when I thought we'd got a dead engine, it gave a couple of coughs and started turning over. Nothing too dramatic at first with just a couple of cylinders firing, but at least it was trying. "Don't open that throttle any more just yet." She complied and, one by one, the old jugs kicked in until the boathouse was full of exhaust smoke and we had a full eight firing away. With the engine settling down to a throaty rumble, I shouted for her to bring it back to a nice warm-up tick-over while we opened the other main door before dying of asphyxia.

With that done, she leaned against the shed-side and ran a hand through fog-dampened hair. "Great stuff, Mark. I don't think I would have got that going on my own." It was an admission enough for Tara Magee and I chose to just nod a smile while we paused to scan outside. It was still thick fog out there and it would have been back to the crew room in my flying days. "Do you reckon you can find Governors in this?"

She nodded. "Shouldn't be too big a problem. I'll just head downriver until we're in the channel, and then it's just 800 yards across."

"Sound's good, so let's go."

Back in the boathouse, the extra light was showing up the Chris-Craft's fine lines and workmanship for the beauty they were. Beneath a year's accumulation of dust and grime, the varnished mahogany and brass deck fittings screamed for polish but, even in that state, the boat seemed as eager as us to get some miles under her planing hull once more. With the engine now settled into a steady purr, we could do just that.

"Okay, Tara, you get behind the wheel and I'll slip the lines."

With that done, I followed her into the cockpit where

she upped the revs to slide us smoothly out into the winter sunshine now breaking through the gloom. Out on the river, we straightway turned south towards its outlet and the Hudson. A quick glance at the gauges showed cylinder head temps nicely stabilizing and oil pressure steady at sixty psi, which was good enough for Tara to ease the throttle steadily open until that OX-5 behind us had changed from a purr to a healthy roar. The result was the Chris-Craft surging up onto the step to produce a rapidly creaming wake that rolled steadily shorewards towards the metropolitan skyline just faintly visible on each side.

We were off to Governors Island, and I only hoped the results would be as good as this exhilarating means of getting there.

*   *   *

I was glad to see the fog thinning to mist by the time we cleared the East River and surged out into the relatively open water of Buttermilk Channel. Soon, Governors Island itself was coming into view, the lushness of its greenery in sharp and pleasing contrast to the urban concrete we'd just left. Seemingly in her element at the wheel, Tara upped the revs even more and headed towards its northern end.

"The main jetty's on the other side, which means we'll have to make a half-circumnavigation."

And so we went powering around, our speedy craft throwing up a rooster-tail of prop-wash and me slightly concerned at the sight of impressive military installations now appearing between the woodland. Perhaps I'd been premature in my relief at losing the fog. By the time the jetty came into view and we slowed for our approach, even the mist had cleared enough to make us feel as exposed as a black panther sneaking across a snow-covered baseball diamond. Thankfully, as Tara brought us in towards the piled wooden jetty, no-one had, as yet, challenged our visit and the several other boats already moored alongside seemed to indicate more general use than I'd expected.

"Probably, staff and students from the flying school," I offered as explanation as I leapt ashore with the lines, pleased our mission was so far going unhindered.

Tara shut down the launch's engine and climbed up onto the jetty to join me. "So far, so good, but we're going to run into someone eventually. What explanation will you give then?"

"Simply that I'm here to enquire about some flying."

"What flying?"

"Perhaps a bit of re-training. It *is* eight years since I poled anything."

"Training paid for with what?" Miss Magee was maintaining her realistic approach to everything. "The way I see it, right now you haven't enough to fly a kite."

"No, but I can dream."

We set off towards what was clearly the island's old wartime flying-training field. On our right were wooden barrack blocks, now-empty, but ahead was a row of buildings comprising a couple of hangars and some wooden offices and, beyond them, a long grass airstrip running south-east/north-west. We headed towards the buildings and the gladsome sight of some biplanes already being wheeled out of the hangars. Curtiss Jennies.

As we reached the flight-line, a helmeted instructor pilot and his pupil were walking out to one, the IP demonstrating with his hands the maneuvers they'd be covering that morning and the pupil doubtless wondering if he'd ever get the hang of this whole crazy business. External checks completed, they were soon climbing into their cockpits, a mechanic standing ready to swing the prop while we took a seat on a nearby bench to watch a procedure that had once been a daily part of my own life.

"Switches off and throttle closed," ordered the mechanic.

"Switches off and throttle closed," confirmed the student.

"Sucking in." The mechanic turned the prop a good eight times.

"Throttle set."

"Throttle set."

"Contact."

"Contact."

The mechanic took hold of the upper blade of the big wooden prop with both hands and pulled firmly downwards. There was a cough and a splutter as the OX-5 fired, and then the exhaust smoke was drifting back in the propwash as the engine gradually picked up on all eight jugs. As it warmed at low revs, I watched the elevators, rudder and ailerons all moving in different directions as the student checked the flying controls. And then he was waving away the chocks and giving a burst of power to get the Jenny slowly rolling towards the threshold of the south-west runway, lurching along in a series of gentle curves so he and the IP could see either side of its long nose.

Then they were lining up with the runway and slowly opening the throttle, and I could imagine the pupil working hard on the pedals to keep his aircraft straight as the prop-torque tried to swing it to the left, getting the tail up into flying attitude as they bounded down the grass strip gaining flying speed.

Back in 1912, the OX-5 had been the first mass-produced US designed aero engine, certainly not the most reliable and, even for the Jenny, a bit low on power, but it still did the job fourteen years hence and, halfway down the strip, the Jenny was getting airborne, building up speed and finally climbing away.

I watched it gaining in height for whatever exercises the IP had planned. The pupil would be intent on listening to his instructions above the roar of the engine and the rush of the slipstream, doing his best to learn the skills necessary to survive in the unforgiving realms of the sky.

Tara turned to me smiling. "Bring back memories?"

It certainly did, and as I watched the Jenny bank into a climbing turn, the purr of its engine seemed to envelop me like a blanket of nostalgia as I was transported back into those heady days of 1916 and miles away to the *Ecole Bleriot* at Buc and my own first initiation into the joys of powered flight.

*   *   *

Close by Versailles, this French aviation school was where Lee and I found ourselves in the spring of that year, the momentous battle on the hills of Verdun-sur-Meuse now in full swing, and us grateful we were being spared a share of the carnage. Not that flight training wasn't taking its own greedy toll of young life but, with the innocence of youth, we all accepted that as a fair price to pay for entry to this newest of man's endeavors.

Before exposure to those dangers, though, came weeks in classrooms learning theory of flight and map reading and, in the workshops and hangars, getting our hands on aircraft rigging, engines and machine guns. With our Legion training and experience, the latter came easily to both Lee and myself, and my own love of anything mechanical made the technical training a pleasure rather than a chore. Being more artistically inclined, that was all new to Lee, but I helped him out on the mysteries of compression ratios and ignition timing and a month saw us both passing that phase and getting flying proper.

Or at least we got to sit in and handle an aircraft on the ground. For our birds were clipped wing Bleriot X1 monoplanes, the same kite that Louis of that name had first crossed the English Channel in 1909. Even with full-size wings, their original 25hp Anzani three-cylinder semi-radial engines had always struggled to get man and machine into the air, but our 'Penguin' versions were never intended to do even that. Instead, they'd been modified to simply initiate us into the joys of high-speed taxiing. Although assigned an *instructeur*, this lucky chap never actually flew with us, but simply offered advice as we practiced fast runs along the strip with the tail up while getting the feel of the controls. When we'd got the hang of this we were let loose with a 45hp engine to feel the aircraft getting light on its wheels and airborne for a few seconds before we closed the throttle and returned to earth without running out of strip. Finally, with full-sized wings, we were sent off for a complete circuit of the field at about eight hundred feet.

We all approached that step with some apprehension, though in Lee and my case, an element of competition to be the first. My motor-cycling had certainly prepared me for handling vibrating machinery and speed, but Lee had done plenty of horse-riding in his youth which put him almost on equal par. Added to this was his artistic temperament, which seemed to express itself now in an empathy with this new element and a natural 'feel' for flight.

As it was, we both completed our *tour de piste* on the same day, after which we had three more weeks of exhilarating solo flight, building up our hours and confidence as we went higher and further and took more and more risks. Then, with 100hp Bleriots, we completed two cross-country flights of

150 miles, impressively termed *le grand voyage*, were awarded our brevets and promoted *caporals*. Now we finally felt ourselves real *aviateurs* and truly members of the *Aeronautique Militaire*.

Then it was off to Avord for advanced training on aircraft more akin to what we would eventually fly in combat. There were a miscellany of types available here, mostly machines surpassed in the ever-more frantic race for aircraft supremacy. As it was, the Nieuport 10s assigned to us – single-seaters with 80 hp Gnome Lambda engines – seemed scientific wonders compared to our old Bleriots, and more like the *aeroplane de chase* flown by the first pilots to be designated aces and who were now hitting the daily front pages.

I think we all had dreams of joining in their glory, and our flying now was focussed on doing just that by learning a whole new ball-game of stalls, spins and aerobatics taught by *instructeur*s who were combat veterans, teaching from experience how to bring trouble to the enemy and how to get out of it when they returned the favor.

Now we felt we were really preparing for the fray, going off alone to practice slinging our craft around and finding out for ourselves just how far we could stretch its limits to breaking point. And then one did!

I'd got about five hours in the Nieuport 10 now and was feeling myself a bit of an ace already as I practiced combat maneuvers, which in those early days were limited to steep turns, spins and loops. But I'd heard of one German ace called Immelmann who was already making a name for himself with some extreme turn to which he'd given his name. The way I understood it, the *Immelmann turn* entailed making a pass at the target and then pulling up into the first half of a loop but, on the top, instead of falling through in the normal way, actually rolling the aircraft level, to end up facing the bewildered quarry head on and guns blazing. This bit of stunting had already cost several allied lives and, it seemed to me, the best way to avoid joining that number was to learn the trick myself.

So, with five thousand feet below me and a clear sky ahead, I tightened my safety belt, stuck the nose of the old Nieuport down for extra speed and then eased back the stick into the first part of a loop. There was the now familiar sensation of being pushed into my seat by the extra forces generated and the earth turning on my wingtip as I went up through the vertical, speed bleeding off and me feeling the old kite up and over the top until an inverted horizon started appearing over the nose. Normally at this point, with speed recovering, I would have checked the wings were level for the second half dive. Today though, I just allowed the speed to build up and then brought the stick hard over to instead half-roll her back to level flight.

That, at least, had been the aim. Perhaps I hadn't got myself enough speed before the roll. Perhaps I'd used too much aileron. Whatever, before I was even halfway through, the Nieuport gave a sickening lurch and fell away. With all control lost and me hanging suspended in my safety belt, everything loose in the cockpit went tumbling earthwards. I prayed I wouldn't soon join them and slowly the blessed old bird responded to my pleas by gathering some speed and falling away into a steep dive. I got control of my nerves and the aircraft again at about the same time and eased us back into level flight, but with the aircraft seeming to handle somewhat strangely. Scanning my array of wire rigging soon told me why: to my horror I saw that with every input I made to the controls, the whole port lower wing was moving slightly on its centre section. That weightlessness I'd experienced falling out of the *Immelman* was clearly more than the Nieuport 10 was ever designed to take and the forfeit now was a wing all set to depart forever and my life with it.

I gingerly tried a bank into the gentlest and slowest of turns back towards Avord airfield, my haven just a few miles away. Next was to ease back the power and bring my stricken aircraft into a glide as though it were made of glass. With just the sound of the wind in the wires now, I descended earthwards, my ears pricked for the slightest sound of a catastrophic CRACK and my eyes constantly scanning the wing that was now flexing alarmingly in the ever-more turbulent lower air.

Steadily I descended to three thousand feet ... two thousand feet ... one thousand feet ... five hundred. There were thankfully few aircraft in the training circuit and it wouldn't have made any difference if there were, because I was coming straight in to get these wheels back on the blessed earth as soon as I possibly could.

But I was too high. In normal circumstances, a bit of tight maneuvering would have soon got rid of that extra height, but that was out of the question with this frail collection of spars all set to fly apart. The alternative though was an overshoot into the rough ground beyond the field, and that seemed equally unacceptable. I was left with just one option, and that was a sideslip.

Crossing controls was a rough, but effective, way to get rid of extra height on an approach. I'd used it just a few times before and figured that if I did one now to the right with my port wing in the lee of the slipstream, I might just bring it off. I rolled the aircraft down onto its starboard wing and gave it full left rudder to keep it straight.

That surplus height certainly started winding off as we went sideways downward, the slipstream on the right side of my face and the aircraft all askew to its desired direction of landing. But I was in the right part of the strip now and could bring everything level with stick and rudder. I centralised both and, as I did so, heard that ominous crack I'd been dreading.

Immediately the aircraft rolled to port and I knew that wing had finally given the ghost and detached completely.

I'd rolled almost completely onto my port side as we hit the ground, the Nieuport then changing from a wounded bird into a spinning fiery wheel as we rotated across the field, the ship disintegrating around me and the first flash of exploding fuel as the ruptured tank shed its contents over the still-hot engine.

Semi-conscious, I vaguely sensed the heat and crackle of what could now well be my funeral pyre. Part of the cockpit side and God-knows whatever other bits of the aircraft had got me trapped as I heard voices yelling orders in French, and one American saying, "Okay, Mark, we'll soon have you out."

It was Lee, ignoring the heat and flame around him to feverishly pull away the imprisoning wreckage, unbuckle my belt and haul me clear.

Then I was lying in blissfully cool grass, pulling myself back to consciousness from the bang I must have given my head, and Lee bending over me with a relieved smile.

"Looks like I won't be helping myself to your girlfriend list just yet."

I wiped away the trickle of blood from my bashed nose. "If I keep putting my face through the wringer at this rate, it won't do me much good anyway." I gave his arm a grateful squeeze. "But thanks, Buddy. Now I owe you for a second life-save."

He wrinkled his nose. "Don't worry, you'll get to save mine before this war's through."

*   *   *

"I'm guessing not all those memories are good."

Sitting there on that bench, Tara must have seen that anguished glaze in my eyes.

"No, not all of them." I told her of my training crack-up and owing yet another life to Lee.

"I can see how you feel you should help him now, but you won't by doing too much day-dreaming." She nodded towards the airfield buildings. "If there's anything to learn here, isn't that where we'll find it?"

"Probably." I could see she was still thinking this whole expedition a waste of effort and she might be right, but not before I'd at least tried to prove it otherwise. So I led her towards the hangar where, in spite of the cold, the doors were wide open to reveal a Jenny with a mechanic working on its un-cowled engine. I left Tara outside watching the other Jenny's return landing while I approached the mechanic, trying to look as knowing and nonchalant as possible.

"Nice old bird."

He nodded without turning from his work. "Yep, and they did great work training the fly-boys, but they're getting tired these days." He kicked an oil pan under the engine, undid the sump bolt and let all three gallons of the black lubrication come pouring out.

"Problem with this one?"

"Nar." He shook his head while pausing to wipe his hands on a piece of cotton waste. "Just a scheduled hundred hour inspection." Although he'd answered matter-of-factly, there was just a hint of suspicion in his voice at this unknown questioner. "Can I help you, mister?"

I took the hint. "I believe an old buddy of mine is connected to this place, so thought I'd stop by and talk to him about a bit of flight training."

"Who's your buddy?" It was asked more as a challenge than casual interest.

"Carl Miller."

"Oh, right. Well, you're out of luck there because Carl took off for South Carolina only yesterday."

"Took off! You mean he's a pilot?"

"One of the best. Bit of an ace in the war, I believe." That look of suspicion returned. "If he's that big a buddy of yours, I'm surprised you didn't know that, mister."

It was time for some serious hedging. "I haven't seen him since our college days ... and a pity I won't today."

"Yeah, and not sure when he'll be back." He nodded towards the flight office. "But if you need to talk to someone about flight training, Captain Ludlow's the man to see."

"Captain Ludlow?"

"The Chief Instructor. He's not flying until this afternoon, so go see his secretary and she'll fix you up."

"Okay. Thanks."

Tara tagged along with me and soon we were entering the low single-story wooden building and making ourselves known to the efficient-looking woman manning the entrance desk. While she went off to check with the Chief, I took the opportunity to scan the framed photos lining the office walls. They were mainly group images of what must be past training courses, and in the third I saw something that confirmed my suspicions and made this morning's visit well worthwhile. It was much the same as the others: a half-dozen or so pupils standing suitably posed with their instructor in front of a Jenny. Except in this one their instructor stood a good two inches above his pupils and with not a hint of humor breaking through his scar-lined face. Meunier, or Carl Miller, to give him his real name, looked older and more like the man in that newspaper photo than the hardened legionnaire I'd last seen in No Man's Land, but it was him alright. I was about to call Tara over for a look at the man I was sure had murdered her brother, when the secretary returned and I alone was bidden into the inner sanctum.

My previous experience of *instructeurs* had been of military gods standing way above us mortals, but Captain Ludlow seemed a human-enough character as I was shown into his office. It wasn't an overly large room, but with its own share of framed photos and certificates surrounding a slightly damaged propeller displayed on the side wall. As I entered he put down his pipe, stood up and offered a friendly, firm handshake.

"Harry Ludlow. Pleased to meet you ...?"

"Mark ... Mark Kingsley."

He ushered me into the seat opposite and sat down himself, relighting his pipe and offering me a cigarette from the silver box on his desk. "How can I help you, Mark?"

I lit up from the offered light. "Thanks. Actually I'm just feeling out what it would take for me to do a bit of flying again."

He took on board the last word with a slight raise of the eyebrows. "You've done some flying before?"

"Some, yes. Over in France during the war."

"You served in the U.S. Air Service?"

I shook my head. "I'm afraid not. All my flying was with the *Aeronautique Militaire*."

"The French!" Those eyebrows had now done a full pitch heavenwards. "But you're a U.S. citizen?"

"Absolutely. Third generation with a grandfather who fought under Grant."

"Which means you must have been in the *Escadrille Lafayette*?"

He'd made the innocent mistake everyone else did when meeting one of the yanks who'd thrown in their lot with France's fly-boys.

"Not quite. Only thirty-four of the original volunteers had the honour of flying with *SPA 124*. There were over two-hundred of us all told and most of us were assigned to regular French escadrilles. I was with the 66th."

"Flying what?"

"Nieuport 17s for starters, and then we got SPAD 7s." I nodded towards one of the framed photos showing a lean figure in the uniform of a U.S. Air Service captain, standing in front of one of those sturdy last-named pursuit ships. "I see you got some time in on those mean machines yourself?"

"That's right. In 13s with the 94th Aero." He seemed glad to be able to explain his own role in the conflict, though the machines he was flying hadn't exactly filled him with joy. "The SPAD was certainly a handful for us new guys, and the ones the French handed over to us were pretty beaten-up ships by the time we got them." He peered at me through a haze of pipe-smoke. "So, you didn't transfer to our Air Service when the U.S. came into the fray?"

"I'm afraid not. By that time I'd got used to the French's pretty informal way of doing things and knew I'd have a hard time adapting to the hidebound ways of the AEF."

"So, you're not overly concerned with rules and regulations?"

I wasn't sure how best to answer that one, and in the end chose honesty. "I prefer to use my own common sense."

That response might well have ended many an interview right there, so I was relieved when Ludlow instead gave a warm smile of understanding. "A man after my own heart." He nodded outside to a Jenny taking off. "And now you feel like getting flying again?"

I did, but knew there was one big problem. "Just a pipe dream. I doubt I could afford it."

He smiled again. "Flight time in our Jennies cost six bucks an hour and another dollar for instruction."

"That confirms it then." I went to stand up. "No way I could pay that sort of dough."

But he waved me back down into my chair. "How many hours did you fly out there?"

"Just over six hundred."

"And you'd genuinely like to fly some more?"

"You bet but, like I said, I don't ..."

"... have that sort of money," he completed for me. "I know, but there might be another way." He caught my bemused expression. "Let me explain how it works."

*   *   *

"So, how did that go?"

There was a hint of suspicion in Tara's question as we exited the flight office and made our way back to the jetty. Perhaps she'd already detected a slight spring in my step.

"Better than expected. I've actually been offered a job." I gave her the complete run-down on my conversation with Henry Ludlow, his offer of refresher training and some work to follow.

"Doing what?" That suspicion was still evident.

"Not sure at this stage. Ludlow said he'd explain more once I've done the checkout and shown I really can wing it with the best of them."

"So, I'm right in thinking your heart is only half in the law and that it's only taken a whiff of the cockpit again to have you shaking the moths out of your flight helmet." She paused in our stride and turned to face me. "I guess this means I can say 'goodbye' to any help from you finding my brother's murderer and that your friend and client had better start preparing himself for a trip to Sing Sing's hot-seat."

"Not at all." I was a bit stung by the harshness of her words even though they might have held an element of truth. "The whole idea of this morning's exercise was to get ourselves some evidence. I know for sure now that my first suspect is connected to this outfit, and getting a job here myself will allow me to dig that much deeper."

"For what?"

"For a motive at least. But I'm convinced now this whole business goes a lot deeper than any of us suspected."

She started walking again, which at least gave me some hope she was accepting the situation. Her next question confirmed it. "But why would Miller Air Services want to employ someone they only met five minutes ago? There must be a bunch of you ex-flyboys wandering around looking for work."

"Yep, but not many ex-Lafayette troops. The way Ludlow explained it, he was looking for a bit of a Maverick prepared to go the extra mile for something he believed in."

"Doing what, for goodness' sake? Surely even a half-ass lawyer like you can see this whole thing stinks."

"It's certainly intriguing," I agreed, "which makes it all the more important I find out what it's about. And the more suspicious it gets, the closer I'm sure we'll be to finding out why your brother was murdered."

"Perhaps." That begrudging false doubt was as close as Tara Magee was going to come to seeing things my way. "So, when do you start your new job?"

"Not exactly a 'job', Tara, but Ludlow has scheduled me for a check the day after tomorrow. If that goes okay he'll explain more about what they have in mind."

"But surely you'll need some sort of qualification won't you?"

"Not yet. Legislation is already going through to get flying formally licensed, but that won't happen until the end of this year, by which time I'll be all set to qualify automatically."

"Seems like you've got it all worked out. And for the long-term as well."

"Just making sure I've got a meal-ticket for the years ahead.

Let's face it, clients aren't exactly battering my door down for legal advice, and something tells me this country is in for even harder times before they get better." We'd reached the jetty now, the Chris-Craft bobbing there alongside, which raised another question with Tara.

"Okay, but how are you even going to get here tomorrow?"

"Miller's have their own little ferry boat running to the island."

"Hmm, there must be more money in flight training than I thought." She paused before hopping aboard the launch and smiled. "Well, one way or another, things seem to be working out for you, so perhaps some little celebration is called for. How about supper tonight?"

I frowned regretfully. "Sorry, Tara, but Lee's Grand Jury hearing was scheduled today. I'm not expecting any good result and I may need to go see him. Can I call you when I know the situation?"

She gave her best imitation of indifference, but I was cheered to see just an inkling of regret. "Okay. Perhaps to-morrow evening instead. If you're flying the day after, at least you'll have the condemned man's traditional last supper."

*   *   *

CHAPTER FIVE

Darkness had already descended by the time I got back to my office, called the 48th Precinct, and got put through to Chief Nolan. Like I fully expected, the news wasn't good.

"Sorry, Mark, but the jury found there was a case to answer and your client got indicted for trial."

"Any date?"

"Two weeks from now."

I was staggered. "That soon? They're in a hurry aren't they?"

"The DA managed to get a slot in the next session, and saw no reason to drag it out longer than needed."

"Except to give me time to prepare an adequate defense."

There was a grunt at the other end. "The way Shreeve sees it, you won't have much of one anyway, so why waste time."

"Given that time frame, he might be right." I was up against determined forces here and there was no point in arguing. Right now I had other concerns. "How did Lee take the verdict?"

"Pretty stoically."

"Is he still with you?"

"Nope, he's already been transferred to the county jail."

Which at least kept him within striking distance of my office. "Will I be able to see him this evening, Pat?"

"I don't see why not. If you like I can make arrangements."

"Yes, please. And one more question, Pat. The address that witness gave your patrolman ... did that check out?"

"Nope." There was a pause at the other end and I got the firm impression this was one bit of information Chief Nolan was loathe to admit. "Turned out to be a false one."

"Not too good a witness then, Pat."

"Not one we can produce in court. He was probably some guy cheating on his wife and somewhere he shouldn't be."

I knew better, but now wasn't the time to show my hand of cards, especially as I didn't even have a full deck myself yet. Instead, I thanked Pat, hung up and then got connected to *Winifred's Welfare* to tell Tara I definitely wouldn't be making supper this night.

*   *   *

This wasn't the first time I'd been to the County Jail on 177th Street and Arthur Avenue, never an experience I relished at the best of times and one I sure as hell would have gladly swapped for that supper date with Tara Magee.

Not that she hadn't been totally understanding when I called to explain. In fact I got the impression I'd actually scored a few points by putting my client before pleasure. So, after settling on some meeting on the morrow instead, I walked the few miles to my evening interview with Lee.

At the jail I found Chief Nolan had been as good as his word and smoothed my visit. After a few brief preliminaries, I was straightway led by a guard along brightly lit passageways to the room normally used for regular prisoner visits.

This was outside normal family visiting and Lee was sitting there alone and looking pretty dejected. I took the seat opposite him across the plain table, glad we'd got the place to ourselves except for the guard watching over us from a reasonably discreet distance. The situation didn't inspire much smiling, but I tried a cheering one just the same. "Sorry about the indictment, Lee, but something both of us were probably expecting."

"Yeah, from what I heard, the DA pulled out all the stops to get me hooked." He ran a distracted hand through thinning hair. "Not that it took too much effort on his part, with that patrolman giving evidence of finding me red-handed. Apparently the jury had considered the facts, given their verdict, and got me indicted, all within a couple of hours."

"That's Grand Juries for you." It was time to put that behind us. I pushed across the standard smoke and lit us both up. "How is your new accommodation?"

"I've had worse."

I could imagine. "At least you're warm."

He nodded somewhere vaguely northwards. "I'll be a whole lot warmer when they take me up the river and strap me into Old Sparky."

This sort of defeatism wasn't going to do either of us any good. "You mustn't think like that, Lee. I'm already following up leads to prove your innocence." I told him about my visit that morning to Miller Air Services, that Meunier was, in reality, Carl Miller and that I was on his trail. I didn't rub salt in the wound by saying I was doing that by getting some flying again, but stuck to what would encourage him. "All I need to do now is track him down, establish the motive, and we've got ourselves a defense."

"Well, let's hope you do." He didn't seem convinced of the wisdom of my plan. "But why in hell would some guy we only knew incidentally a decade ago, want to murder a nice guy like Richard Magee?"

I sat back. "I've been thinking on that one myself, and I'm sure it relates to Richard's time as a POW. We know Meunier was a traitor. What if Richard actually met or saw him in Germany, recognised his likeness in that newspaper photo, and threatened to expose him for what he was? That would surely put the cramps on his father's Senate election hopes and give them both a motive for extreme action."

"You think the father, Wilson Miller, is actually *involved* in all this?"

"Who knows, but he's the one with most to lose. His son's a trained killer, he's obviously ambitious for power, and we all know that can drive a man to carry out extreme acts."

"But how come they involved me?"

"Probably just opportunism. They knew you were aware of Meunier's treachery, and Father Richard could well have told them he was meeting you that night. So they planned the whole thing around that time purely so you could carry the rap and rid them of two threats in one foul swoop."

He nodded. "Yeah, makes sense, but surely that leaves you all set for elimination too?"

"Possibly, but I can take care of myself."

"Better if we get them before they get you." He sat back and blew some smoke upwards. "But how the hell will you prove any of this with Richard now dead and gone?"

"I'm working on that one."

"Good, but it'll need to be in less than a fortnight, which is when they're talking about my trial date."

"Don't I know it, but tomorrow I'm going to try and talk the DA into an adjournment."

"Good luck with that." He stubbed out his cigarette in the cheap metal ashtray and rolled despondent eyes. "I've never met the guy, but somehow he seems to have zeroed in on me like I was Public Enemy Number One."

"That's only because he wants to use you as a stepping stone to his own vaulted ambitions."

"Which won't be harmed by protecting the interests of a prospective Senator."

"Possibly." I lit him another smoke and inhaled a slow drag on my own as I took that thought on board. "Are you sure Richard never mentioned an encounter with someone he suspected of treachery when he was a POW?"

"No, nothing."

"Hmm, perhaps his spiritual good nature made him hold short of pointing a finger without due cause."

"Until he saw the likeness of the man in that piece in the *Tribune* and then threatened to expose the whole thing."

"Exactly."

"But, what if you can't find Carl Miller, alias Meunier? What if he's skipped the country completely? You say he's a pilot. Perhaps he's already flown to Mexico or somewhere else?"

I stopped him right there. "Don't go painting too many devils on the wall, Lee. We'll get him *and* the truth before long and then you out of this mess." Perhaps I was talking a bit more optimistically than I felt, but he needed encouragement and the remembrance of good times past. "This isn't the first fix we've been in, remember. We always got out of them before and we'll get out of this one."

"Yeah, but it was me getting you out then." He gave a demanding look. "I guess you owe me a couple."

I could understand his predicament hazing memories, but I needed to get the balance sheet right on that point. "I only owe you *one*, Lee, remember? But I'll do my damndest to get you off this, and then I'll have more than paid my dues."

But he seemed reluctant to acknowledge that and we parted perhaps just a little coolly.

On the walk back to the office I wondered if I'd been a bit touchy myself. Lee was in a damn-awful situation and entitled to be feeling the stress of it all. Just the same, I was surprised he'd forgotten that time in mid-summer 1916, when this whole story, and his future, might have changed forever.

*　　*　　*

By that time we were operational in our assigned French unit, flying out of Souilly, a temporary airfield supporting the 2nd Army's's ongoing blood-bath in the interminable Battle of Verdun just a few miles to the north.

Not far away in Behonne, fellow Americans in N124 *l'escadrille Americaine*, were already making a name for themselves, but their ranks had already been filled by the time Lee and I completed our flight training. Hence, we took our places in a regular French squadron, *Escadrille* N66, flying pursuit ships under a great CO, *Capitaine* Dominique Barcat.

Our machines now were Nieuport 11s, much superior kites to the 10s of our training days, powered by the sweet 80hp Le Rhone rotary and a delight to fly, though gradually being replaced by 110hp 16s in a new brown-green 'dead leaf' camouflage. Inevitably, these replacements were swiftly snapped up by the more senior members of the *escadrille*, though we soon heard grumbles that the marginally improved performance from the larger engine was more than offset by balance problems from its extra weight. Added to that, they still had that weakening circular section joint in their lower wings, so Lee and I were quite content in our 11s as Barcat mentored us into front-line combat flying and gave us our first taste of dog-fighting the German *Jastas*.

In the frantic pace of war though, time for instruction was limited and experience soon gained, and just days had our CO rostering us for regular patrols with other squadron pilots. Here we more-or-less followed the leader, getting in a shot from our single Lewis gun whenever we could, but essentially just trying to stay ahead of the game by following the hard-earned maxim that 'it was the one you didn't see that finally got you'. That way we lived to fight another day, though many of our comrades didn't, meaning us two 'new boys' soon found ourselves sent as a pair on patrols of our own.

In some ways this was what we'd always wanted, though the satisfaction of flying as an all-Yank team was now tempered by a new ambition. In our training there'd been a race to be the first to solo and I'd narrowly won that one. Now Lee seemed intent on redeeming himself by being the first to score a kill. That, to me, seemed something fate would decide as we took it in turns to lead our two-ship forays across the Meuse River.

On these patrols, we inevitably ran into enemy Albatros B11 recon aircraft, usually escorted by Fokker *Eindecker*s. The latter were particularly feared, not for their manoeuvrability, but for the fact that they could fire straight ahead with their new synchronised machine guns. With those they only had to aim their aircraft whereas we, with our single Lewis machine gun mounted on the upper wing, had to position beneath our target to get in a shot. It was also much more difficult to change the drums of our .303 calibre ammo, with the result that any encounter we made with the enemy usually ended with us fighting our way back against the prevailing westerly wind without either of us scoring that first kill. That all changed though early one morning in late July.

We'd been slated for first patrol, which meant rolling out of our camp beds at the crack of dawn and having a quick swig of stimulating coffee before then joining our hard-working, but very bored, *mechaniciens* out on the flight-line. A quick check of the aircraft, start and warm up, and then out to the field edge for a formation take-off. At least at this sunrise hour flying conditions were usually cooler and smoother, giving us beautiful glimpses of mother earth as we climbed to our patrol height of around sixteen thousand feet.

But this morning even that pleasure was somewhat

dimmed by heavy mist, bordering on fog, that made even basic control somewhat tricky as we struggled to maintain ground reference before finally breaking out on top. Over the Meuse, the fog, if anything, seemed to have thickened, and I could imagine the divisions of infantry below us awakening to yet another day of slaughter while blanketed in impenetrable precipitation. It was probably also the reason our enemy flyers seemed to be having themselves a lie-in, because we met no air opposition, allowing us to penetrate further over their lines than we had ever done before.

Perhaps too far, because it wasn't long before the rising sun started to burn off the fog below and we realized we had a long way back to our side of the lines. Lee was leading that morning and I was glad when he finally signalled for us to turn back. At least, in these still conditions, we weren't battling against the dreaded westerly wind and, as we headed homeward, my concern at finding our own field and landing was eased by the last of the fog now turning to translucent mist. We stuck our noses down to swap height for speed and an even quicker crossing of the lines. Thankfully, there was still no sign of the *Jagdstaffeln*, but just before we reached the Meuse we did see another form of aerial activity.

Nearly a mile before the line was an enemy observation balloon, slowly ascending as its ground-crew took advantage of the still conditions to get it winched high enough for the observer in his basket to start telephoning corrections to the guns for their morning barrage.

These artillery bombardments were very much a part of the Verdun scene. The Germans had brought up twelve hundred guns to start the battle, theorizing that a continuous onslaught of shells would be the most economical way to inflict maximum casualties. The French had replied in kind, resulting in over ten million shells being eventually fired in the course of the three-hundred day battle and accounting for over sixty percent of the nigh-on three-quarter million casualties. Observation balloons had therefore become a vital part of the action and this morning yet one more was about to play its deadly part.

Flying off Lee's wing, I saw he'd spotted the sinister sausage with its black Maltese cross, at exactly the same time as me. More disconcerting was that his pointing finger had now turned to the clenched fist signal for attack followed by an immediate wing-over as he headed downward straight for it. As his wingman, I had no option other than to follow, beset as I was with horrible doubts.

These were based on several serious factors. For one, balloons were valuable and, consequently, their sites were protected by generous anti-aircraft weaponry only too ready to stop any attacking aircraft in its tracks. Also, balloons were not that simple to shoot down. A burst of machine gun fire might well puncture them, but to get them exploding needed incendiary ammo, which we weren't carrying that morning. Some of our new 16s had been equipped with rockets for the purpose but, again, our old 11s still only had their single Lewis gun to try to pepper them ... if we got that close.

None of this though seemed to be daunting Lee. As we tore downward, I could almost sense the way his mind was working. He was probably disappointed at not encountering any enemy aircraft and the chance of being the first to score, but now he had something else in his sights and, like a dog with a bone, he wasn't about to let it go.

He might have no choice though, because enemy observers in their baskets were the first to be equipped with parachutes and this one, at the first sight of our attack, had wisely taken to his while the ground-crew frantically started winching down their precious balloon. Now it was a race to see who'd be first and I felt the slipstream whip past ever-more chillingly as Lee stuck his nose down further in his desperation to win.

The balloon was filling both our windshields now and I was wondering if the old Nieuport's wings would give in before the ground-fire even started coming up. With his Lewis gun angled up at the usual forty-five degrees, Lee had dived below the descending balloon and was already opening up at extreme range. All I could do was stay in close to him in the hope of at least drawing some of the fire when the ground defenses opened up.

Except they weren't, which was puzzling to me, but obviously encouraging to Lee as some of his .303s started hitting home. Now he was so close to that great grey floating elephant that for a moment I wondered if he'd even got target-fixation and was about to ram it. And still no ground fire. Why? Then, in that last manic split-second I suddenly remembered crew-room chat I'd once heard of how the Boche sometimes booby-trapped their balloons and ...

Suddenly, my recollection turned to appalling fact as there came the mother of all detonations and the balloon disappeared in an incandescent fireball. Even the roar of my le Rhone was momentarily overwhelmed by the thunder-like explosion and my sight, by its resulting flash. As the Nieuport shuddered and flicked like an autumn leaf in a gale, I gripped the stick in a desperate battle to stop the aircraft pitching and rolling itself to oblivion. After what seemed a lifetime, I found myself almost on the deck, still flying, the le Rhone mercifully still running and my wheels just inches above field grey figures diving for cover to avoid instant decapitation.

At least that might have temporarily taken the self-satisfied grins off their faces at finding some dumb-ass fighter jocks all set to walk right into their trap. I should have realised that, with no *Jagdgeschwader* operational, this was the perfect opportunity and ... but no time now for self-recrimination as I shook myself back to reality and the Nieuport into controlled flight while at the same time trying to see what had happened to Lee.

At first I couldn't find him and feared he'd already speared in. Then I glanced further away to the north and saw his aircraft, still airborne and slightly above me, but describing a series of ever-tighter downward turns. I again closed with him in tight formation and saw why. His aircraft was black with smoke from a blast that had effectively stripped off large areas of its fabric. From the wings, long shards of canvas now fluttered in the slipstream while the *empennage* control surfaces seemed all set to become a flying skeleton. He was still flying, but only just and with little control. Certainly, there was no way he would ever reach our lines and whether he would ever land safely *anywhere* looked horribly doubtful as he battled just to keep it right side up. And then his faltering engine gave its last gasp and all other options suddenly went the way of his luck.

That luck though had just given him one last gram of hope: an area of shell-holed, but reasonably open ground a few hundred yards from the balloon site into which he might just pancake his failing craft. He'd obviously spotted it too, because the aircraft was sliding its way downward towards it with Lee crossing controls to slip in with whatever control he had left. Just over its outer edge he began to flare, but the elevators weren't up to it and instead his wheels struck hard, the ship bounced once, twice, and then came down again on one wingtip, spinning the Nieuport around even as it hit, tearing off one wing, but incredibly staying upright. As the still-turning prop splintered into a thousand flying darts and the engine-mounts crumpled, I prayed the le Rhone wouldn't end up on his legs in the cockpit.

It didn't, and neither did it catch fire. At least not immediately. Instead, as I circled at low level, I watched Lee scramble clear just seconds before the whoof of igniting benzene had him diving for cover in a nearby slit-trench. I glanced beyond the crash-scene to where mean-looking soldiery were already doubling from all directions. I pushed my Lewis up until it was aiming just over my prop and dived down towards the larger group. A good burst had them diving earthwards, with some staying down for good. Those who did jump to their feet again now speeded up their advance, all the time firing as they ran. I'd doubtless just lost them some good buddies and filled them with a firm resolve to extract revenge.

I made a quick assessment of our chances, steep-turned on my wingtip, brought back the power and headed down. Lee's crashed Nieuport was blocking one end of the landing ground but, with no wind yet, I could perhaps get mine down the other way. It was still going to be a tight fit and Lee's quick stop by turning his aircraft over wasn't one I intended to copy if I was to get to him before the Boche. No time now though to weigh the pros and cons, and so I came winging on down, slowing to just above the stall while all the time sensing, rather than seeing, enemy fire now striking home. I touched down with just enough room for a landing run, using bootfuls of rudder to avoid the worst of the shell-holes and praying one of my wheels didn't find an unseen one.

They didn't and I ended up close by Lee's crashed machine, still rolling fast but using full rudder and a good burst of power to swing the Nieuport around so sharply that she heeled enough to dig in the outside wingtip. Back with the power now to come to a standstill with a yard of loose fabric dangling, but nothing that would stop us flying as long as Lee got his ass in gear before those grey-clad guys in coal-scuttle helmets got to us first. I heard a clang from up front as one of their rounds struck home on the engine cowling. Another might still get my tank or the prop and then it would be curtains for both of us.

Then Lee came running from his near-by slit-trench, limping slightly from some bash he'd taken in the crash, but making impressive speed nonetheless. He needed to if we were to get ourselves out of this hell-hole in one piece. Above the clatter of the idling rotary I yelled for him to hurry while squeezing myself tighter into the port side of the Nieuport's small cockpit. He jumped up onto the starboard wing and squeezed in beside me.

"Thanks!" I saw the word mouthed rather than heard it, and no time now for any others because the enemy were already on the edge of our landing ground, firing on the run, which thankfully spoiled most of their aims. Two were taking their time though, already lowering their MG08 light machine gun onto its bipod, feeding an ammo belt into its breech and dropping into a firing position behind it. Another second and those hundred rounds would be spraying my kite and us with deadly effect.

An immediate take-off now was only going to present them with an initially slow-moving, beam-on target for those lethal 7.92 rounds. That left me with just one extreme measure that would either buy us time or stop our clock for good. I jammed in full left rudder and pushed the stick forward while at the same time gunning the engine. The result was the aircraft spinning around to face our attackers while at the same time getting its tail up into flying attitude and then more some. The question now was whether my prop would hit the ground and shatter before that Lewis gun on my top wing was down enough to start spitting its own reply.

I didn't wait to find out before I clenched the trigger handle, let fire a good burst and had the satisfaction of seeing a trail of my own .303s go scything across the ground between, taking down more soldiery and finally ending up in the laps of that machine gun crew. Then, with the engine still at full-power, back with the stick before the prop hit, full right rudder to align us with that one strip of clear ground, and we were tearing along it, sped on our way by a fusillade of angry shots from behind. The shredded wing-tip didn't exactly help, but we just about scraped over the far boundary before becoming airborne, holding our nose down for more speed, and then steep-turning away back to our own blessed lines.

I glanced sideways to Lee, crouched there beside me with no helmet, wiping his bloodied nose while his streaming blond hair whipped itself into tangles in the slipstream. Neither of us even tried to speak. Perhaps he was already totting the score. That decoy balloon had self-destructed, but I had little doubt he'd claim it as a first kill. For myself, I couldn't care less. My own thoughts right now were simply on the big cup of French coffee laced with a generous brandy that I aimed to murder within minutes of landing.

I guess, in wartime, we all have our own priorities.

*   *   *

Back in the grim present, my first priority next morning was an interview with Bronx District Attorney, Gary Shreeve. This wasn't an experience either of us would find particularly joyful, seeing as we'd crossed swords several times before and with each occasion only hardening my conviction that here was a man who'd stop at nothing to get what he wanted, regardless of how many lives he ruined in the process.

Thirty-something years old, fastidiously dressed, but with a pointed foxy face and, probably, the cunning to match, Shreeve had never struck me as someone dedicated to justice. Instead, his ardor seemed more directed towards getting as many people as possible either strapped into the hot seat or behind bars for good. With the aim of at least delaying Lee joining that dubious tally, I put in a call to his office.

When I finally got through, the DA's secretary had clearly

been schooled in the art of deflecting unwanted intrusions to her boss's day, so I didn't waste time asking for an appointment, but only checked if he was in court that morning. When she admitted he wasn't, I hung up and headed straight for his downtown office, expecting another battle-royal to get past his flunkies, and instead being surprised by an immediate order to be shown in.

Shreeve's office was what you'd expect from someone with aspirations: antique mahogany desk and a chair behind it that looked more complex than any of the fighters I'd flown. As I walked in he brought it from full-recline to upright while offering a limp hand and insincere greeting. "Kingsley, good to see you. What can I do for you?"

"Your agreement to an adjournment of the Vennington trial." I sat down unbidden on a far-less grand visitors' chair that, probably by design, put me at least four inches below his.

He eased his own back enough to look down at me contemptuously. "That's for the courts to decide. Have you tried them yet?"

"Not much point, seeing as the first thing they'll do is check for your concurrence."

"And why would I agree to that?"

"To give me reasonable time to prove my client's innocence."

"In your dreams, Kingsley, seeing as yesterday's Grand Jury didn't take too long in deciding there was a case to answer."

"Only so they didn't have to wait too long to collect their day's pay."

He frowned. "For a lawyer, you seem to have a strangely negative opinion of our Grand Jury system."

"You mean by giving the power of indictment to a bunch of citizens pulled off the street, who have no training in law, but with their blood well and truly up from reading pre-conceived accounts of the crime in their local rag." I paused in my grumbling to look around his office, its walls covered by numerous framed diplomas, certificates, and photos of him shaking hands with the great and the good. Wilson Miller's wasn't yet amongst them, but probably soon would be once he'd achieved the senatorship our DA was doing his best to support. "And I guess a swift judgement here won't do your career any harm, will it Shreeve?"

"And wasting your time pursuing some mythical defense won't do yours any good, Kingsley. Everyone wants this case over and done with as quickly as possible, and you'd do well to remember that."

"Is that a threat, Shreeve?"

The snide laugh he gave me back was one totally devoid of humor. "Lord no, Mark. Just friendly advice."

"Well, thanks, but forgive me if I put my client's life ahead of what few trinkets the legal profession might, or might not, throw my way." I decided to quit this fooling around. "Have you any contact with Wilson Miller?"

"Who's he?"

"Our senatorial candidate, whom I'm surprised someone as politically astute as yourself hasn't heard of."

Our DA's eyes narrowed as he leaned towards me. "But *you* obviously have, and you'd be well-advised not to do anything that might hinder his path to The White House."

"Ah, so that's where he's aiming for, is it?" I stood up to go. "And, presumably, when he eventually gets there, he'll be all set to appoint a new Attorney General."

Shreeve shrugged. "Who knows, but I believe in opening doors, Kingsley, like you'll do with mine right now as you get out of my office."

With nothing else to say or achieve, I did just that, while comforting myself that it hadn't been a totally wasted encounter. If nothing else, I now at least knew the forces I'd pitted myself up against.

*   *   *

Still inwardly seething, I headed straight back to my office. With facts to investigate, a defence to plan and a trial to handle in two short weeks, I needed to clear my very small cluster of case-files in the interim.

One of these was a relatively simple property transaction passed to me by Betty Devinsky, a real-estate agent on the same block floor as me. Being office neighbours, we enjoyed a mutually convenient professional association, though Betty sometimes gave the hint that she would have liked a closer one outside of office hours.

A somewhat homely girl with a nature to match, I liked Betty a lot but, in spite of her engaging smile and natural blonde curls, I'd always managed to keep our relationship on purely friendly terms. She'd never seemed offended at my excuses or in any way curtailed the crumbs of legal work she regularly dropped my way. I had some questions relating to a current crumb, and so knocked and entered her office before even unlocking mine.

"Hi, Mark, great to see you. What brings your welcome presence this dreary morning? More typing or one of my deals?" Betty helped me out by typing up all my letters and court documents for virtually zero recompense, but still managed to make me feel genuinely welcome.

"Just a few points to clear on that shop purchase I'm handling for your client."

"You mean the deli for Mr Morgan? Let me get his file." She stood up, popped on her glasses, and while fingering her way through an impressive drawerful of cases, said casually, over her shoulder, "I hear you're involved in that dreadful killing at St Winifred's."

Even for the Bronx, Father Magee's killing was pretty

exceptional and I should have known better than to think that all the details hadn't already spread across the borough. "That's right, defending the man accused."

"Someone has to." It was a response typical of dear Betty, who was usually the voice of reason on any subject even if, like in this case, she probably had little sympathy for the accused. "Anyway, whatever the outcome, I'm sure it's keeping you busy. A pity you weren't here to see your visitors."

"Visitors?" I'd already checked I hadn't any appointments before going to see the DA. "You mean I actually missed some potential clients?"

She came back and plopped the file onto the desk between us. "No, I don't think they were clients as such. Just two men in smart suits." She frowned. "Strangely, they just seemed to want to know about you."

"Me?" Already alarm bells were ringing. "Who were these men, Betty? What exactly did they ask?"

"Oh, just general things like, how long you'd been in practice here, and what sort of clients you had."

"And what did you tell them?"

"Just that I knew you as a very fine person, but that if they needed personal details, they should talk to you direct."

"You did just right, Betty, but did they leave their cards or anything?"

"No. I asked them to, but they said they'd be in touch." She frowned again. "Strange sort of guys, really. Sort of official-like."

As I left her office, I gave as nonchalant a shrug as I could manage. "Probably guys from the DA's office checking how big a threat I represent for the prosecution."

Back in my own, there was at least one good item in the post: a check for fifteen bucks from a client who I'd managed to get off a drunk and disorderly charge months ago. At least now I'd be able to take Tara Magee for another meal without too much financial restraint.

Buoyed by that bit of professional advancement, I rang Shreeve to protest at his sending goons around to check me out. He naturally denied instigating such a thing.

I knew our DA well enough to know there was no level to which he wouldn't stoop to win a case. So why did I have the feeling that this was one of those unique times he was actually telling the truth?

*   *   *

"So, who do you think these men were?"

Needing a break from the tedious legal backlog I was wading through, I'd called Tara to suggest supper on me that evening, only to find she was busy at *Winifred's* until late that night. In fact, even this call was delaying her getting out for supplies, but she did cushion my disappointment by suggesting we meet up near the grocery store. And so here we were, at a Dyre Avenue coffee shop, me explaining the strange events of the morning and her wanting a take on the whole business.

"Your guess is as good as mine, Tara. I thought it might just be Shreeve trying to get some inside info on my line of defense, but now I'm not so sure."

She took a sip of her coffee. "The DA seems very keen to get a conviction, but why the urgency to put away some down-and-out who could well be innocent anyway?"

"I'm trying to figure that one myself. Shreeve is an ambitious bastard and he might just see this as an easy step up, except ..."

"What?"

"That something tells me this all goes far deeper than that. That there are forces behind the scenes here very keen to have Lee Vennington pay the price for the real murderer, and the sooner the better."

"The Miller Corporation?"

"They're the most likely candidates."

"Hmm." Tara sat back and shook her head. "I've been racking *my* brains to fathom why Richard, of all people, could be involved in whatever this is. No luck so far but, for my own peace of mind, I'm going to keep trying."

"You and me both, Tara, but this scheduling of Lee's trial for just two weeks doesn't give us much time."

"And you don't think it worthwhile applying for an adjournment?"

"Nope. Normally I would have just gone straight ahead in spite of Shreeve trying to warn me off, but now I think everything and everyone is stacked against it."

"Then we need to get ourselves in gear, Mark." She leaned forward. "While you're learning more when you go flying tomorrow, I'll be doing a little digging of my own."

"And how do you propose to do that?"

"By paying a visit to the Miller's main office, where I've arranged a meeting on the pretext of discussing a donation to *Winifred's Welfare*." She gave an impish smile. "Perhaps a bit of feminine charm and intuition will give us something more to go on."

I was feeling more wary. "We still don't know what we're dealing with here, Tara, so don't go sticking your neck too far out."

"Why not? Richard did, so I can too if it gets his murderer."

For the first time ever, I took her hand. "Just don't go opening up a can of worms for yourself."

"Only enough to have the worms giving us the information we need." She gave my hang agravation of this whole affair more worthwhile than I could ever have imagined.

"I'm not saying I don't need some help right now in finding some basis for Lee's defense."

We'd both finished our coffees and the waitress came and

refilled our cups. As Tara added some cream, she said, "You obviously went through a lot together with Lee Vennington."

"Yep, war is a place where you make true friendships. He did save my life a couple of times and I still owe him one."

"Only one?"

I explained the two times he'd saved my neck and the balloon action rescue I'd managed for him. It seemed, if anything, to leave her more bemused than ever.

"My goodness, Mark, I would have thought wartime experiences would have gone beyond simple balance sheets of who owed what."

"I agree, but Lee didn't seem to see it like that, being the highly competitive person he was. That whole balloon business seemed to leave a real bad taste in his mouth, seeing as instead of being credited with a kill, he got a roasting from our CO for losing a Nieuport, while I got a commendation for saving a pilot."

"As you deserved." She squeezed my hand again. "Lee should have been grateful for still having his life and freedom."

I shrugged. "War does change people."

"Just the same, there's a difference between healthy competition and ingratitude." She paused to stir her coffee, obviously mulling over what I'd just told her. "Was he always obsessively competitive about everything?"

"Pretty much so, and more and more as the war went on."

"Including girls?"

I gave a little chuckle of pleasure at this hint of personal interest. "Not much time for that, Tara. There *was* a girl, but that was all one-sided on his part."

"Go on."

I took a sip of coffee and sat back. "It was in late 1916. By then we'd been flying operationally with N66 non-stop for six months, badly in need of a break and grateful when *Capitaine* Barcat sent us on a long-weekend leave to *gay Paree*."

"Where you met a girl?"

"Sort of."

Was it a whole ten years now since we'd swaggered down the *Champs-Elysées* and the *Bois de Boulogne*, feeling smug in our uniforms as NCO pilots in the *Aeronautique Militaire*? Strange how, in my mind, everything back then, even in the midst of the worst war the world had ever seen, seemed infinitely more light-hearted than my present incarnation. As I recounted that weekend to the only bright spot in my current world, I willingly let my thoughts glide back to a time when life was for living, no matter how short that life might be.

*   *   *

It had been our first time back in Paris since my hospitalization in the *Jean-Antoine Villemin* just a year before. A lot had happened in those twelve months, and even this city, which I remembered for its sparkling gaiety in those glorious pre-war days, now seemed edged in mourning after all the appalling losses at Verdun and The Somme. Undeterred, though, and with extra francs in our pockets from the ever-generous Doctor Gros, Lee and I had found ourselves a comfortable-enough billet close to the South Bank and set out to reacquaint ourselves with old haunts.

With the stringencies of war, there turned out to be rather less choice of fayre in the *cafés* and *patisseries* we took delight in revisiting, but it was one way of escaping the winter weather and, at least this time, as we shook off our rain-soaked greatcoats and ordered the drinks, we could enjoy admiring glances at our pilot's brevets from the locals and sweet smiles from the pretty girls. Relaxing for the first time in months and simply enjoying the moment, it was on our second day in a nearby wine bar that Lee met the girl.

I say 'girl' when, in fact, she seemed close to forty and with a figure that had seen better days, but those dark sensuous eyes that glanced at us from under a shock of thick black hair were clearly still capable of seduction, as evidenced by the much younger man sitting drinking with her at the corner table.

He was a somewhat thick-set character wearing a sullen face, a patch over his left eye and a uniform I couldn't immediately identify. While I waited at the bar for our drinks, I saw that Lee had paused to talk to them both and was already getting some enticing glances from the woman. By the time I joined them, wines in hand, he was already in deep conversation.

"Mark, meet ..." Clearly, his bubbling chat hadn't extended to introductions and he paused to cast an admiring and questioning glance at the woman.

"Margaretha." She smiled a sparkling smile that must have melted many a previous sucker's heart. "Margaretha MacLeod, but my friends call me Margreet."

Her English was good, though voiced in the husky resonance of a seductress and with a Flemish accent at odds with her surname.

"MacLeod sounds very Scottish to me."

"Ah, yes, but that was my married name even though my husband was Dutch, as am I." She seemed keen to avoid any presumptions on my part by quickly adding, "But Captain MacLeod and I have been separated for over thirteen years now."

"She's a dancer," added Lee, anxious to show he'd already done a recon of the target while keen to avoid my getting into a conversation of my own.

"*Was* a dancer," corrected Margreet with a patronizing smile. "For eight years I specialised in sacred eastern dance at the *Musée Guimet*, but now I devote myself to helping the war effort." Perhaps, by bringing comfort to the likes of the officer beside her, who she now felt she should introduce. "Oh, and please meet Captain Vadim Maslov of the Russian Expeditionary Force."

As we shook hands I realized why I hadn't been able to place his blue-grey uniform with its broad epaulettes and impressive array of medals. It was Lee, though, who voiced our confusion.

"Russian! I didn't know Russia had men serving here."

"There were over forty-four thousand of us," explained Maslov, speaking up for the first time. He had that de-pressed-sounding Slavic voice that we'd encountered before in the Legion, and edged now with obvious discontent. "We were sent here in April this year at the request of the French Government. Now one in ten of those brave men have already fallen in action."

I took in the scarring around his wide face and the black patch over his left eye. "It looks like you've seen some yourself."

He nodded. "I was a fighter pilot, but this last summer, some Boche got me in a dogfight."

"Too bad," I looked for words of comfort, "but at least you're still alive."

"As alive as a man can be without his sight," he countered, dejectedly.

"His other eye was damaged too," explained Margreet, placing an obviously-loving hand on his. "But at least he still has me."

I could see she held genuine affection for this Russian officer young enough to be her son. I noticed also an immedi-ate shadow cross Lee's face. Then he jumped up and grabbed both their glasses. "Let me get you another ..." and, as an afterthought to Maslov, "... and for you too, Captain?"

As he went off on his mission, Margreet turned to me. "You are both pilots yourselves?"

"Yes, *pilotes de chasse* … like Captain Maslov here," I quickly added, to keep her jaded *beau* in the conversation.

"Ah, what dangerous lives you lead." She nodded towards Lee just getting the drinks at the bar. "You and your young friend are both in the same *escadrille*?"

"Yes."

"And where is that based?"

But I was saved from having to say that was something we couldn't talk about, by Lee's return. He handed Margreet her large glass of *Beaujolais* and Maslov his vodka and clinked his own against them. "Here's to health, long life and enduring friendship." I noticed he was looking into Margreet's eyes as he proposed the latter and kept them there even as she took her first sip. It was a slightly uncomfortable situation, my seeing for the first time a side to Lee I never had before. Not that two years of war had ever given us much chance, but I was sad this first encounter was with a woman I had little doubt was something of a maneater.

Maslov too had obviously noticed a certain *frisson* between the two. He stood up and for a moment I worried there was going to be a scene, but instead he nodded outside and said, "I need some fresh-air."

He went to feel his way and I realized how bad the injury to his eyes was. Making the excuse of wanting a breather myself, I tactfully guided him to the door and soon we were standing outside, beneath the *cáfe*'s rain-spattered awning, lighting up our *gauloises*. He had his back to the window, but over his shoulder I could see the two inside making ever closer chit-chat and Margreet writing something on a page from her small notebook and handing it to Lee. I was sure it had to be her address and felt I needed to make some peace-offering to Maslov. "Don't worry. We'll be returning to the front tomorrow."

"Ah that I was fit enough to join you." He shrugged and

glanced back inside. "And what is happening in there is something I am well-used to. Just tell your young friend to be careful, that is all."

*   *   *

"So, did Lee see her again?"

"Oh yes." Tara's question brought me out of my lengthy diatribe. "From then on he disappeared any time he could get off base and I suspected it was Margreet making her way to see him."

"I'm surprised a foreign national like her could travel so freely in a war zone."

"I know, but later I found out how."

"Which was?"

But I shook my head. "It's a long story, Tara. I'll explain later."

She gave me one of her suspicious looks. "Could it have something to do with what's happened since?"

"I can't see how. Just forget it for the moment."

I could see she wasn't satisfied, but she just shrugged and quickly changed the subject. "Where are you getting the boat to the island tomorrow?"

"Down at the Battery Park ferry dock. The flying school have their own boat doing a shuttle service."

"Lucky for you then, because Miller's office is also in Manhattan and I can give you a lift there in the car."

"Great, but where exactly is their office?"

"East Village, apparently just off Second Avenue."

"Hmm. I expected them to be in some swankier part of the state than that." It had given me one idea though. "Look, how about we rendezvous somewhere locally when we've finished our day and then I can treat you to that supper I promised?"

She smiled cynically. "And that way, Mark Kingsley, you'll have yourself a lift back as well."

"I was thinking more we could share our day's experiences. And, besides, I'd just like to see you."

I was expecting another cynical remark, but instead she smiled sweetly and said, "Okay, that would work well. There's a nice little seafood restaurant I know down near Pier Fifteen at South Street Seaport. We could meet there when you hit the mainland again."

"Sounds great."

"Good." She pushed away her cup and stood up. "Thanks for the coffee, Mark. Be at *Winifred's Welfare* at seven-thirty tomorrow morning for the lift in."

"Will do."

We went our separate ways, me not looking forward to an afternoon clearing my desk of the legal backlog, but very much to the morrow. And not just for the flying.

*   *   *

CHAPTER SIX

The old Jenny's rate of climb wasn't ever going to catch any homesick angel, but eventually I was back at three-thousand feet in a reasonably clear area over the Hudson and all set to enjoy my first aerial freedom in a decade.

It was certainly less congested here than my dawn journey in with Tara when the early-morning traffic had slowed us enough for me to start having second thoughts about the whole plan. Perhaps she was right and this was just an excuse to get near airplanes again instead of my using valuable time to construct a real defense for Lee. Whatever my doubts, though, I kept them to myself and gave her a heartfelt kiss as she dropped me off at Battery Park.

"Thanks for the lift, Tara."

"You're very welcome." She said that very quietly and close enough to my ear that, even in the morning freeze, I felt the warmness of her breath, the scent of some discreet perfume, and then the wondrous sensation of her lips on mine way beyond any polite peck of farewell. "Enjoy your flying and stay safe."

"I will." Truth be told, my immediate instinct had been to get back into that Dodge in pursuit of something even more exciting than flight. Instead, I simply returned that blissful kiss for as long as decorum allowed, hitched my bag over my shoulder and made the superhuman effort to step back. "See you at Pier Fifteen at five."

"I'll be there."

And then I was standing in that cold Hudson River wind, watching her drive off for her own appointment fourteen miles back north-east and suddenly feeling very, very alone. Nothing for it now but to press on with the plan, and I headed down to the ferry slip, pulling up the fur collar of my old flight jacket as I went.

Last night's resurrection of this old kit from its battered trunk in the corner of my office, impregnated as it was with the aroma of leather, sweat and high octane benzene, had certainly been emotive. In the battered leather bag now slung from my shoulder was also my old helmet and logbook, the latter, the only proof I'd got of a past skill that might still be there, or so rusted as to be almost worthless. I'd soon know as I made my way down to the wooden jetty where I could already see an open workboat lying with its engine rumbling.

Fifteen minutes had me clambering out at the island jetty and another ten at the flight line being welcomed by Harry Ludlow. He was as friendly as on my first visit and was soon briefing me on what my check would involve. "We'll climb out to our playground over the Hudson, do some general handling at altitude and then come back here for take-offs and landings. Then, if you're okay, I'll send you off for some consolation on your own." An exciting thought and, as I strapped myself into the Jenny's rear cockpit, I felt all the old instincts returning and pretty confident the skills would as well.

Ludlow handled the start-up, taxied us out and did the take-off and then, as we climbed out over the old military facilities on the north end of the island, his voice came through the speaking tube into my helmet, telling me to 'take control'. For just a second, as I took the stick in my hand and feet on the rudder bar, I felt like a raw first-timer, but then the *feel* was there again and it was almost without thinking that I rolled into a climbing turn as Ludlow pointed the way to go.

At three-thousand feet, I levelled off for some gradually steeper turns, managing to keep things balanced with no slip or skid, before some slow flight, stalls and then a couple of spins each way. Ah the joy again of tumbling earthwards, but this time without having to keep one wary eye open for 'the Hun in the sun'. When Ludlow told me to head back to the field, I had one request of my own. "Okay to try a loop?"

"Sure, go ahead, but make sure you've got at least seventy-five on the clock first."

"Will do." I opened the throttle to full, stuck the nose down to get those vital knots and eased the nose up and up until Manhattan was appearing again above my inverted nose and we were sliding down in the second half, throttling back the engine and leaving it there as I made a steep gliding turn back to Governors. Then down to circuit height of eight hundred feet and the daunting prospect of my first landing in ten years.

Downwind leg parallel to the runway, turn base leg and throttle back when it looked good for the glide approach. Then the turn to finals to line up with the south-west runway. Down we came, me feeling myself tensing on the controls, but glad to see the glide working out well for touchdown on the threshold. And then, as the blades of grass took on definition, I eased back the stick to flare just a few feet above the surface, taking care not to balloon back up, but holding off in a three-point attitude until I felt the rumble of those wheels touching mother earth and the need for swift use of the rudder to keep her running straight. At the end of the landing run, Ludlow said, "Good one. Now, back to the threshold and do it again."

I did, and then some 'touch-and-goes' where you open the

throttle straight up on the landing run for another take-off. After four of these, he told me to taxi in and drop him in front of the hangar without switching off. There, he climbed out, secured his straps to avoid them fouling the controls and shouted in my ear above the rumble of the engine, "Okay, you don't seem to have forgotten much. Go off and amuse yourself with some airwork and them come back for a few more rollers."

I obeyed joyfully, climbing back up into the blue yonder above the Hudson where I made up for ten lost airborne years by flinging the dear old Jenny about as much as she'd take, finishing off with a barrel-roll on the glide before back down for a half-dozen take-offs and landings. Then, taxiing in and shutting down and sitting for a contented minute, as the engine tinkered and cooled, thinking how, once again, I'd returned to earth solely by my own endeavour and relishing the sense of satisfaction that brought.

Heading for the flight office, I also thought how Lee's appalling situation had transformed my own dreary life in the last few days. Now I was keen to find out what the next ones held.

*   *   *

Harry Ludlow greeted me with a steaming mug of coffee. "Well, how did that go?"

"Great. A few cobwebs to shake off to begin with, but the old instincts soon came creeping back."

"I don't think they'd ever gone. I could see you were back in your element the second you strapped in." He nodded towards his office. "Come on in. There's a couple of people you need to meet."

I followed him in to where two men in smart suits sat just to one side of his desk. One was older than the other and stood up as Ludlow went to make the introductions. "Mark, this is ..." but I already recognised this stocky figure with the granite jaw and silver-grey hair cut in a crew so short as to be almost bald, "... Wilson Miller."

The father of the man I fully-intended to indict for murder smiled warmly and took my hand. "Good to meet you, Kingsley." He indicated Ludlow. "The chief here reckons you fly pretty good."

I shrugged. "I walk away from most landings."

"And that you're a lawyer."

"I'm afraid so."

"But that you'd like to get back into aviation."

"Possibly. Airplanes and flying seem to be where my heart still lies."

"Perhaps not all your heart."

Did he mean what I thought he did and that he knew about Tara? If so, how much more did he know? I took the seat Ludlow was ushering me into and the offered cigarette and sat back to see where all this was leading. It didn't take long, withWilson Miller not the sort to mince his words. "Well, Kingsley, I'd like to offer you a job with Miller Air Services. A job that would make use of both your flying and legal experience."

"Doing what exactly?"

"Setting up an operation for us overseas, for which I've invested in some Stout 2ATs. Have you heard of them?"

"A single-engine, high-wing monoplane designed and built by the Stout Metal Airplane Company but, according to *Aero Digest*, a bit underpowered with the old 400 horsepower Liberty engine."

Mr Miller nodded. "Yep, but only with its full load of six passengers or 1500 pounds of freight. And, anyway, the plan is to soon replace them with something a whole lot bigger and better." I raised my eyebrows and he continued, "You may or may not have heard that Ford Motors have bought out Stout, are going into the airplane business themselves in a big way and, later this year, plan to roll out a large new three-engined transport."

"Already being called the 'Tin Goose' on account of it being built entirely of aluminium," I recalled from my magazine reading. "So, how would I fit into this new setup?"

"Initially, to check out on the 2AT, which they've already started delivering to a small base we have on the Savannah River. You could check out on one there before it's dismantled for onward transport."

"Dismantled?"

"Yes. The base has its own dock facility but the river isn't deep enough for ocean-going freighters. So, after dismantling, the aircraft are loaded onto barges which take them downriver to Savannah Port where they're then trans-shipped."

"To where exactly?"

"Somewhere." Wilson Miller gave a small smile at his own deviousness. "You'll find out soon enough, Kingsley, but not before you've signed up with us."

I took a long draw on my cigarette and let the smoke curl upwards with my thoughts. "Wherever that final destination is, Mr Miller, it'll be too far away for me anytime soon, seeing as I have a defense brief for a trial in two weeks."

"The Lee Vennington murder case."

I gave a nod of approbation. "You obviously keep abreast of local news, Mr Miller."

"Only if we're interested in the parties involved."

Was he referring to me or his own son? Perhaps both, and was this job offer simply an inducement to back off. If so, I had to make a stand of sorts. "I can't abandon my client, Mr Miller, and lose him his only chance of an acquittal."

"From what the DA's told me, there isn't much chance of that, Kingsley, whoever's defending him." Then his slightly commanding tone eased somewhat. "But there's no reason you can't get checked out down there and still be back for your trial."

"I don't see how. The Savannah River's the border between South Carolina and Georgia and eight-hundred miles from here. Just getting there and back is going to take a week."

"Not if you fly." It was Harry Ludlow stepping in for the first time. "You could use one of our Jennies and be there in a couple of days and back in time for your trial. It'd be fun trip."

"Especially if you took your Miss Magee along for the ride," added Wilson Miller with a conspiratorial grin.

So, they did know about me and Tara. I couldn't decide whether to be shocked, offended or excited at a possible new dimension to my love-life. In the end, I chose to retain some shred of professionalism by seeking confirmation on the most important point. "But you'd be happy for me to still defend Lee?"

"Of course, but how does Miss Magee feel about you acting for the man who murdered her brother?"

I tried to ignore this extra disclosure of personal knowledge and simply answered, "Like me, she's not convinced they've got the right man."

"Take it from me, they have." Miller sounded genuinely sure, but his manner then again became surprisingly understanding when he leaned forward and said, "I know how you feel, Kingsley. You and Vennington were old wartime buddies and you want to be there for him now. In fact, I tried to help Lee myself by taking him on as a form of advisor on post-war trauma. But it seems I was wasting my time and money. I guess every defense counsel likes to believe in their client, but the guy's obviously as guilty as hell, so don't go squandering all your talents on a lost cause. Instead it's time to be thinking of your own future and what *we* have to offer you. Like a salary of ten thousand dollars a year."

"Ten …" I tried hard not to slaver at this figure, twice what I should have been earning as a lawyer, four times what I was currently scraping in and a whole world away from what I'd ever get for Lee's defense. "That's *very* generous, Mr Miller, but I owe Lee Vennington more than just money. Besides, he's a veteran who did his bit for the country and deserves justice in return."

"Not in this case, he doesn't." It was the shadowy Mr Smith now speaking up for the very first time. Up until now he'd just been sitting there eyeing my responses while I tried to work out his place in this whole setup. With his dispassionate expression, emotionless voice and piercing eyes, he didn't seem a man I'd particularly enjoy working with, especially when he said, "You need to understand, Kingsley, that certain people have a sincere desire to see your client put away for good."

I was quite sure those 'certain people' were facing me right now, but shutting this particular door wasn't going to help either me or Lee. I turned back to Wilson Miller. "I need to have a think about this."

He nodded. "Sure, but don't take too long."

"How long is 'long'?"

"Twenty-four hours." He took out a card and handed it across. "Here's my personal number. Call that direct when you've made your decision, but give serious consideration to what you'd be giving up if you turned me down." Once again he smiled the disarming smile that I knew must have closed many a deal. "The law isn't any kind of life for a man like you, Kingsley. But this could be fun, not just for you, but also for that nice girl you've got yourself. Take her with you to the Savannah. It'll help her get over her brother's loss and give an insight into the new life you both could be taking."

He stood up and I did the same. "Okay, Mr Miller, you'll have my answer by this time tomorrow."

"Good."

We shook hands again and I followed him back to the flight office, noticing for the first time as we went, two framed photos on the corridor walls. They were of large airships in U.S. markings. I paused to study them. "Heh, *Shenandoah* and *Los Angeles*."

Wilson Miller's eyebrows did a momentary rise. "You have any experience of airships, Kingsley?"

It wasn't the time to go into that indelible memory. Instead I said, "Only enough to know that millions of cubic feet of hydrogen over your head is a pretty dangerous way to fly, as evidenced by *Shenandoah*'s own sad demise last year."

"That was nothing to do with the gas." There was an edge of defensiveness in Wilson Miller's voice. "The ship broke up in a storm, but she had helium instead of hydrogen, which is why she never caught fire or blew up."

"You sound like you have more than a casual interest in the subject, Mr Miller."

He nodded. "Miller Industries have been involved in aviation from its earliest days. When they discovered helium back in 1903, our chemical division immediately saw its potential as an inert lifting gas and we straightway got working on its use for airships."

"I bet the Germans would have welcomed that in the war."

He shrugged. "We all would have, but it's hellishly expensive and supplies are so limited that it'll only ever be available to U.S. users."

"Well, thank goodness airplanes don't need it." With that, I thanked Miller Air Services for the morning's flying and their generous offer, took my leave and headed back for my dinner date with Tara Magee.

In my own mind, I'd already decided which path I was going to take, but winning her support might be the toughest part of this whole deal.

"Let me get this right. You're planning to accept a job overseas with the very outfit you think might be involved in my brother's murder?"

I'd met Tara as planned at the *Fisherman's Inn* on Manhattan's South Street waterfront, fully expecting to have to use every bit of my advocacy skills to make my case.

With the inn yet to be filled with late-night diners, we'd got ourselves a window table from which I now watched the steadily-flowing East River below already becoming veiled in resettling mist. From distant New York Harbor there came the eerie wail of ships' horns warning it would soon be deepening to fog. But not as chilly as the east wind now blowing across our table!

"I know, Tara, but the whole idea of this exercise was to find the truth, and getting into Miller Industries is the only way we'll do it." It was a time for conciliation. "Okay, things seem to have gone a bit faster and become more involved than either of us expected, but this way we'll surely uncover what's going on sooner and I'll have a defense for Lee."

"If you actually get back for his trial."

"I should do, seeing as they're going to let me use a Jenny. And, it's even better than that, because they're happy for you to come along too."

That made her sit up. "What, me, fly all the way to South Carolina?"

"Yep, and the Jenny will have dual controls, so I can start giving you some flight-training on the way."

"My goodness." I could see that conflicting emotions were already coming into play. "This Wilson Miller certainly knows how to make tempting offers." She laid down the menu she'd been studying. "Somehow, though, all this seems just too good to be true. Are you quite sure, Mark, that this job offer isn't just a honey trap to stop you pursuing his son and ensure that Lee takes the rap instead?"

"It's a definite possibility I've considered." I sat back and frowned. "But something still tells me that all this goes a whole lot deeper than that." I absently fingered my menu. "And even more so since I met the enigmatic Mr Smith."

"So, who do you think he is?"

Before I could answer, the waitress came to take our orders, at least giving me time to marshal my thoughts and for the atmosphere to ease.

"I'm still not sure, but he seemed to be calling the shots even more than Miller. At first I thought he had to be from their personnel department, and then, later, perhaps the company lawyer, but now I don't think he was either."

"Who then?"

I shrugged. "It's pure supposition, but somehow I got the impression he was government of some sort."

"Government!"

"Yeah, and even more so with this new overseas operation they're gearing up for all sounding a bit shady. Wilson Miller certainly isn't the sort to risk money without some guaranteed backing and perhaps it's our own government providing it. Smith certainly seemed stiff-necked enough to be the man overseeing something like that."

She gave a nod of understanding. "I can see the likes of Wilson Miller only too ready to get himself a lucrative government contract, especially with him now campaigning for senator."

"And it wouldn't be their first handout from Uncle Sam anyway, because I also found out that for several years they've been supplying helium for U.S. airships."

"Which makes it all the more unlikely, Mark, that the family could in any way be involved in my brother's murder."

"On the contrary, with a government contract in the offing, they'd be hell bent on ensuring that no skeletons ever got out from that particular little cupboard."

"Okay but, from what you tell me, this Smith character seemed equally determined that Lee Vennington go down for Richard's murder. Surely the government wouldn't want to be involved in anything so sordid."

Right there, she'd put her finger on something that had been worrying me. "Good point, Tara, and that's just one of the mysteries in this whole strange business that I need to get to the bottom of. But the only way I'll do that is from the inside, which makes accepting this job offer all the more vital."

"So, you don't actually intend going the whole way to the overseas assignment?"

"No, of course not, but I'm sure their Savannah River base is where son Carl took off for, and going there ourselves is the only way we'll track him down and bring him to book." The waitress arrived with our seafood choices, providing a welcome excuse to redirect the questioning. "So, how did your own investigation at Miller headquarters go?"

She smiled for the first time this evening. "Pretty good. I got to meet their man in charge of public relations, put on my most flirtatious persona and got, not only a healthy donation to *Winfred's Welfare*, but also a full run-down on the history of the Miller dynasty."

"Did you now?" I paused in forking a mouthful of shrimps. "Go on, tell me what you found."

This time she didn't even need to check any notes. "Well, let's start with Wilson's father, Johann Mueller, who was born in Prussia in 1828."

"Prussia?"

"Yep. Back then, what we now know as Germany was a collection of independent states, but with some factions already pushing for unification. The resulting conflict of loyalties was obviously going to end in some sort of fracas, prompting young Johann to up-sticks and emigrate here in 1852."

"Okay, but did you say 'Mueller'?"

"Yep, and he kept that name when he first settled in New York, and even when he moved on west to Texas a couple of years later."

"So, old Johann, was a frontiers man?"

"Very much so. He settled initially in Galveston where there was a large German population, set up in business as a blacksmith and soon gained a reputation for good and reliable service." Tara paused to dig into her lobster. "At that time though, it was California where men were making their fortunes in the gold-rush, and Johann set off there in 1855, basing himself in the boomtown of Columbia to try his luck."

"And did he find it?"

"Yep, in the form of a glistening seam that set him up for life. With his new-found wealth, he then headed back to his original Galveston home to expand his blacksmith business into a full-blown engineering setup, but not before also ploughing some of his gold earnings into another small industry in the small town of Sonora."

"Doing what?"

"General engineering in support of the mining operations. It seems he had an inventive bent in designing, developing and, ultimately, producing various technical breakthroughs in such things as cranes and windpumps."

"Hmm." I nodded, admiringly. "Old Johann sounds like he was an enterprising type and my guess is he had some sort of engineering background before he ever emigrated. How about the family angle?"

"Ah, in that he wasn't quite so successful." Tara's mouth gave a little downturn. "Like many people's lives at that time, it wasn't without its sadness. In 1858 he married Janice Wilson, but a year later she died in childbirth having their son, who was christened Wilson in her memory."

"Our corporation president and senatorial candidate, and who obviously Anglicized the family name to Miller?"

"But inherited both his father's business acumen and technical expertise. The family enterprises were prospering and Wilson was sent off for a good engineering-based education before coming back into the businesses in Texas and California. And then, after Johann's death in the mid seventies, Wilson expanded their operations even further afield."

"Where, exactly?"

"Gradually back eastwards. By 1892, he'd set up concerns in Nebraska, then into Illinois and, finally, into New York. But he'd also gone back to Califormia and set up a small concern in Oroville, a town sixty miles north of Sacremento."

"A chemical plant?"

"That's right." She gave me a quizzical look. "How did you know that?"

"Just connecting to what they told me this morning. Do they still have that place?"

"I believe so. It's only a small facility employing about twenty men. Is it important ?"

"It might be, because I have a crazy theory that all those locations are linked to something I'm just starting to speculate on."

"Which is?"

"I'll explain that later. For now, tell me what kind of research they were doing in these other places."

"All sorts of futuristic concepts, but with an increasing emphasis on aviation." She smiled. "According to the man at Head Office, it was only an accident of timing that prevented the Millers from beating the Wright Brothers as first aviators."

"If they hadn't already done it."

Tara frowned. "What do you mean?"

"Never mind. You said 'Millers', so I guess you're also referring to Wilson Miller's son?"

"That's right, Carl born in 1886, but my man didn't seem to want to talk much about him."

"And probably with good reason, because I think this Carl is the one who murdered your brother."

That was enough for her next forkful to freeze midway to her mouth. She lowered it again and pushed away the plate. "Good heavens. Can you prove that?"

I shook my head. "Not yet, other than that I know his background, that Lee recognised him that morning at Saint Winifred's, and his description fits the man who initially reported the murder to the patrolman."

"You'll need more than that."

"I know, which is why I need to make this trip to the Savannah River, find Carl, and get myself some evidence." The waitress came to collect our plates and I ordered coffees. When she'd brought them back, I leaned closer to the girl I was finding not only beautiful, but intelligent as well. "And having you with me would be the real icing on that particular cake."

She gave a roll of those endearing blue eyes. "Very tempting, Mark, but I couldn't leave *Winifred's Welfare* for all that time."

"Not even if it meant giving up the chance of some flight training?"

"Me? Learn to fly?"

"Why not?" Seeing the glimmer of excitement in her eyes, it was time to pull out all the stops. "I've seen what a great driver you are, Tara, and know you'd ace it. So, why don't we make the most of this plan and achieve something together." I gave her a conspiratorial wink. "Come on, live your life."

She gave a little gulp. "I'm not sure, Mark."

"Not sure of the idea or me?"

"Oh, I think I could handle both." She smiled, reached across the table and put a reassuring hand on mine. "I do like you. It's just that it's all so sudden." She gave an extra squeeze. "Let me sleep on it and we'll take it from there. And, talking of home ..." she was glancing outside to where vapors of deepening fog were already drifting up the East River. "... I guess we should get motoring back before that gets any thicker."

"You're probably right."

She gave another of those impish smiles of hers. "But nothing to stop you coming in for a late-night coffee ... with one condition."

"Which is?"

"That you tell me what whole strange story that devious mind of yours is evolving that could possibly lead to Richard's murder."

*   *   *

It was gone ten and *Winifred's Welfare* battened down into its night routine by the time Tara wheeled the *Roadster* into the shelter's adjacent alley and let us in by a side door.

"We have a rule that everyone has to be snugged down by nine-thirty," she explained quietly as we tiptoed up the stairs to her apartment, "so better our poor inmates don't see me sneaking in after a night on the town."

"It's still only late evening, Tara, and you must have some staff on duty?"

"Just a night manager and a couple of attendants," she whispered over her shoulder while silently unlocking the apartment door and ushering me into the fond-remembered room with its books and memorabilia lit by just one shaded standard lamp. I was glad she didn't switch on more. "Coffee?"

"Yes, please."

It was the kind of room you instantly felt at home in, not so tidy as to diminish the atmosphere of warm cosiness created by subdued light and her feminine touch. Soon she was joining me on the sofa with two mugs of freshly-brewed coffee, warming her hands around hers as she curled up at one end, chin resting on her knees and her eyes telling me it was a time for explanations.

"Right, now tell me what the Sherlock Holmes of The Bronx has managed to deduce so far."

This was the closest we'd ever physically been and not the best situation to have my mind at its most deductive, but I took a deep breath to steady my pulse and a good mouthful of coffee to arrange my thoughts. "Well, it all relates to those locations you mentioned regarding Miller's early years."

"What, Galveston and then Columbia?"

"Yep, and before that, when he was in California and later, in Nebraska and Illinois."

She took a sip of coffee. "A long way from here, Mark. Are they really that significant?"

"Only in their order and timing. At first I couldn't think why, until I remembered something I'd read about in accounts of early aviation."

"Which was?"

"Airships."

She raised curious eyebrows. "What, you mean the big Zeppelin things the Germans were so keen on?"

"And still are, but I'm talking about some mystery airships that were seen over this country long before those big monsters ever reached that stage of development."

Tara frowned over the top of her coffee mug. "When was this?"

"1896, starting on the dark evening of 17 November over Sacremento."

"California again?"

"Yep. Darkness had already fallen when witnesses reported seeing a strange bright light, suspended below some dark mass, moving slowly over the city from east to west at a few hundred feet. Some even reckoned they heard human voices."

"Were there *any* airships operating at that time?"

"There'd been some early experiments in Europe and here in New Jersey, by a medical doctor called Solomon Andrews who flew a directionally controllable balloon called the *Aereon* in 1863. But that was nothing like the cigar-shaped craft shining something like a searchlight that they saw thirty-three years later."

"That's *if* they 'saw' anything." Tara took another sip of her coffee and smiled, skeptically. "Surely that light could just have easily been a bright star or planet, or even a Chinese lantern released by some mischief-maker. That could be enough to get everyone's imagination fired up."

I nodded. "That's what disbelieving voices said at the time, except it reappeared five nights later, but this time going west to east *against* the wind. Then, just a few hours later and ninety miles up the coast in San Francisco, it reappeared and seen this time by hundreds of citizens, including the mayor."

"So, who or what do they think was responsible?"

I shrugged. "There were several theories, though the most interesting came from a respected San Francisco attorney called George Collins. He reckoned he was actually representing the inventor, who'd constructed the ship at a secret location just sixty miles north of Sacramento at Oroville."

"Oroville!"

"Exactly, so you're starting to see the Wilson connection."

"Tenuous as it is so far," she admitted, begrudgingly, "but you've got me intrigued, so go on. Did this attorney give any more details?"

"A few, including revealing that the airship's components had been manufactured in the east and then shipped to Oroville where it was assembled in a hundred and fifty foot barn."

"Pretty specific."

"Indeed, except that a few days later he withdrew his statement completely and endured ridicule as a result."

"But *you* think he was telling the truth?"

"I do, but that he'd opened his mouth a bit too freely for his clients, who then ordered him to retract his statement. Amazingly, though, that didn't stop William Henry Hart, another San Francisco attorney, and past attorney-general of the state, stepping forward to say there were actually two airships and the plan was to use them to bomb Havana. Then Hart too withdrew his statement and said nothing further."

"Presumably, leaving the whole thing as something of a mystery," surmised Tara, finishing her coffee. "So, apart from the locations, what connection does any of this have to the Millers?"

"Plenty, because ever-more airship sightings started coming in from other states. Most significantly for us, though, was an early report from Texas where a man called Tucker wrote to the Galveston Daily News explaining how he'd earlier met the young pilot and inventor in Lake Charles, Louisiana, and that the pilot's name was Wilson."

"Wilson!" Tara put down her mug and sat up a little straighter.

"Yep, and then in April 1897, a brewing agent in Texas, called Ligon, reckoned he was arriving home near Beaumont at eleven at night with his son Charley, when they saw a light in a pasture a few hundred yards away. When they went to investigate they found four men gathered around an airship. The leader said they needed some water and even introduced himself as ..."

"Don't tell me. Wilson again?"

"Correct, and this Wilson told them they were returning from the Gulf and heading for Iowa. And then, a few days later, four local dignitaries were playing dominoes in a hotel in Conroe, Texas, when their game was interrupted by two men saying they were from an airship and needed water. The players were naturally skeptical until they went and saw the ship lift off and head on its way, brilliantly illuminated by electric light. But, not far it seems, because later a farmer called Frank Nichol from near-by Josser, reckoned he looked out of his window and saw an airship. When he went to investigate, he was accosted by two men carrying buckets and asking for water."

Tara gave a wry smile. "These early aeronauts certainly seemed to need a lot of water."

"They did indeed, either for ballast or perhaps something to do with the gas being used to lift the ships. Anyway, it didn't stop there in Texas, because on April 24th, some frightened Mexicans in Eagle Pass ran to the house of the local sheriff to report another landing on the banks of the Rio Grande. Then another sheriff called H.W. Baylor in Uvalde was alerted by a bright light and voices behind his house. Investigating, he found an airship and four crew taking on water. The leader introduced himself as Wilson and said they were on a trial run and asked him not to make their presence known. But he did say he'd known a former sheriff called Captain Akers in Fort Worth and asked to be remembered to him. When Sheriff Baylor followed that up, Akers confirmed the association."

"So, several authentic-sounding identifications," acknowledged Tara, "except it sounds like 'Wilson' was actually this pilot's surname."

"Not necessarily." I sat back. "Okay, this guy introduced himself as 'Wilson', which is a common enough surname, and over the years since, everyone has just assumed that's what it was. Looking at it from our perspective, though, it could just as easily have been his first name. In fact, if he was trying to keep his operation secret, in all probability, that's all he would have given."

"And you think *that* Wilson is now our senatorial candidate and head of Miller Industries?" Tara ran a hand through her hair, now loose and shining in the subdued light. Then she sat back frowning, as though trying to recall something of her own. "It's certainly an intriguing mystery, Mark, but all that about phantom airships somehow strikes a chord in my own memory. I'm sure I've read something about that myself."

"Really!" I was glad she didn't think me completely off my rocker. "Where was this one?"

"That's the trouble, I can't remember except I think it was long ago when I was still at school. Hopefully, it'll come back to me, but in the meantime, you still haven't told me how all this airship business led to Richard's murder."

"Right, but before I go spinning you that theory, there's a couple of points I need to check with Lee tomorrow."

"When you're also going to tell him that you're off on a flying spree for a week."

"That's right," I gulped slightly, "and which I know isn't going to be received at all well."

"But necessary if you're to find the key to his defense."

At least she was now voicing my own convictions, and perhaps this was a good time to push the other carrot. "And I'm still hoping you'll be flying to the Savannah River with me?"

She smiled sweetly. "Like I said, let me sleep on that one."

"Ah, yes, sleep." I shrugged. "How nice that must be."

"Meaning?"

"That I never seem to get a full night of it without it being plagued with nightmares."

"Of the war?"

"Yep. In some ways it was the most fulfilling time of my life, but one still filled with vivid memories and happenings that seem hard to shake off."

"I do understand, because I know Richard was haunted by those same demons." She edged closer and took my hand. "I know it helped him to talk to me about it and I could do the same for you if you wanted."

"You wouldn't want to be bored by all my old war stories," I said, giving a laugh to lighten the mood before glancing at my watch, "and right now I need to get going and things sorted for a week away."

"Not if it's back to that miserable office of yours for even more nightmares." She squeezed my hand tighter. "Perhaps we need to get working on those demons sooner rather than later." Her voice had become soft and compassionate, creating the joyful sensation of feelings starting to match my own, especially when she added. "Stay here tonight and let's see if we can give you something nicer to dream about."

As curative prescriptions go, I couldn't have found any better in this whole universe and, without further words, I took this wonderful girl in my arms for what I hoped would be a long and mutually blissful course of treatment.

*   *   *

CHAPTER SEVEN

"I hate to bring us back to reality, Mark, but what are your plans for today?"

It was next morning and later than it should have been, wintery sunshine already filtering in through the apartment windows and the enticing aroma of frying eggs coming from the open kitchen along with Tara's question.

I made an effort to come down to earth. "Call Miller Air Services and tell them I'm accepting their job offer. Then I'll visit Lee and update him on what's happening."

"Which won't be the best news he's heard this week."

"Or the worst."

"Even so," she placed two platefuls of eggs and some buttered toast on the table and sat down beside me, "are you really sure this is the best way to go?"

"It is if we're ever going to uncover what's actually going on."

She frowned. "You said 'we're'."

"Right, because I know you're as keen as anyone to convict Richard's murderer. The only question now is whether you're flying down there with me. Did you come to any decision last night?"

"I didn't have time to think of much at all last night." She smiled as she stroked my arm. "What I am now sure of, though, is that I want to be wherever you are."

That was all I needed to know, but instead of jumping for joy, I just about managed to control my excitement and mumble, "So, you're coming?"

"Of course, though only to ensure you don't stick your neck out just that bit too far."

"I won't if your neck's right there with me."

"Glad to hear it, because I'm as sure as you are that we're dealing with ruthless people here who won't stop at murder to achieve their aims."

I nodded agreement. "Yep, but we need to find out just what those aims are, and we won't do that playing it completely safe."

She removed her hand so we could get eating, but there were other factors she obviously wasn't happy about. "This job you're accepting sounds a bit suspicious to me."

"I know what you mean but, according to them, it's a legit overseas contract."

"But they didn't actually say *where* overseas?"

"No, and I got the feeling it was Mr Smith's presence that kept that information under wraps."

"Hmm." She poured some coffee and frowned. "From what you've told me, there's something about that man, whoever he is, that I don't like. I think he's the one you need to watch out for."

"Amongst others," I said, thinking also of son Carl when I finally tracked him down.

"Quite." She gave another of her resigned smiles as she stood up and started clearing the table. "Anyway, we both need to get going if you're off to see Lee and I'm to make arrangements for leaving *Winfred's Welfare* for a week."

I took the hint, quickly finished my eggs, and fished out the card Wilson Miller had given me. "First though, to call the big man and tell him I'm on board and that you're flying with me to the Savannah River."

With those entrancing thoughts, I got the operator to put me through to Wilson Miller.

*   *   *

Decision given and gladly received, another hour saw me returning to the county jail for my meeting with Lee. It would have been a daunting prospect, had my spirits not been raised by the way other plans were working out. Miller had even said he'd be happy to pay all of Tara's expenses while we were away, which made me wonder again if this whole thing was simply a way of getting us both well away from New York for the trial week.

And the very next day due, he told me, the freighter imminently arriving in Savannah Port and the need for me to be checked and the aircraft dismantled and shipped. I'd have protested at such short notice if it hadn't been for the euphoric thought of winging it over the horizon with Tara for a whole week. She too seemed just as excited at the prospect and not daunted at the task of sorting more-immediate arrangements for the shelter while she was away.

But, if I needed something to bring me down to earth, the penitentiary with its clanging doors, stomach-churning odours and atmosphere of hopelessness, was certainly the place to do it. As a guard once more escorted me along those dismal passages, I consoled myself with the thought of how blissful my own outlook now was and how it might help Lee. That still didn't stop me feeling some guilt, though, and even more so when we reached the meeting room to find him already waiting and looking more dejected than ever.

I knew my current plans weren't going to be received with an abundance of enthusiasm so, after the now-obligatory issue of cigarettes and enquiries as to his general well-being, I got straight to the point by telling him I'd accepted a job with Miller's.

"You mean you're dropping my case and going over to the other side?"

"No, of course not, Lee, but we know that the man we once knew as Meunier is actually Carl Miller and the real murderer. Getting our hands on him and bringing him back for justice is your only hope." I looked directly into his skeptical eyes. "You do understand that, don't you?"

"Would it matter whether I did or not?"

"It would to me." I leaned closer and lit up his *Camel*. "Lee, we have to face the fact that we're dealing with more than just evidence against you here. As it is, the whole justice system seems intent on your conviction, encouraged, I'm pretty sure, by more far-reaching, sinister powers."

I thought he'd demand to know who or what, but instead he simply blew an ascending cloud of cigarette smoke up into the room's chilly atmosphere. It reminded me of those thunderclouds we used to dice with over the Western Front and almost as forbidding as he asked, "If you do lay hands on Meunier, what then?"

"Somehow get him back into New York jurisdiction. If nothing else, Pat Nolan wants him as a witness, but my intention is to then lay enough doubt before a judge to get us an adjournment and, eventually, have him indicted in your place."

Lee gave a humorless laugh. "You always were the optimist, Mark. Do you really think we have a chance of that, with everyone determined to have me fry at Sing Sing."

"Not everyone, Lee, but it's the *why* that I'm trying to figure." I lit another *Camel* of my own and took a deep drag. "You got *any* idea?"

He shook his head. "Probably because he's the son of a

senatorial candidate and I'm a down-and-out loser who's best placed to take the rap in his place?"

"I knew you in better times, Lee." I wasn't convinced by his self-effacing analysis, but now wasn't the time for ego-boosting. "And, anyway, I'm not so sure the father is that squeaky clean either, but I need something more than conjecture. For starters, do you happen to know which POW camp Richard ended up in?"

"What's that got to do with it?"

"Just a theory. Did he tell you?"

"He did, and I'm trying to remember." He frowned while looking up into his nicotine cloud, as though for inspiration. "Yeah, it was Cologne ... that's right ... Cologne .... I remember him saying how he caught a glimpse of the cathedral there when he first arrived by train."

"I didn't know there was an *Offizierlager* in Cologne."

"There wasn't, but they had a hospital for wounded allied prisoners in the *Kaiserin Augusta Schule Lazarett*. I guess they figured Richard, being a padre, would be of more use there than in a regular camp."

"Doubtless, but there was something else in Cologne as well." The sourness in my voice made him suddenly realise that just the mention of that Rhineland city had brought back vivid memories of my own.

"Oh, of course, I forgot, that's somewhere you were as well, wasn't it?"

"Close by and only briefly, but a visit I'll never forget."

"I can imagine." He seemed to be at least making an effort to show something like empathy. "That was a long time ago, Mark, but I'm still sorry you had to go through it."

I shrugged. "The luck of the draw." But I was letting my own personal feelings surface, which was something no lawyer should ever do. "Anyway, recollections apart, I'm glad that's where Richard was."

"Why?"

"Because it fits right in with my theory as to the motive for his elimination and why we might still get the real murderer in court."

*   *   *

"So, how did that go?"

Back in Tara's apartment, her question came on top of a welcoming kiss and heart-warming smile.

I managed to give a more subdued one in return. "As well as can be expected, though I suspect Lee's beginning to realize he's got no Clarence Darrow defending him."

"No, but he's got a good friend instead."

I shook my head. "I'm not even sure if the 'friend' bit still holds up."

"How come?" She looked genuinely perplexed. "What happened to all that brotherly comrades-in-arms-for-ever stuff you told me about?"

"Just another casualty of the war, I guess, or at least a consequence of it in the shape of Margreet McLeod."

"The Dutch woman you met in Paris? *She* came between you?"

"Yeah, but not in the way you think. Personally, I couldn't stand her, but Lee was besotted and *that's* what came between us." I sat back and sighed. "I learned the hard way that the quickest way to lose a friend is to tell him something he doesn't want to hear."

"And you told him what you thought of Margreet?"

"Yep, but only as a good buddy would for his own sake. The chump was making a complete fool of himself over a woman a full nineteen years older, but clearly an experienced seductress who had him completely hooked. Every chance he got, he was creeping off from camp to a local hostelry to be with her, and coming back more smitten than ever."

Tara frowned. "I'm amazed your officers allowed it. Surely there were regulations."

I shrugged. "Actually, the French were pretty broad-minded about that sort of thing. As long as we were back by dawn and ready for that day's ops, they accepted cheap wine and liaisons with local girls as a good way to take our minds off imminent mortality."

"But you say this Margreet was from a neutral country, and yet was able to wander around a war-zone at will." Tara leaned forward and frowned. "How was that allowed?"

"Quite. I challenged Lee myself on that very point and he came back with the amazing story that she was somehow linked to French Intelligence."

"You mean, she was a sort of spy?"

"That's what Lee reckoned, and later events showed he was right, but not the way he thought." Now wasn't the time for remembrances, but future plans. "Are you all set for an early start tomorrow?"

She nodded. "Pretty much so. I'm all packed and sorted for my deputy to run *Winifred's* while I'm away. How about you?"

"Likewise. I stopped by my office on the way back and arranged for Betty Devinski to check my mail."

"Good, so plenty of time now for you to give me your theory on how the Millers might be connected to Richard's murder. You said you needed to check some things with Lee first so, did you, and did it help?"

"Yes on both counts, so let me give you my own take on things. Of course, it's all surmise, based partly on fact and some of it purely suspicion."

"As long as it's not too far-fetched." She sat back on the sofa. "So go ahead. I'm all ears."

"Okay, well, for starters, we know the Millers were originally Muellers from Germany and that after they'd emigrated here they always chose to live in communities of mainly German extraction."

"Which is understandable," concurred Tara.

"Agreed but, more to the point for us, there's strong evidence that, early on, they became involved in airship design and chemical research and that they still own a chemical works in Oroville that produces helium for U.S. airships. All very worthwhile and respectable, but what you don't know, Tara, and I haven't told you, is that the family has a link to treachery through Wilson's son, Carl."

That certainly made her sit up. "How do you know that?"

"Personal experience." I gave her a brief run-down on my own brush with Carl, alias Meunier, in the Legion.

"My goodness, not the best of backgrounds for the son of a senatorial candidate." Her eyes were wide by the time I'd finished, though she still seemed loathe to accept the reality. "But are you really sure it was Carl who Lee saw in the church when Richard was murdered?"

"Absolutely. And he completely matches the description of the man who reported 'the disturbance' to Officer Burroughs. Chief Nolan now badly wants him as a witness but, having given a false name and address, he seems to have mysteriously disappeared."

"Okay, but what motive could he have for killing Richard?"

"I'm working on that, but I'm pretty sure it was something your brother saw when he was a POW in Germany ... something that just a week or so ago, came back to haunt him."

"The newspaper piece on Wilson Miller's election hopes and that photo of him with Lee?"

I nodded. "Has to be. This morning Lee confirmed that your brother's POW time was spent in Cologne, so it must have been there that he saw something he shouldn't have."

"Something? What?"

"A man, or men, who he might have suspected as being Americans collaborating with the enemy."

She shook her head. "He certainly never mentioned it to me, so why would he stay silent about something as serious as that?"

"Like he said, he wasn't completely sure, didn't want to make false accusations and probably felt some things were best forgotten. Back then the public were celebrating a final victory and the last thing they needed to hear was that some of their countrymen had been less than honourable. But, if what I'm surmising is correct, when he saw Wilson Miller's photo in the paper last week, he recognised the strong resemblance to the man he'd seen in Germany, realized the father of a traitor was now having the effrontery to run for public office, and knew he had to act." I took Tara's hand. "From what you've told me, your brother wasn't a man afraid to grasp the nettle, so I can imagine him contacting Wilson Miller direct, telling him he knew the family secret for what it was, and advising him to step down from election."

"And instead got himself silenced for good." Tara wiped away something from the corner of her eye. "But you still have no proof, Mark, and accusing Wilson Miller of being associated with treachery is one big step. Have you considered other scenarios? Could it have been that Lee found out that son Carl was the Meunier you'd once known as a traitor, and then told Richard. That would surely have been damaging enough to his father's election hopes to take things into his own hands."

I nodded. "A possibility, but remember it was Wilson's photo in the paper and he might well have been a party to his son's treachery as part of an orchestrated plan."

"A plan for what? What did they hope to gain?"

"Money. Lots and lots of money." I sat back, trying not to

sound too much like a college lecturer briefing first-year students. "You have to remember, Tara, that Germany was then engaged in full-scale Zeppelin bombing operations against Britain. But those deadly aerial monsters were kept aloft by millions of cubic feet of highly-flammable hydrogen, making them death-traps for their crews. The British had started getting their air defenses together with incendiary-armed aircraft capable of flying higher to intercept. Now it was the Germans who were starting to count the cost, with each raid being marked by one or more of those costly airships going down in flames. The solution for the Germans would have been to use non-flammable helium, but that was only to be found here in the U.S. and we weren't going to export any, even before we came into the war. But what if Miller Industries, way back in those early mystery airship days, had discovered and developed a safer alternative?"

"You mean something that needed lots of water, like in those reports you told me about?"

"It's a possibility. Helium is an expensive substance whereas hydrogen is produced cheaply from water, so perhaps the Millers found a way to make that non-flammable. If so, it would have been a discovery virtually priceless to Germany and its Zeppelin fleet."

Tara shook her head. "I can see how fortunes could have been made from such knowledge, Mark, but aren't you perhaps letting your imagination get the better of you with all this conjecture? And anyway, how come you, an airplane pilot, knows so much about Zeppelins and airships?"

"Ah, that's another story that I'll tell you later." I'd had enough of wartime memories for the moment and needed to think along more immediate and pleasing lines. "But, talking of airplanes, there's something else we need to discuss now."

"Which is?"

"How you fly them, because, remember, I promised to teach you en route, and tomorrow will be your first lesson."

"Oh, gosh!" Her face lit up with excitement before creasing into a slight frown. "But why now?"

"Because the open cockpit of a Jenny trainer is a lousy classroom and the more we go through here, the more you'll understand when you're in it."

So, I got started on explaining the fundamentals of flight and what she'd be putting into practice on the morrow. It took her mind off the sadder aspects of our mission, and the questions she shot back showed she was well up for this new experience and determined to make the most of every minute. We had a dawn start planned, so I didn't drag it out too long, but she had one final question. "Just how long is this trip going to take us?"

"A couple of days, if the weather's reasonable. The old Jenny's no speed-bird, but with the forecast north-westerly wind helping us along the way, twelve hours flight-time should see us there."

"So, one night-stop along the way?"

"Yep, but where that is will depend on how far we get the first day." I shrugged. "Rather than have a fixed plan, we'll just truck along and then find some convenient little place *en route* where we can land and have ourselves a snugly night."

"Sounds fun to me." She grinned mischievously. "I'm thinking learning to fly will only be part of the excitement this trip is offering."

Amen to that, but I was hoping there wouldn't be too much of the adrenalin-pumping kind, seeing as I'd be carrying someone becoming ever-more special. For now, though, I put those concerns to one side and guided us to bed for what I hoped wouldn't be a full night's sleep.

*　　*　　*

"Okay, Tara, how do you like it?"

"Wonderful."

This was not pillow-talk, but early next morning and with a biting cold slipstream already chilling our contented bodies. We were climbing away from Governors Island on the first leg of our long flight and shouting into the aircraft's speaking tubes as the only voice communication between the Jenny's two cockpits. It was good to hear her enthusiastic reply and see her helmeted head in the front cockpit, turning to show as broad a smile as the slipstream allowed.

I smiled back and banked into a turn to take us south of the city and on to the coast, at the same time levelling at eight hundred feet as stratus overcast started flitting past our wingtips. I'd told Harry Ludlow that Newport News would be our midday refuelling stop, and between here and there, we'd be hugging the coast for the first three hundred miles and needing our first gas-up in half that. Where, remained to be seen, loathed as I was to waste time diverting to some other en route airfield. Instead I planned on doing it the old barnstormers' way of just finding a handy regular gas station on some quiet road and landing in the nearest field to top up the Jenny's twenty-one gallons.

Weather would be another factor. I'd checked the east coast forecast, which wasn't brilliant on this winter morn, but good enough to scud run all the way. Keeping low would also give us a slightly higher temp and keep the icy blast of the Jenny's sixty knot slipstream just about bearable. Back over the Western Front in winter, we'd had to stay high to avoid the Archie guns, but now my priority was making things as tolerable as possible for the girl in the front cockpit. There she sat, huddled in fur-lined flight gear, wisps of recalcitrant hair already fluttering defiantly outside her helmet and a gauntleted hand giving me yet another thumbs-up. She seemed happy enough now, but there was a long, cold way to go and already I was looking forward to our first landing for fuel and the chance to restore circulation. In the meantime, I could take her mind off the cold by giving her a first try at aircraft handling. We were well clear of the city now and already picking up the coast. I shouted into the voice tube, "Right, take the stick in your right hand and put your toes on that rudder bar."

"Okay."

She remembered my briefing of the night before and I felt some input going on the controls as I lightly followed through on mine.

"Just keep her like this, using the stick to hold the nose and wings level, and only use the rudder to prevent it yawing."

Immediately the nose went up slightly and then dipped just as suddenly as she over-corrected. "My goodness, it's like a bucking bronco!"

"Yep, airplanes are more sensitive than cars. Just think in terms of *pressure* on the controls rather than moving them. And rest your right arm on your knee and just use your wrist."

"Okay."

I felt the inputs through my controls already becoming more finely tuned and the aircraft flying more steadily as it responded to her delicate feminine touch. As suspected, she was going to be a natural pilot, and I happily let go of my stick completely. "Just keep checking the altimeter and that eight hundred height."

"I'll try."

Further on, though, passing Atlantic City and with Cape May just visible ahead, holding that height was becoming ever more problematical as we clipped the lowering overcast. Out west the sky was darkening with threatening snow showers, probably triggered by those far-off Appalachians. "Just ease her down, Tara, and keep us out of this clag."

"Will do." She lowered the nose just enough to slide off

height while the increased slipstream made me look forward more than ever to our first stop.

By the time we cleared Delaware Bay we'd be needing that landing, as much to avoid the advancing weather as for gas. "Keep her going down Tara, and try a turn out over the ocean. If this cloud base keeps lowering we might need to get right down on the deck."

I was tempted to take back control, but our chat the night before had covered how an aircraft turns and so she gingerly rolled in just a few degrees of bank and allowed the old trainer's nose to accordingly swing steadily to port. "That's great – just a bit of back-pressure to prevent the nose from dropping – okay, roll out now and hold it there." Soon we'd cleared the beach and were down to a couple of hundred feet over that rolling Atlantic, but not so far out that we couldn't stretch a glide back to land if the old OX5 V8 gave trouble. "Okay, now just follow the shoreline."

Another thumbs-up with her free hand and along we went, she seemingly happy in these deteriorating conditions and me content to let her keep poling while I scanned ahead. Not long and Cape May itself was disappearing to starboard and we were out over the ten-mile wide bay. "What now?" asked an unflustered voice from up front.

"Head just a little more to the right so we pick up the other side and the road to Seaford."

"Okay."

Thankfully, the waters of the bay were choppy enough to provide good reference, but I was glad when the southern arm appeared through the murk. We coasted in, solid ground just a hundred feet beneath us now and time for me to retake control. "Okay, I've got her. When we reach the road, keep your eyes skimmed for a gas station."

"Okay."

I headed even further west to ensure we picked up the

road and minutes later the blessed highway appeared. I turned thankfully along it with just the odd flakes of snow beginning to sting my cheeks. Then Tara excitedly yelled through the voice tube, "I think that place ahead has pumps outside."

As we steep-turned overhead and looked down, there, sure enough, rotating on our wingtip was a clapboard garage with gas-pumps. The surrounding fields weren't the best for a landing, but one across the road might just be long enough for our needs. With no spare time to be picky, I brought back the throttle and kept the turn going until we were in a banked and descending turn straight onto a final approach for landing. As luck would have it, that north-west wind was freshening with the approaching storm, hopefully giving us a shorter landing.

It needed to be. That field now looked barely long enough as I chopped the throttle completely and dropped us hard and firm onto its threshold. As the Jenny's spoked wheels hit and rumbled, I worked hard on the rudder to keep us straight, but already the far hedge was starting to fill the windshield and I gave a good bootful at the end to swing us clear. Graunching round with the outer wing almost clipping the rutted surface, we finally came to a stop with the prop turning only feet from the hedge and with the gas station just across the road. I shut down the engine and peace descended, but with it, ever more snow as the storm matched our arrival. I sighed a silent sigh, clambered out and stretched cold and stiff limbs before helping Tara do the same.

"My goodness, that was an exciting last few miles." She pulled off her helmet and goggles before shaking out flattened, matted hair. "For a while there I did wonder how and where I would ever feel solid ground again."

"Yeah, well the trick is actually avoiding that solid ground until it suits you." I took her in my arms for both love and warmth. "Anyway, we need to be away again just as soon as this snowstorm clears, so let's go get ourselves some gas."

"A big mug of coffee would go down even better ... and I think I can see just where we might get one," she added, indicating across the road to what looked like a regular diner beside the garage.

"Right, well let's get fuelled first and then breakfast on Miller Air Services."

There was a field gate close by and we crossed the road, Tara clearly savouring the thought of food and warmth, and me remembering another landing way back in those war years that had been in strangely similar weather. I hadn't known it at the time, but it was my last in a pursuit ship with the old *escadrille*, but one which marked the start of an experience that would change my life out there forever and the cooling off of my friendship with Lee.

Right now though, my first priorities were fuel, warmth and that large mug of coffee.

*   *   *

"Ah, nectar of the gods." Tara had just taken a first sip of coffee before sitting back contentedly in the blissful warmth of the diner. Outside, the snow was now driving horizontally, whitening buildings, hedges and the old Jenny, which we'd thankfully refuelled before the elements did their worst. I sat back too, knowing we were in the best place in this weather and content to make the most of it.

The gas-station attendant had been a cheerful enough soul and more than happy to have his day interrupted by two cold flyers. With aviation still new enough to excite instant interest, he'd willingly helped us carry cans of gas across the road before also giving us the benefit of his own local weather lore. It would be an hour or so yet, he told us, before the snow-storm passed, which at least promised a relaxing break-fast. So we'd promptly headed for the diner, shed our flight suits, warmed hands around steaming mugs and ordered scrambled eggs.

It should all have been ideal had I not still been feeling pangs of guilt at the thought of my client back there in the county jail awaiting trial for his life. I kept telling myself that this whole adventure was to find and apprehend the real perpetrator, but that clearly didn't hide my true feelings from perceptive Tara, who eyed me now over the top of her mug.

"You're thinking about Lee, aren't you?"

"Yep." I shrugged. "It's a sad fact of life that the happier you are, the more guilt you feel for those who aren't."

"And *are* you happy?"

I reached across and took her hand. "Very much so."

She squeezed mine back. "Me too, and I know the obliga-tion you feel to Lee, but you mustn't spoil what we have with pointless guilt. You're doing what you think is best for him and the end will surely justify the means."

I remembered using that phrase myself in more than one court case but, somehow, it didn't seem to help. Instead, my conscience kept telling me that all this was just a selfish excuse to return to a life I loved rather than helping an old comrade. Was I simply running away from the truth?

Tara seemed to read my thoughts. "But were you really such good friends in the end, Mark? You said yourself that he'd taken umbrage at your disapproval of his woman-friend, but I suspect it went a bit deeper than that."

I nodded. "You're right. I wasn't going to bore you with the whole story, but perhaps I need to for you to understand the big picture."

"I think perhaps you do." She squeezed my hand encour-agingly. "This was when you were both still in the Lafayette Flying Corps?"

"Yep, and still in Escadrille N66 which had become SPA66 in late 1916 when we re-equipped with SPAD Sevens." For a second, my thoughts drifted back to those sturdy pursuit ships, trickier to fly than our old Nieuports, but able to take far more punishment, faster in a dive than the Fokkers and blessed with interrupter gear for the two Vickers machine guns. That invaluable improvement allowed us now to aim straight at the Boche machines and for both Lee and myself to up our scores to four kills each. One more would have got us 'ace' status, and Lee seemed hell-bent on that laurel, though I suspected it was more to impress Margreet than any great sense of duty."

"So, Lee was still seeing his Dutch floozy?"

"Very much so, and slipping away to be with her any chance he got. He hit one glitch, though, when we started taking it in turns for a week's attachment to Luxeuil, flying escort to the bomber outfit there. With Margreet installed in the local *auberge*, Lee talked me into covering his stint, but it only got him a week's reprieve before I was back at Souilly and him detailed to replace me the next day. I thought it would do him good anyway to get away from Margreet's clutches for a bit, but he was already uptight at having to go and I aroused his anger even more by telling him how I felt."

"The start of your falling out?"

"I guess so. I tried to get his mind off it by asking about an unfamiliar aircraft I'd noticed on the other side of the field when I landed. It was a Morane Saulnier MS 1112, a two-seat high-wing monoplane that the French used in a variety of roles. I thought it must have diverted to our field due to weather or fuel, but Lee explained it had arrived a couple of days previously under mysterious circumstances and that the two crew were billeted down the road at a local inn instead of being messed with the rest of our escadrille. All very intriguing, and unfortunate for Lee, because that inn was the very place he and Margreet were currently meeting."

Tara smiled. "A bit awkward."

"More like a tragedy for Lee, seeing as he'd be gone for a week and the seductive Margreet was already chummy with the French pilot, having managed to squeeze out of him discreet details of his mission."

"Which was ...?"

"Neither she nor Lee would say, but the whole thing went from intriguing to downright scarey the next morning when I found out for myself. I was out on the airfield early to wish Lee 'good luck' before he headed for Luxeuil. As it was, he'd already taken off, but the Morane crew were there checking their aircraft for a short pre-mission air-test and the strange passenger was learning start-up procedures. They could have got mechanics to swing the prop, so I guessed they'd later be landing somewhere with no technical support and that had to be some place on the wrong side of the lines."

"No wonder they were so secretive."

"Yeah, but quite amusing to me, listening to the French pilot gabbling on about switch and throttle setting and then going to swing the prop himself. He began by turning it over to suck in fuel, but the switch must have been 'on', causing a cylinder to fire, the prop to kick over, and him rolling off to one side yelling all sorts of Gaelic blasphemies."

Tara's eyes widened. "Was he badly hurt?"

"Not really. Just a broken arm, and I thought the whole debacle a bit funny until later that morning I was called into *Capitaine* Barcat's office. Then the joke definitely soured when I found the Morane crew also there, the pilot with his arm in a sling and looking very sheepish, and his strange passenger appearing more sinister than ever. It didn't look good for me, and the C.O. straightway confirmed it by telling me *I* was taking over the mission."

"To do what?"

"Drop the strange passenger well into enemy territory."

"You mean he was a secret agent?"

"Yep, and probably a Belgium, though he never said and I was never quite sure."

"But why you?"

"According to Barcat, because I'd rescued Lee from that balloon-bursting fiasco and showed I was good at landing in short spaces. That was definitely going to be needed on this mission but, if things went wrong, my working knowledge of German could also come in handy."

I paused as the waitress brought our eggs, and we dug into a few delicious mouthfuls before Tara said, "This was going to be dangerous."

"You're damn right it was, because getting caught on a spy-drop mission got you shot along with your agent. And that seemed an even likelier prospect on this little caper when I found out where we'd be going."

"Which was ...?"

"A Zeppelin base just north-west of Cologne at a place called Bickendorf. Apparently the allies already had a spy there sussing what further airship developments the Boche had been making, but it was time to get him out and do a switch with my agent."

"An important mission then?"

"Very. By this time those zeps were giving the British a really hard time, targeting industrial areas, but not being too fussy if their bombs also dropped on civilian residential areas. The result was a knock to British morale and twenty thousand personnel and a hundred aircraft tied up on home defense. But the Brits had organised good tracking procedures, developed better incendiary ammo and sharpened their night-fighting skills and now it was the zeps starting to bite the bullet."

"So, why the need for this spy mission."

"Because the enemy were desperate to stop losing their precious airships and Bickendorf, it seems, was where they were experimenting to find the solution. The agent we had in place there reckoned the Boche were close to cracking it, so we needed to get him back with his information and replace him with someone to gather more."

Tara had finished her breakfast now, replacing hunger with a curiosity as to where this story was going. "What you're saying is that their 'solution' might have been one already developed by the Millers?"

I nodded. "It would certainly fit my theory. If the Miller Corporation had found a way to make non-flammable lifting gas, the Boche would have paid a fortune for the secret. Not hard to imagine Carl going over to offer it and perhaps even Wilson himself later going to negotiate."

"And you think it was one of them who Richard saw in Cologne and then later recognised in that newspaper photo?"

"That would certainly go a long way to explaining this whole mystery."

"It certainly would, but if the allies were so sure that this Bickendorf place was that critical, Mark, why didn't they just bomb it?"

"Actually, the Brits had tried in 1914. But, back then, the port of Antwerp was still in our hands and the front line much further east. By the time my secret mission was launching, Antwerp and all of Belgium to the Marne River was in enemy hands, making a return flight way beyond the range of any bombers."

"So, how would you get back?"

"I wouldn't. The leg to the rendezvous was going to be a hundred and fifty miles, almost all of it over enemy territory. The Morane had an operational range of about two hundred miles, so it didn't take too much calculation to work out this was going to be a one-way trip."

"You mean they were treating you as expendable?"

"Not quite, because after the rendezvous, they reckoned I

might just have enough fuel to reach neutral Holland. That meant internment for the rest of the war, but certainly better than the alternative."

"And, as you're here now, presumably that's what happened."

I shook my head. "Not exactly, but that's another long story, Tara, and one we don't have time for now." I nodded outside the diner to where the snowstorm had finally passed, leaving in its wake, a countryside white and gleaming and with just a smidgen of sunshine starting to break through the overcast. "We need to get going while we have the chance to make Newport News for midday."

"Okay, let's go." She pushed away her empty plate, stood up and was enthusiastically pulling on her flight suit as I went and settled our bill. Five minutes later, and we were at the Jenny hastily brushing snow from its wings.

*   *   *

"Throttle set."

In her cockpit, Tara opened the gas a notch and repeated, "Throttle set."

"Switch on ... contact."

"Switch on ... contact."

I'd avoided the same mistake as that Morane pilot by giving her a good briefing on start procedure, sucked plenty of juice into those eight cold cylinders, swung the prop and rejoiced in the old OX5 immediately kicking into spluttering life.

With it firing on all cylinders, I made a hand gesture for her to close the throttle completely, pulled the old oil cans I'd borrowed from the gas-station as temporary chocks, jumped into the rear cockpit and strapped in. With checks done and engine warmed, I then swung us around and trundled to the far corner of the field, thankful the snow wasn't too deep, but enough for me to know that getting airborne was going to be nothing if not another nerve-strummer.

For things had been tight enough getting into this pasture in what had been a healthy breeze. Now that wind had eased and wouldn't be helping us much on takeoff, other than to allow a slightly longer run by going diagonally across the field. I could feel the snow giving some drag to the wheels and to keep our momentum going, I didn't stop when we reached the far corner, but straightway gunned the Jenny round and into the take-off roll.

Normal technique would have been to immediately get the tail up into flying attitude, but I needed the wheels out of that snow as soon as the power could haul them, and so left the tail down so the downward thrust of the prop would work its magic and pull us clear. It was a technique we'd often used in snowed and muddied France and it worked now as, half-way down the field, I felt the old bird breaking free and finally getting airborne. Close to the stall and with the far-hedge getting nearer by the second, I gingerly eased the nose down, swapping attitude for speed without running the wheels back on.

Even so, those knots were building horribly slowly and, only inches off the ground, I knew there was no way we were going to clear the far hedge. But there was a small gap about ten degrees right of our nose and I rolled a degree of bank towards it, the Jenny on the edge of a stall and one wheel almost back on the deck. With that blessed opening now ahead, I reached it with just enough time to roll level, roaring through with the lower wings just inches above the gate posts and my knuckles almost as white as the next open field ahead.

I used that lovely open expanse to hold the nose down,

build our speed, and then wing away in a climbing turn up into that fresh Delaware air on course for Newport News. In the front cockpit, Tara's head stayed resolutely ahead and I could imagine her just starting to breathe again while reassessing her opinion of my flying. I couldn't blame her and told myself that those old wartime split-arse ways had no place now with the girl I loved right there sharing it with me. This time, and not for the first time, my guardian angel had seen me through, but how many more lives had I got left?

I could only hope the next few days wouldn't have me finding out.

*   *   *

CHAPTER EIGHT

With Tara's increasingly apt and gentle touch holding a steady two-thousand feet, we kept on tracking down that Eastern Shore with me map-reading our progress in near-perfect flying conditions. Here aloft, the wind had remained north-westerly, again giving us a healthy groundspeed and every chance of reaching Newport News without another stop between.

For the first time this trip I truly relaxed, only having to give Tara the occasional instruction as she quickly learned to think ahead and use only small corrections for height and heading. With the snow-covered land gradually sinking astern, it was good being able to follow our route on my map and pick out various landmarks along the coastal way. I could also afford to let my mind wander back again to that whole desperate mission and the sunset that had found me and the agent on our way to whatever awaited us deep in the enemy's own backyard.

*   *   *

It was after dusk that we'd taken off from Souilly, climbed to eight thousand feet and set course for the Rhine. Earlier in the day I'd flown and familiarised myself with the Morane and learned its handling which, after the SPAD, had seemed somewhat elephantine. Heavier on control and certainly lacking the fighter's maneuverability, it did have the advantage of a lower stall speed, permitting a slower approach and landing and the capability of putting down and stopping in a few hundred yards. And that was what this night's mission was going to be all about.

I'd taken my secret agent passenger along with me on my familiarization in the hope it might let me get to know the man better. But he'd stayed characteristically taciturn and I never did even get to know his name, poor devil. The few words he uttered in his Belgium-accented French gave the impression of complete foreboding for the night ahead, an apprehension I sadly shared. One thing I did leave out was another prop-swinging session. Assuming we ever made it to our rendezvous, I had no intention of shutting down the engine or loitering a second longer than I needed.

And so, there we were, climbing to cross the lines, the sun already setting over the cold war-torn landscape and me contemplating the fact that, one way or another, this was the last time I would ever see Souilly. To distract me from that thought, I concentrated on following my course to Cologne, an interesting exercise in itself, given that my night-flying experience so far had been limited to creeping back to base after late afternoon patrols and landing with the aid of hastily lit flares. There would be no such aids at the other end of this trip, and map-reading my way in the darkness was another new experience. Thankfully, this night had been chosen for its full-moon and, as I levelled at eight thousand and turned for the lines, I was glad to see the battle-scarred land below bathed in beautiful lunar light. How I'd fair landing at the other end was something I'd only find out when I got there. I'd been told to only expect a short few blips of a lantern to signal all was well for the rendezvous and after that it was up to me.

That was still an hour and three-quarters away though as I set course over the Meuse River with the bloodbath of Verdun just to the north and the front line below. Down there, thousands of men on both sides would be hunkering down in their trenches for another night battling the bitter cold of a northern winter and just a few would be preparing for night patrols into No Man's Land. Compared to that, I counted myself almost lucky to be up here in the peace of the night sky, unmolested by enemy aircraft, and with only the odd exploding starshell to remind me that this was the scene of the worst war man had ever contrived.

Another thing I was glad to see was our healthy ground-speed. In normal operations we'd always cursed the prevailing westerly wind that in any dogfight had us continually drifting back over the enemy's home patch. Now it was helping our mission on its way by a good fifteen knots and soon had us over German-occupied Luxemberg and then Hunland itself. On our port wingtip, the vastness of the Ardenne forest was bathed in moonlight while far below, the lights of small hamlets and villages gave an almost reassuring sense of normality to the scene.

But life down there wasn't normal. We knew from allied news reports that the British Navy's blockade of Germany was taking a serious toll on its food supplies, resulting in strict rationing and the deprivation of its population. At the same time, allied bombing of industrial areas was causing inevitable civilian casualties, including children, and any airman ending up facing that population could hardly expect a warm reception. That was another reason to avoid capture this night, though I sought to neutralise guilty thoughts of innocent deaths by reminding myself of those the Zeppelins were inflicting on England and why our own mission was so vital.

I glanced at my watch and, by the light of the moon, saw we'd been flying for an hour and a half. Then I looked ahead and picked out a ribbon of brightness that was the River Rhine winding eastwards into the heartland of Germany, but here turning more north towards the dark mass of a built-up area that had to be Cologne.

I didn't intend to fly over the city itself and alert their defenses, but I did want to make a positive identification and position check. And so I held my heading a short while longer until I could see the twin spires of a magnificent cathedral rising up beside the glinting steel of a large railroad terminus. From my pre-war days of European wandering I knew this was indeed Cologne, but what did concern me was a thick mist already starting to roll in from the Rhine. It could soon be covering the whole of the valley area and the sooner I got down, offloaded my agent, and set course for Holland the better. I swung slightly north to skirt Cologne's western side and on to what I hoped would be our rendezvous.

According to my briefing, the zep base was about eight miles north-west of the city and our r/v, alongside a large wood four miles west of that. As an initial fix, I started scanning for the base itself which the Brits had failed to find in their own 1914 attack. Back then they'd been unsure of its position and thick mist had prevented an extensive search. Seeing that eerie precipitation now turning to fog and spreading relentlessly along the valley, I wondered if I was doomed to the same lack of success. Then, in the moonlight, I saw a large open area and, in its centre, a huge shed that had to be an airship hangar with smaller sheds located around the perimeter. Quickly scanning west of what had to be Bickendorf, I eventually picked out the large wood with a small field running beside, turned straight towards it and was instantly rewarded by the quick flash of a light on the edge of the wood. Our contact had heard my engine and they were ready and waiting.

But if they had heard it, so too would the Boche and speed now was of the essence. I didn't even allow myself the circling recon I would have liked, but chopped the throttle and headed straight down. Though horribly short, the landing area looked reasonably level and I was glad of the bright moonlight, but concerned about the fog creeping insidiously towards the field. By the time I dropped the Morane down only just the right side of the boundary hedge, it was already covering the far end close to the wood's edge from which another quick flash told me where my man was waiting. I kept the landing roll going and only when I had just enough room to swing the Morane round did I kick in full rudder and yaw to a halt right where a figure was already emerging. From the cockpit behind me, I sensed rather than saw the agent already climbing out.

But, glad as I was that he wasn't wasting any ground-time, alarm bells were already starting to ring as the man running towards us in the moonlight became more recognisable. Only when he was twenty yards away did I see he was dressed in the field-grey uniform of a German officer. And behind him other soldiery were also materialising. In the split second it took me to realise this whole operation had been blown, the officer was five yards nearer, holding a pistol and close enough for me to see his face.

Without even pausing to check whether my agent was in or out, I instantly shoved the throttle full-open, booted the nose of the Morane round and, with the tail up, went roaring back down the field. Deliberately holding the nose down for faster acceleration, I went careering towards what was now the far hedge, only lifting the nose over it at the last second with jagged holes already appearing in my cockpit side and the crack of others striking more solid parts of the high wing. I glanced back, glad to see the agent was still with me, huddled low in his seat while, well astern now, a ripple of flashes from the wood's edge showed the pursuing enemy letting loose a final frustrated fusillade. Levelling at just a hundred feet, I turned onto a rough heading for Holland.

And then, just as quickly, the smell of gasoline and a fine spray of the stuff into the cockpit told me the Low Countries were going to be as unattainable as anywhere else beyond the next half mile. Those parting shots had holed our gas tank and the rate it was now emptying spelled engine failure or fire anytime in the next few minutes. I needed to put down while there were still some landing options, and desperately scanned the surrounding fields for one as far from that unfriendly reception committee back there as I could possibly get.

The only one offering even a chance of a controlled landing was an infinitely small one halfway between our old r/v and the zep base itself. This was no time to be picky and I headed straight into it, side-slipping off some height and scraping over a high hedge to thump the wheels down onto what seemed a furrowed field. That slowed us quickly, but not enough for the far hedge to be already filling my small windshield. I slammed off the engine switches even as we hit the hedge and the ditch beneath, and still fast enough to pitch the Morane onto its nose with the graunching lurch of the collapsing landing gear and the sickening staccato crack of a splintering prop. We came to rest almost vertical, fuel still spraying out and the still-hot engine all set to ignite into a funeral pyre. With only seconds left, I leapt from my cockpit while shouting to the agent to do the same.

Instead he did nothing and a quick glance told me why. This nameless figure who'd lived in the shadows had now died in them and would never be springing anywhere again. Whatever had taken him down that dark and clandestine trail had ended right here, slumped in the cockpit with a bloody ring of shattered brain tissue showing where one of those 7.92mm Mauser rounds had struck him fair and square in the head.

No time now though to even consider the vagaries of life and luck, as I ran for the field's side hedge, with no immediate plan other than to put as much space as possible between me and my soon-to-be incinerated machine. There can't have been much fuel left in its tank, but what there was suddenly went up with a head-rattling *whoof* that, if nothing else, effectively denied Boche intelligence anything they might have gleaned from the wreckage, including the poor agent. On the negative side, this flaming beacon would soon be drawing the ambush party to my crash-site like moths to a candle and I didn't intend being here when they arrived. I took off across the field at a speed I hoped would put as much distance as possible between me and them.

Keeping off the lanes and on the other side of hedgerows, I doubled along, listening for the sound of approaching enemy while casting my mind back to those few desperate seconds when they nearly got us.

But it was the officer leading them that was mainly filling my confused and bitter thoughts. I'd only had a fleeting glimpse of him as he'd led them out of the wood, but that had been enough to recognise a face already indelibly etched in my memory.

I didn't have the slightest doubt that it had been my old nemesis, Meunier.

*　　　*　　　*

With my body and soul back in the Jenny, cruising at two-thousand feet down Chesapeake Bay, I came back to the immediate present as Tara turned and pointed to the large populated area appearing just ahead of the nose. With a start, I realized I'd lost miles in old remembrances and that it was Hampton Roads area with Newport News immediately ahead. I tried to give the impression that I was quite aware of our progress by giving a thumbs-up, a knowing smile and indicating for her to lower the nose and start losing height. Soon the Jenny was sliding down at a whistling eighty while I grabbed my map and checked for the airfield.

It was where it should be, nestling there on the edge of the Bay, and at twelve hundred feet we came overhead, checking layout and landing direction before letting down into the circuit and turning finals. Flaring just feet above the grass, I managed to touch down in a reasonably good three-pointer before letting the landing run merge into a fast taxi that took us towards the large barn-type hangar and the near-by refuelling point. Shutting down the engine as we rolled to a stop, I wasted no time in climbing out to stretch stiff limbs. Tara was soon down beside me, pulling off her helmet and goggles and shaking hair loose as she unbuttoned her flight suit. "Boy, it's good to feel a bit of sunshine on my face again."

I agreed and was stripping off my own flying gear when a smiling figure in oil-stained coveralls and an old campaign hat came out to meet us.

"How can we help you?"

"Fuel, please."

"Fill right up?"

"Yep, right to the brim. We've got a long way to go."

"No problem."

Like most airmen, he was a friendly soul and was soon filling the ship's twenty-one gallon tank, seemingly keen to talk and giving the old trainer a friendly slap. "A few years now since we were operating Jennies from here."

"Right. Didn't this used to be the Curtiss Training Field?"

"Yep, 'til twenty-two, an' then, mores the pity, they went an' closed it down." He shook the last drips from the nozzle, wiped around the tank and rewound the hose. "During the war, though, thousands of guys got their wings here, includin' the great Eddie Rickenbacker himself."

I nodded to his old campaign hat. "I'm reckoning you got yourself some time in France as well."

"Sure did ..." Beneath the coveralls, his back perceptively straightened with that old pride. " ... an' in Rickenbacker himself's 94th Aero."

"The famous 'Hat in a Ring' squadron."

"The very one." That scrap of knowledge was enough for him to eye me as a possible comrade-in-arms. "You out there too?"

"Yep, but with the LFC."

"The Lafayette Flying Corps." His eyebrows did a momentary rise. "We had some of your boys with us in the 94th, and welcome they were too, with all that combat time. One of our first commanders, Major Huffer, was ex-LFC and we even had Major Lufbery from the *Lafayette Escadrille* itself." He glanced at me with just a hint of suspicion. "You didn't transfer to our Air Service when we came in, though?"

I smiled and shook my head. "No. Probably too used to the French's casual way of operating to start again but, anyway, by the time they started accepting *Lafayettes*, I was well out of Europe and fighting on another front." Enough of me, though, because I was hoping this veteran might just plug some of the gaps in someone else's story. "But a good friend of mine did transfer to Uncle Sam's Air Service. Perhaps you knew him. Lee Vennington?"

"Vennington ... Vennington ..." He took off his hat and scratched his slightly balding head. It was a long shot on my part, but the Air Service had been a close-knit group and, sometimes, long shots work. As, it seemed, did head-scratching, because his eyes suddenly widened with recall. "Yeah, I remember him now – *Captain* Vennington – came to the 94th in early eighteen 'bout the same time as Lufbery." He frowned as more recollection returned. "Nice guy, but didn't last long though."

"Really. Why was that?"

"Aw, just one of those things that sometimes happen in wartime."

He obviously didn't want to elaborate, but there was no way I was going to let him off the hook now. "What sort of 'thing'?"

He shuffled slightly. "Well, sad business, but he accidently shot down a Frenchie."

"He shot down a *French* aircraft!" I hadn't been ready for this one, but now wasn't the time for wearing my lawyer's hat. Instead I made an effort to keep it casual, as one airman to another. "How the hell did that happen?"

"Just a misidentification, he reckoned. Said he was returning on his own from an evening patrol when this Nieuport 17 suddenly dived on him from astern. Later, when he had time to think about it, he reckoned the French guy must have just done it for fun to give him a fright but, right then, as the machine went through his sights, he gave an instinctive burst from his 30-cal Marlins and sent him down in flames."

"Jesus! He must have been devastated when he realized what he'd done."

The mechanic nodded. "Yep, and our HQ and the French weren't too happy about it either. Of course, there was an inquiry that decided it was all a sad mistake and that no-one was really to blame."

"So, that was the end of it?"

"Sort of, officially, but we soon learned that Mr Vennington had been taken off ops and sent to some ground job in the Forty-second."

"Poor old Lee. So, he never did get that fifth kill to make him an ace."

"No so long as you don't count friendly aircraft, he didn't." He smiled at his own grim humour and, when he didn't get one in return, glanced at the fuel pump gauge and said, "Close on thirteen gallons. Any other way I can help you?"

I was shocked that Lee hadn't confided in me, and had to force myself to put this revelation to the back of my mind and get on with the job in hand. "There is, actually." I nodded roughly south-west. "We'll need to night-stop somewhere about halfway to the Savannah River. Any ideas of a good place, reasonably quiet and with accommodation close to a field big enough to take a Jenny?"

He stroked his chin. "Hmm, I might know just the place you're seekin'. A nice little town we did a weekend of barn-stormin' once. You got your map?"

Fetching it from the Jenny, I came back, spread it out on the pump cover and watched while his oil-stained finger traced its way to a dot halfway along our route to the Savannah River. "This small town here's Wellingville. A friendly place and right on the railroad from Washington to Charleston, so easy to find. Nice hotel on the edge of town with a big field opposite that we flew out of. Should serve you right."

I did a quick measure of the distance, which turned out to be just over the hundred and seventy-five mile range of the Jenny, but a glance at the Newport News wind-sock showed some north still in the breeze that would help us on our way. "Sounds good, as long as they have a gas station there."

"They sure do ..." he paused to make a quick calculation of his own from a table in his pocketbook, "... and your refuel here came to two dollars eighty-nine."

I took out my roll of greenbacks and peeled off three bucks. "Here, and keep the change."

"Thank you kindly sir." He threw a quick salute and, while he went off to his shack for my receipt, Tara sidled closer.

"That story he told you of your friend Lee shooting down a French aircraft …do you think that really happened?"

"I'm sure it did, Tara, but you have to put things into the context of aerial combat over the Western Front. Out there we were constantly expecting the worst to happen and it was only a matter of time before it usually did. Nerves were stretched to the limit and if some French jock chose to jump him, I can understand Lee letting loose first and thinking second."

"Okay, but it's strange he never told *you* about it, Mark. Apart from being an old buddy, you're now his lawyer. Doesn't it make you wonder what else he hasn't told you?"

"There's a lot that still doesn't make sense, Tara, but the mech saying that Lee got shoved back with the ground-pounders in the forty-second does explain how he got to meet your brother. And, if his conscience over downing an ally was eating into him, I can see him turning to a priest for some sort of absolution."

"Meaning my brother was one man who knew his secret. Do you think that might have some relevance in Richard's murder?"

It was a thought, but I was spared further discussion by the return of the mechanic with my receipt. "Here you go, sir." He nodded to the Jenny. "If you're ready to go I'll get you started."

"Great."

We pushed the aircraft back off the pumps and soon settled into our cockpits to enjoy the convenience of someone else getting us burning and turning. Once warmed, he pulled the chocks, gave us a final friendly wave and then we were taxiing out for take-off, completing the checks and opening the throttle for North Carolina and the third leg of this long flight.

We climbed away to the south-west in smooth and clear

flying conditions with me handing Tara controls and throttle soon after take-off and her climbing us steadily upwards as we crossed the state line from Virginia into North Carolina. With a full fuel load, that climb to two thousand took us a full ten minutes, and then I was pulling out the map and fingering our way along the course to Wellingville.

With that blessed wind still on our tail, our ground-speed was still a good eighty-five mph and, if it held the same for the morrow, just one more hop could see us reaching the Savannah River base by midday. And, before that, was the idyllic prospect of a night in some small-town love-nest with Tara Magee.

I should have been basking in the contentment of it all going gloriously to plan, but for an insidious little niggle that seemed determined to take the edge off my bliss. Back in my old flying days I'd learned the danger of worrying about *possible* problems to the neglect of the immediate present, and trained myself to let the future take care of itself. I tried to apply that same discipline now and enjoy this flight with a girl I loved.

As if understanding my thoughts, she turned and gave me another of those joyful smiles and I smiled back as the miles slid by and I picked up the 'iron compass' of the railroad guiding us effortlessly on the way to our nightstop.

But was it was also taking us ever-nearer some indefinable threat my instincts told me might be waiting at the other end.

*   *   *

CHAPTER NINE

That railroad track was holding a pretty straight south-westerly course to our intended nightstop, which was just as well, seeing as my hope of reaching it on one tank allowed no en route deviations.

In a way, that straight-lining was a shame, because I'd been hoping to follow the coast just that little bit further and pay my respects to the flat dunes of Kittyhawk where, twenty-three years earlier, Wilbur and Orville had catapulted their 'Wright Flyer' into history as the first ever powered flight.

There'd been several times since when I'd wished they'd never decided to get out of the bicycle business, but now wasn't one of them as, up there in smooth clear air with that tailwind winging us ever nearer our next night of togetherness, I kept my thoughts clear of future problems and our fuel just the right side of critical.

Only just, as it turned out, with two hours and fifteen minutes seeing us finally banking over Wellingville, which turned out to be a neat little community of white clapboard buildings clustered about a tree-lined leafy square. The railroad ran through a small station on the west edge of town, and what was obviously our intended small hotel sat on the eastern. I was relieved to see that the promised field still lay across the road opposite and long enough to take this aerial interloper already low down and circling for landing.

By the time I'd side-slipped in and rolled to a stop, inquisitive figures were already appearing on the road and giving us cheerful waves. Shutting down, we both waved back, glad to see that this little township seemed friendly and welcoming. That impression was heightened further when a burly figure came striding towards us with a broad smile and outstretched hand.

"Bill Raymond – Mayor – welcome to Wellingville." He glanced with concern at the Jenny. "Not a problem, I hope?"

"No, everything's fine." I nodded towards the hotel across the road with its hanging sign rather grandly proclaiming it to be THE PRESIDENTIAL. "We just hoped we could get a room there for the night."

"Good choice." He gave a proprietarily smug smile. "Happens to be owned by yours truly and run by my sister and her husband, and I know they'll be glad to accommodate you."

As indeed they were when Mayor Raymond personally ushered us in, introduced us to his sister, and I signed the register as *Mr and Mrs Kingsley*. And, when I mentioned the need for gas, her equally accommodating husband offered to run me to a station in his small truck.

And so, while Tara escaped to our room for a refresh and shower, ten minutes had me motoring in and being proudly shown Wellingville's small but pristine Town Hall, church, library and school and, further on, the sheriff's office which, apparently, had been told by the mayor to keep an overnight eye on the Jenny. Eventually, on the far edge of town, we rolled into the gas station where the friendly owner filled five five-gallon cans. The aircraft's tank would take four, but the final leg on the morrow would be right at the limit of our range and getting an extra one for possible unforeseens seemed a good idea. Back at the Jenny, willing hands helped me top the tank and stow the extra can on the wing, and then I was thankfully heading to join Tara in our room.

I found her lying on the big colonial-style bed in a spotlessly clean room, the furnishings of which probably hadn't altered much since the Civil War. She was looking refreshed and delectable after her shower, hair still damp and with lightweight bath-robe clinging enticingly to her lean but shapely figure. By contrast, after a day in flight-gear and my recent refuelling, I felt decidedly grimy, but that didn't stop me dropping on to the bed beside her and resting for the first time that day. "Well, here we are. This is my first time in the Carolinas. How about you?"

She smiled that endearing nose-wrinkling smile of hers and shuffled closer. "Same here, but somehow I knew I'd read a story set in North Carolina. Now I remember what it was and that it was the same novel in which I'd read about a mystery airship."

I sat up on one elbow. "A *novel?*"

"Yep, and pretty good one too entitled *Master of the World*, written by no less than the great Jules Verne. It was given to me as a prize at school."

"Jules Verne wrote a book involving mystery airships?"

"He did, and one you obviously haven't read yourself."

"Not that one, but how did it involve North Carolina and mystery airships?"

"From what I recall, it was based loosely on strange lights seen regularly up in the north part of the state near the summit of the Brown Mountain. Apparently this so unnerved the locals that they got the government to send a USGS scientist up there to investigate, who reckoned they were just train and car headlights. Verne, though, used it as background for his story in which the lights were from an airship built by a mad scientist in his secret base in Table Rock near Morganton."

"An *airship!*"

"Yes, but don't get too excited, Mark. Like I said, it was just a work of fiction."

"But one which might have more than a smattering of fact behind it."

She stroked the side of my face, soothingly. "All fiction has that, Mark. For the moment, let's enjoy being here in this friendly town and just hope we find everyone at the other end as kind."

"Amen to that." Clearly she was having the same strange foreboding as me regarding our final destination but, like her, I was determined not to let anything mar this moment of peaceful contentment, with nearly six hundred miles behind us and a night's pleasures yet to come. I sensed we would both have liked to have had a little foretaste of that pleasure, but there was something else I needed to do before even showering. Reluctantly, I got back on my feet. "I hate to do this, Tara, but I need to see if I can use the hotel phone before the work day ends back in The Bronx."

"To call ...?"

"Betty Devinski in the office above mine. She's promised to collect my incoming mail and I need to find out if there's any trial instructions from the courts that I need to know."

She winked mischievously. "Glad to see you haven't completely abandoned your legal responsibilities."

"It at least eases my conscience. I'll be back soon."

In fact, sooner than I anticipated, because five minutes had me back in the room and with Tara detecting my less-than-cheery expression. "That was quick. Wouldn't they let you use the phone?"

"Oh yeah, and the landlady put me through to the town exchange, only for them to say they had no lines available for long distance."

She shrugged. "Ah well, this *is* a small town and, I guess, these things happen."

"I know but, somehow, I got the feeling I was being thrown a curve."

"How come?"

"I'm not sure, but let me shower and you get dressed and then let's go eat."

*   *   *

"So, what makes you think there was something odd about not getting that line?"

We were sitting facing each other in the town diner, a typical small-town eatery with long counter, utility-style tables and manned by a bored but friendly female teenager who'd poured us coffees and took our order for burgers and French-fries.

I sat back and shook my head. With evening shadows now lengthening, we were the only diners in the place, so I didn't have to be too discreet. "Hard to put my finger on it, but one thing that was odd was that the woman on the switchboard first asked my name."

"Perhaps that's normal procedure down here."

"Perhaps, and it might just be my imagination, but somehow I got the feeling the whole thing was a stitch up."

"But Mark, we're in rural North Carolina and even *we* didn't know we'd be here until you asked that mechanic back at Newport for a good place to stay. So there's no way the little rinky-dink Wellingville telephone people could in any way be prepped to stop you calling out."

"There is if you remember Newport News was the one place we planned to refuel en route. All someone had to do was talk to airfield personnel – in our case, the mechanic who'd refuelled us – to find out where we'd be night-stopping."

She shrugged acceptance. "I guess it wouldn't then have been difficult to get word to Wellingville to deny us any outside line, but don't you think you're getting unreasonably paranoid, Mark?" She paused as the waitress delivered our meals and then waited until she was well clear before leaning closer. "Okay, so they, whoever *they* are, *could have* if they wanted, by why on earth should they?"

"I don't know but, whatever, it's a worrying turn of events." I nodded at our platefuls of food. "Let's enjoy our meals while I mull it over."

And so we dug in and when we'd finished I ordered coffees as one way of avoiding having to explain the grim solution that was beginning to form in my cynical mind. Besides, I had more immediate concerns. "The thing is, Tara, given that someone is keen to ensure that all contact with our old lives is lost forever, I can't help having bad vibes about what may lie ahead once we get to the Savannah River tomorrow." I stirred in some cream and took her hand. "I think too much of you now to get you further into God-knows-what. It's great having you with me, but I think the smart thing would be for you to bale out while the going's good and head back to New York and safety."

"And how about you?"

I shrugged. "I've come too far now to make a one-eighty. I have to see this through to the bitter end, if only to get the last few pieces in my jigsaw of life."

"Yeah, well, I don't intend you finding those pieces alone." She squeezed my hand back. "So just accept there's no way I'll be jumping ship either. Don't forget it was *my* brother who was murdered, and I'm as keen as you to find out why and by whom. If that requires a bit of risk-taking, so be it." Then she pulled her hand away and sipped her coffee slowly before giving an encouraging smile. "And anyway, you promised to teach me to fly on the way, remember?"

"I know, but like I said, right now I'm wondering what mess were actually flying into."

"Okay, but it's not the first flight you've done where you weren't sure of the ending is it? A few hours ago you were telling me of some secret mission you'd been handed in France." She put down her cup and leaned closer. "So how about you finish telling me how that worked out."

I grimaced over my cup. "Like I said back then, it's a long story."

"We've got the time, so get telling."

"If that's what you want."

It wasn't difficult picking up the story, seeing as I'd been reliving some of it on that last long leg. So, while she lingered over her coffee, I described that business of blindly flying into what was obviously an organised ambush, getting out of it by the skin of my teeth, losing my agent his life, ending up with a burnt-out machine and on the run deep in enemy territory.

She listened without interrupting, and with varying degrees of reaction, but it was the identity of the man I'd recognised back at the drop point that really had her mouth dropping. "You mean it was Wilson Miller's son, Carl?"

I nodded. "Not the slightest doubt, and the same man I'm sure is now down on the Savannah River and all set to ensure I never do get to defend Lee."

"And you think I might also figure on his elimination list?"

"Only because they'll be sure I've already told you my suspicions." I finished my coffee, sat back and lit a smoke. "I was surprised from the first at them being so keen to have me bring you along on this trip. If what I'm surmising is correct, it makes me all the more determined I carry on alone."

"Well, no chance there." She pushed away her empty cup and signalled our waitress for refills. "Right now though you're going to tell me how the hell, back in 1916, you got out of Germany alive."

"You'd never believe me if I did."

"Try me."

"Okay." I waited until we'd had our cups refilled, stubbed my smoke, and then got recalling times that joined so many others in plaguing my every sleeping moment. Once again, she listened intently to a story that, as I related it, seemed almost unbelievable to me. But it was true, every word of it, and as I took my mind back to those frantic moments of putting as much distance as I could between me and my burning machine, it was all as vivid in my mind as that desperate time it happened.

*   *   *

Stumbling across ploughed fields and along low hedgerows, I'd forged on, trying to remember my Legion training at escape and evasion and wishing that the forty *Gauloises* a day since hadn't taken such a toll. I'd not eaten since departing Souilly, so hunger too was now joining the stark realisation that I was on the run in enemy territory, fifty-two miles from neutral Holland and not a clue as to how I'd get there. I paused beside a derelict farm-shed for a breather, a quick smoke and some sort of plan for the way ahead.

In my pre-flight planning for this operation I'd allowed sixty minutes of flight-time for crossing the border to safety. Now, each of those minutes would equate to an hour of walking, given that there'd be periods of lying low, foraging for food or catching a quick sleep, assuming, of course, that I didn't allow myself to get caught in the meantime. Wistfully mourning the relative ease with which an aircraft would have carried me into safe territory, I couldn't help fantasizing on simply stealing some Boche aircraft to still do just that.

But was that really such a madcap plan? The objective of this mission had been an enemy airship base. Perhaps there

200

were aeroplanes on Bickendorf as well as Zeppelins. Okay, infiltrating such a high security base wasn't going to be child's play but, presumably, my agent had been planning getting in, so why couldn't I? I thought back to some scoundrel I'd met in the Legion, and remembered him saying that if you were on the run from the law, the one place they wouldn't look for you was in a police station. The same was surely true of the Zeppelin base lying just a few miles east of me now. I glanced up into the night sky to where Polaris marked true north, orientated myself to a star at right angles and set off in that direction.

One thing slowing me, though, was the Rhine fog I'd seen creeping across the countryside as we flew in. Now it was settling on the land around me, thankfully deadening my footsteps, but turning the outline of every tree and bush into the menacing image of an armed German *Fusslatscher*. But it might also help me infiltrate the base, and I pressed cautiously on.

Being radiation fog, it was only feet thick and my compass star above was still clearly visible. I followed it for another hour and was beginning to wonder whether my instinctive nav really had held true when an image ahead stopped me dead in my tracks. It was the dark, forbidding, but also glorious, sight of a huge shed rising from the encircling vapor. It had to be the mighty Bickendorf airship hangar, but it was still a quarter mile away and a few more cautious steps through the thickening fog brought me up against a high barbed-wire fence that I realized must be the airfield boundary. There would doubtless be sentries patrolling this perimeter and, ever more warily, I edged along it, searching for some form of entry.

What I did come across was a narrow railroad track entering the airfield through a gate. That gate was closed, but not for much longer because, even as I stood on the track, I suddenly felt a slight vibration through my feet. That surely meant a train was making its way along the line. Then I heard the shriek of a steam whistle some way off from the direction of Bickendorf town and guessed that must be the signal for the gate to be opened. If so, this was another place for Mark Kingsley not to be.

Or was it? The thickness of the fog meant that fifty yards down the rail track I'd be completely out of sight of the gate and the possibility of a way into the air station. With a plan forming, I made my way down-track just as the clank of the approaching train and the mournful wail of its steam whistle sounded again, but now that much nearer. Close by the track was a pile of loose shingle which I ducked behind just as the ghostly shape of a small locomotive came hissing and slowing out of the murk. I was thankful to see it hauling mainly flat-bed trucks and a tanker, with a conductor already swinging a red lantern from the van bringing up the rear. It was being answered by another fog-shrouded red light from the gate, presumably by base personnel arriving to open it. With all rolling stock now stopped and the engine engulfed in its own cloud of exhausting steam, the conductor climbed down and made his way to meet them while I ducked even lower behind my shingle pile.

Through the gloom I could now hear some shouted exchanges going on between ghostly figures, while the engineer leaned out of his cab, his charge snorting, hissing and clanking like all locomotives seem to do while stationary. It was now or never. Opposite my hide were two flat-bed wagons carrying what looked like canvas-shrouded engines, drums of oil and assorted other machinery. I crouch-scuttled towards the for'ard one before rolling beneath and managing to jam myself up between the rear axle and the flat-bed itself. A minute later and the uniformed legs of the conductor came scrunching back, the trill of his whistle answered by a toot from the loco and then the clanking of couplings and a jolting jerk as they took up their slack and we moved off.

I feared the gate guards might be checking below the wagons, but that never happened as we trundled over the crossing and on into the base itself.

For better or worse, I was into Bickendorf airship station. How or if I would ever get out was something I was yet to find out.

*   *   *

"So, how did you?"

Tara's question brought me back into the Wellingville diner and the realization that I'd been rambling on for the last fifteen minutes. Now young people were beginning to enter the place for their evening get-togethers and the waitress was giving us we-need-your-table glances.

"Time to go, Tara. I'll tell you more as we walk back to the hotel."

"I can't wait."

I paid our bill and off we set, casually strolling along the pleasant main street of Wellingville as lights shone behind closed drapes and families settled down for another night in their own little world a million light years away from the one I'd just been recalling. But, right now, my immediate thoughts were on our present situation and future consequences.

"Tara, I need to check whether that really was a deliberate attempt to stop us calling New York."

"But surely, if your suspicion is correct, you won't have any more luck now than then."

"Agreed, which is why I've got another plan."

"Which is ...?"

"That I bought an extra five gallons of gas here to guarantee we have enough for that last leg. So, what I'm thinking is that tomorrow we land near enough to a town large enough to have a telephone exchange, where no-one will expect us, and we can try calling again."

"Sounds good to me, if only to put your mind at rest." She came to a stop and smiled. "But don't think changing the subject is going to get you off telling me how you did get out of that base and Germany." She nodded ahead. "So, come on, you can talk as we walk."

And so we did just that, with me at least comforted by the infinitely more agreeable company I was enjoying right then than that I'd been facing back in the Bickendorf Zeppelin base. Talking as we walked, I told her how, after a slow trundle into the base, there'd been much shunting and clanking as we slid into and out of various sidings. From my worm's eye view beneath the flat-bed, I'd caught glimpses of men unhitching different wagons, all the while holding my breath and praying that none of them bent low enough to discover me hiding there.

By that time my limbs were starting to really ache as I held onto the axle with both arms and legs and longing for my own wagon to soon be shunted somewhere and left. Each stop though saw one of the other wagons unhitched, and I was just about clinging on with the last of my strength when we came to another halt, the engine was detached and my wagon was finally at its stop.

With not a clue as to where on the base I'd finally ended up, I was content to simply lower myself onto the tracks, stretch away excruciating cramps and give myself even more time to ensure that all was quiet before I could actually emerge from my hide.

When I did cautiously roll from under the wagon, it was to find I was right beside the huge shed that had first given me my bearings for the base. Now it served to give me cover as I edged closer to it, all the while listening for the footsteps of patrolling sentries. Relieved to hear none, I scanned its length, trying to decide which way to go, only to find each end hidden at ground level by the low-lying fog now blanketing everything around me. But by stepping warily away, I could get some measure of its size and see it was a huge construction rising up like some industrial cathedral topped at each end, not by spires, but by rectangular watch towers. These had to be anti-aircraft defenses, probably installed after the first British raids in 1914. Up there in clear air and moonlight, I could see the glint of several big-calibre machine guns and, even more alarmingly, the coal-scuttle helmets of the troops manning them. Briefly remembering my own days on sentry-go in freezing winter, my heart, illogically, and only momentarily, went out to these poor clods slapping their arms in an effort to beat off the icy temp of the night.

What was more certain was that there'd be precious little sympathy returned if I was spotted. I quickly slid back into the lunar shadow of the shed to decide just what to do next. It was now early morning and, although still in my flying coat, I too was feeling the extreme chill of the night. Daybreak would bring some comparative warmth, but also the heightened risk of detection. How I'd handle that would depend on circumstances. Right then I needed warmth and shelter and began edging along the base of the shed to find some way in.

A stealthy creep eventually found me turning the corner of one end comprised of closed doors huge enough to only be moved by mechanical means or abundant manpower. These must be the ones through which the zeps were maneuvered. For immediate access there was a small personnel door set into one corner, but would this 'eye of the needle' be locked? I gingerly levered the heavy steel handle to find out and felt the door move slightly inwards. What lay beyond? I eased the door open further and quickly scanned inside.

At first I was greeted only by impenetrable blackness, which suited me just fine as I crept in and quietly closed the door behind me. But, as my eyes adjusted, I realized I wasn't in total darkness. Moonlight was beaming in by way of windows set high in the hangar walls and skylights up in the roof, enough for me now to see just what was filling this vast cavern.

It was a sight that simply took my breath away, for there floating above me in the moonlight in all its sinister and formidable grandeur was a Zeppelin, its great cigar-like hull probably seven hundred feet long and completely filling the hangar.

I stood gazing up at its aft end, the huge fin, rudder, tailplane and elevators alone bigger than any aircraft I'd ever seen before. Below and further along the hull, was suspended one of the engine gondolas with its four-bladed prop facing aft. I knew mechanics actually worked and flew in the gondolas, tending and nursing the six 240 hp Maybachs that powered these leviathans. I let my eyes wander further along the vast hull length to where, depicted on each side, was an iron cross, that hated symbol that more than once had filled my gunsight and which now hardened yet more my resolve to find a way back to continue that fight to conclusion.

To do that, though, would need more than resolve, and I continued along the hangar floor, feeling my way past tooling and maintenance equipment while taking great care not to send any clanging onto the floor to awaken some sleeping sentry or working ground crew. Thankfully, I encountered neither, though this would surely not be the case in the morning when I could imagine this hangar probably coming alive with men preparing the ship for its next operation.

And that would doubtless be another bombing raid over far-off England with innocent men, women and children, victims of its indiscriminate carnage. It was such outrages that my own mission this night had been launched to help combat, but one I'd singularly failed to accomplish. Treachery had been the cause of that failure, but that didn't negate the sense of dismay I was now feeling, or that some way and some time, this score would need settling. But how? Was there a way, even now, that I might play them at their own game and achieve something from this night's debacle?

I gazed up again at this latest addition to the Kaiser's airborne terror arsenal. There was a lot of technology there the allies would like to know about and I was in a unique position to get it. Relaying it was something else, but if I got back, so too would that intelligence and I got working out how to actually get inside that zep and start sussing its secrets.

I was now about a third of the way along its length with the aft two midships engine gondolas low enough to almost touch the hangar floor. On the top of each gondola was a hatch and ladder leading up into the hull. There were also windows in their sides with one of the aft ones half-open. Using a nearby crate, I heaved myself up and squeezed inside, finally tumbling down into a small compartment filled with a gleaming engine and the all-pervading odour of diesel spirit.

 So far, so good, and I only lingered long enough to take in the engineer's controls and telegraph dials and imagine the deafening hell the poor devil who manned this station would live through as he fought altitude sickness and arctic cold for hours on end. And the end of those hours might well be the prospect of a blazing plummet to earth as the only way he would ever feel warmth again. It was a scenario that spurred me out of that steel coffin, through the hatch and up the ladder into the hull.

I emerged onto a narrow lateral gangway that led to a longitudinal one seemingly running the full length of the ship. After the confines of the engine gondola, the voluminous interior of the hull here was almost refreshing until I looked upwards and saw what looked like massive balloons. These had to be the hydrogen gas cells containing a few million cubic feet of the stuff and which gave this monster its lift. Just the thought of that lot going up if ignited, had me cautiously continuing along the long walkway towards the bow, noting machine gun ports at intervals along the hull and bombs already in their racks. There had to be at least five tons there, still without their detonators, but otherwise all set for another raid which could well be very soon.

Further along the gangway, just beyond the for'ard pair of engine gondolas, I was surprised to come across what I at first thought was another huge bomb. But this one was suspended from a winch and, in addition to a fin and tailplane, had a small open cockpit and windshield. Then I remembered reading that Hun zeps had what they called 'cloud cars', which were small aluminium capsules that could be lowered by winch from the mothership. By this means, the zep itself could stay hidden in cloud while an observer in the car could either direct the bomb-run or check ground features for navigation. Their navy had ultimately rejected this accessory and its associated winch-gear in favor of increased bomb-load, but the army had kept them which meant this had to be one of their ships, confirmed by the field-grey caps I saw hanging nearby along with fur flight coats and boots. I had some pity for the poor soldiers doomed to man this aerial battlecruiser, but my first priority now was to inspect the control gondola, the command position from where its whole deadly mission would be directed.

I followed the gangway as it rose slightly towards the bow which in turn led to a vertical ladder leading down into what must be my objective. Easing down it, I found myself between another engine in the aft end and a well-glassed area for'ard that seemed more like the bridge of a ship, with a spoked steering wheel and, at right angles to that, another identical wheel that had to be the control for the elevators. This nautical layout was completed by telegraph controls to the engines and a modest chart table, which I hoped might give a clue to intended targets. Unfortunately, it was bare of all maps and charts, but what I did study was an elaborate switchboard, its German placarding showing it to be the controls for releasing the bombs, and definitely of interest to the allies.

I made a mental note of it all before heading back onto the keel walkway and aft to the 'cloud car' where I aimed to 'borrow' one of those fur-lined flight suits I'd seen hanging nearby. Even here inside, the damp cold of the morning was starting to eat into my bones and I needed warmth if I was to stand any chance of sleep before first light. Then I intended finding some airplane in which I could make my escape. It was a long shot, I knew, but all the more vital now if I was going to pass on this hard-learned knowledge to my side.

Back at the winch station and its strange flying egg, I slipped into a suitably large flight-suit and luxuriated in its comforting warmth, aware I was now wearing enemy uniform which made me even more of a candidate for the firing-squad if I were caught. Right then, its warmth seemed to be worth the risk, and I still had my French uniform underneath as some form of legitimacy. In accordance with the old adage that 'you may as well be hanged for a sheep as a lamb', I then helped myself to one of the flying helmets which would come in doubly handy should I eventually find an airplane to steal and have the need to convince some ground crew I was one of their pilots needing my prop swung.

Next job was to find somewhere in this flying leviathan where I could bed down for a couple of hour's snooze. There were places along this keel I could have used, but on the off-chance that some patrol did regular checks, I wanted somewhere well tucked away.

I remembered that further aft along the gangway I'd seen

a vertical ladder disappearing up between the voluminous gas-bags. I wasn't particularly keen to get closer to the most explosive section of this ship, but figured that up there would at least find me a place less open to discovery. A couple of minutes had me climbing the aluminium rungs to a higher level where a working platform between two of the bags promised a good place to rest. There were even some nearby rolls of material that I assumed were for emergency patches. Whatever, they made a reasonably soft bed for me to get my head down, and two minutes had me well into a needed 'eyelid inspection'.

Not that it was a particularly restful sleep. Under the circumstances, it was inevitable I only fitfully dozed until a sudden flash of light had me wide-awake, straightway upright and alert.

For a startling second I thought the whole shebang must have ignited, but that light stayed constant and my senses more rational as a glance at my watch told me that I'd been asleep for hours and that it was five in the morning. Then I realised the hangar lights had been switched on and that it was their brilliant glare now penetrating even the fabric of the hull.

I should have expected the Boche work-ethic to call for early-rising, but this now completely stymied my plan for a dawn recon outside the hangar. Already I could hear German voices bantering like any other close-knit group of comrades and, with my basic German, could more-or-less follow what they were saying. Not that I was able to share their humor as I faced the renewed hazard of discovery right here in the enemy lair. All I could immediately do was find somewhere else to hide that was even more secluded than my current sleep-spot.

On the old military assumption that 'height gives you the initiative' I went back to my vertical ladder and started climbing again, up, up into the cathedral-like voids of the airship's innards.

More walkways, more ladders, and eventually I was climbing the last to what was obviously the top of the hull and where a small opening showed the roof of the hangar just feet above. I climbed through and found myself in what had to be the most precarious duty-station on this whole ship of hazards.

For up there, right on top of the hull, were a pair of recessed mounts, each with its own heavy caliber machine gun and obviously the Zeppelin's answer to aircraft diving to attack. Attached to near-by strong-points were canvas straps and belts, clearly for the dubious security of the poor devils assigned to this worst-of- all jobs on the ship.

It also represented something of a dead-end for me, with nowhere else to retreat should some Boche armorer decide to check those guns. Using them as a means of self defense was also a non-starter, seeing as they were empty of ammo. Besides, even if they had been armed, any last stand I might make here was doomed to about as much success as Custer's. Instead, I needed to find myself somewhere better placed for concealment well away from any wandering airshipmen. I slid back down the ladder into the hull, still staying near the top, but not in a direct track to those upper gun positions. Between the upper fabric and the top of a gas bag, I found a reasonably secluded lair, wrapped myself ever-tighter into the fur folds of the flight-suit and tried hard to plan some sort of alternate strategy for escape.

It was a forlorn mental exercise, as I just as quickly realized I could do nothing until night fell again and the hangar cleared. With that probably twelve hours ahead, I knew I was facing a long cold wait. And then ... what?

I hunkered down, wondering how in the hell I'd ever gotten myself into this damn-awful fix.

*   *   *

"Look, they've even put a man to keep watch on the aircraft."

For an alarming second I thought it was my own sub-con-scious warning me of further danger. Then I realized the voice was Tara's, that we were still walking back to our Wellingville hotel and that in relating my story, I'd again completely lost track of the here and now. I followed her glance to the Jenny and saw a figure hunkered down beside it giving us a friendly wave.

"That's good of the sheriff."

"Or perhaps your mysterious people have also told him to keep an eye on us as well as the telephone exchange." I wasn't sure whether she was being sarcastic or maybe coming around to my suspicions. Whatever, there was genuine em-pathy in her voice when she added, "That really was a horrific experience you related back there, Mark. When you're ready, I want to know how it ended."

"Sure, but not tonight, Tara." I'd had my fill of intrigues past and present and was ready for more immediate and infinitely more pleasurable action. "How about some more of that wonderful sleep-therapy you're so good at?"

She smiled, slipped her arm through mine and guided us into the hotel. "You've earned it, Captain Kingsley but, as your personal physician, I'm thinking I might have to double the prescription."

*   *   *

CHAPTER TEN

Yet another sleep blissfully devoid of nightmares and filled instead with divine experience guaranteed to drive out even the most persistent of demons. Not that the contentment of love, given and received, made it any easier to roll out of bed the next morning and force ourselves to the Jenny for an early-morning take-off. It would have been easy, right then, to abandon this whole crazy jaunt but, like it always does, some indefinable force drove us on to see things through and half an hour after dawn found us again winging south.

With Tara back on the controls, we levelled at two thousand on a south-westerly heading that in an hour had us crossing the state line into South Carolina. That course would keep us just south of the geographical fall line and most of the region's large towns that used the energy of water forging down from the Appalachians to power their mills. Below that line, in the relatively level coastal plain, tamed water fed the agriculture and allowed the rivers to be more navigable. That was why our destination, the Miller base on the Savannah River, lay where barges could be used to transport their aircraft a hundred miles downriver to the Port of Savannah for onward ocean shipping. Even so, it seemed a strange place for a flying base. Why there? Had it a connection to the Brown Mountain lights that Tara had read of in Jules Verne? That was just one of the mysteries I hoped to resolve very soon.

First priority now was to find a suitable field in which to land and transfer that five gallons extra fuel I'd bought in Wellingville. Thankfully, the more agricultural nature of this region was offering several pastures large enough for the Jenny, but what I was also seeking was one close enough to a built up area and populated enough to have telephone connection. Most of the farmhouses we were flying over seemed too secluded to sport any sort of modern amenity but, eventually, one came up, not far off our track, with a nearby small town that might well fulfil our needs.

As would the pasture running beside the straight track leading to a largish farmhouse whose owner, I hoped, wouldn't object to this noisy machine now in a descending turn overhead. And so I glided in, well clear of the two horses nibbling grass on the other side, and soon running our wheels onto its level surface before shutting down as close to the farmhouse as seemed discreet.

Like so many farms, nothing here seemed to happen too quickly and we'd already climbed down and shed our flight kit before a small, ancient wagon came clanking its way down the track towards us. Its driver turned out to be the farm's elderly owner clad in baggy dungarees and floppy hat. As he squealed to a stop nearby, the frown he gave only added to other lines and blemishes on a face weathered from a lifetime of outdoor labor.

Those lines certainly weren't from excessive laughter. "What you people doin' scarin' ma horses?"

I looked towards the nags that might just have moved a further ten yards away with about the same level of excitement as their owner.

"I'm sorry, but we just need to refuel our aircraft."

"So, you won't be here long?"

"Ah, that depends on whether there's a telephone exchange in town."

"There's one at the general store that people can use if they need to." He gave another disapproving frown. "Don't have much use for that kind 'a new-type gimmickry, misself, but I do need some things from hardware, so a few cents for fuel could get you ride in."

I readily accepted, but Tara had other plans.

"Look, why don't I stay here and top the tank while you make your call?"

"Could be a while, knowin' how long them operators take to put ya through," warned our host. He nodded towards his house. "When you've finished ya jobs here, go on up to the homestead, and the wife'll be glad to have someone to talk to and for you to sample her homemade bakin'."

And so, with Tara left fuelling the Jenny, another half-hour found me and my farmer-driver chugging into a small, sleepy township and parking in its equally listless main street. After accepting my full dollar for his trouble and pointing out the general store, my farmer departed on his errand and I on mine.

The storekeeper was friendly enough and, in a sort of private booth equipped with what looked like one of Alexander Graham's early models, I was soon trying to convince the local operator that I really did want a New York number. The procedure itself was anything but swift as she began the tedious process of leap-frogging connections from one main exchange to the next but, after many clicks and whirrs, there was finally a ring at the other end and Betty Devinski's lovely Bronx voice.

"Mark, is that really you?" Her greeting seemed a mixture of relief and near-desperation. "What's happening? I didn't think I'd ever hear from you again."

"How do you mean?"

"You closing down your office like that."

"Me doing *what*?"

"Sending those men to clear out your things. They came yesterday and now everything's gone."

I took a second to digest this incredible news. "Betty, I don't know what you're talking about. You mean these men just walked in and cleaned me out?"

"Not without me challenging them, they didn't. But they had pretty official-looking government orders, and left me no choice."

"Government!"

"Yes, and when I asked if they had your new address, they refused to discuss it, so that's when I rang *Winifred's Welfare* to speak to Tara Magee. I know you're friendly with her now and thought she might know something."

I didn't realise Betty knew anything of my private life, but I should have known that female intuition meant that was one secret I wouldn't keep for long. "Thanks for trying, Betty, but Tara's not there either."

"I know that now." There seemed just an element of hurt in her voice. "In fact, they sounded as bemused as me when they told me she'd gone for good, wouldn't be returning, and that Father Huber had now taken over running the shelter."

"The assistant priest from Saint Winifred's?" This whole conversation was rapidly going into the realms of ludicrousy. "Betty, I don't know what's happening any more than you, but I'll get back to you just as soon as I do."

"Thanks, Mark. I didn't think you'd just up and go for good without saying, and sorry if I handled things wrong."

"You and I are both dealing with things we didn't bargain on, Betty, so no need to be sorry."

I hung up, paid the storekeeper for the call, found my driver already back at his truck and got him rolling us farm-wards just as fast as his clunker would take us.

Back there, I found Tara happily chatting over cookies with his plump and homely wife, though she immediately sensed my less-than-happy demeanor. I thanked the farmer for all his help, told him we'd be fine getting away unaided and ushered Tara out. Clear of the farmhouse and hoofing it down the track, I broke the bad news. Her reaction was pretty well what I expected.

"I can't believe it. You mean some faceless government department has even given over the shelter to that dreadful Huber? But they can't do something like that."

"I'm afraid they have."

"Then we need to head straight back and sort it out."

We were at the Jenny now and I sat down on one wheel. "That was my first reaction too, Tara, but we'd be wasting our time trying to fight forces way out of our league."

"I can't believe this." She stood above me, hands on hips. "You've handled high odds before, Mark, but now you seem ready to just roll over and accept it all as inevitable."

"I do when I realise it's the establishment that we're up against."

She dropped down beside me. "But what on earth is our administration doing getting involved in my brother's murder? Yes, it was unbelievably tragic for me, but there are a hundred such crimes a day in this country, so what makes this so special?"

"I've got my suspicions, Tara, but that's all they are."

"So, are you going to share them?"

"Not just yet."

"And instead, just give up and accept it all?"

"Who said anything about 'giving up'? No, I'm going to carry on as planned and get to the bottom of this once and for all."

"Like a fly into the spider's web. You must be mad. We'd be playing right into their hands."

"Except it won't be 'we'" I put my arm around her. "Look, Tara, it's pretty obvious that certain people are out to ensure this is a one-way trip for both of us."

"With what final destination?"

"I don't know yet, but what I am sure of is that I don't want you there when I do. I seem to have somehow got you into some dire one-way trip to hell, my love, but it's not too late to have you off it before the final stop. So, now I really am going on alone." I turned her so she faced me, expecting tears or even anger.

Instead she smiled. "You are priceless. We went through all this yesterday, Mark, and the reality remains that where you go, I go too. Okay, things seem to be getting more sinister by the mile, but at least, whatever life throws at us, we can face it together."

More than ever, my heart went out to this amazing girl whose spirit was as great as her quest for the truth. I struggled for a response but, in the end, it all came down to three simple words. "I love you."

"And I love you."

Words that suddenly made this whole crazy jaunt worthwhile. What lay ahead was a mystery to us both, but the journey there was turning out to be one of exquisite tenderness and shared endeavor. "As long as you understand that it's my love for you that makes me want to keep you safe, while wanting nothing more than to have you by my side."

She threw her arms around me. "I know and don't try and explain. Richard once said to me that love drives men to take the most uncharacteristic and bizarre directions in life."

In spite of all the emotions then coursing through my being, that one statement illogically struck a chord. "He's right ... but when did he say that, Tara?"

"Strangely, just a few days before he died."

"And do you have any idea what he was basing it on?"

"None at all, other than all his spiritual work dealing with other people's problems." She gave me one of her quizzical glances. "Is it important?"

"Only in what it might imply." I was getting into areas here where even I didn't want to tread and quickly glanced towards the sun already past its zenith. "Time's going, Tara. If we're going to see this through to its bitter end, the sooner we're on our way, the better."

With no more discussion, ten minutes saw us winging out of that South Carolina field for our last leg to who-knows-what. Like Tara had said, it wasn't the first time I'd had little idea of what the immediate future held, but at least now I was doing *something*. Back all those years ago, as I shivered in silence in the upper hull of that accursed Zeppelin, just the sheer inactivity of it all seemed almost worse than the drumming I knew my nerves were ultimately in for. As it was, when that moment came, cold and tedium seemed the least of my problems.

*   *   *

Lying low while trying to stay warm isn't the easiest of pursuits, but back there in that Zeppelin, I had no choice as morning turned to forenoon and work in the hangar contin-ued apace. From my hidey-hole at the top of the hull, all I could do was shiver and listen to all that was going on around me. Somewhere down below were men talking, orders being shouted, machine tools working and all the other sounds of an intense operation in full flow. Above all I listened for the faintest hint of footsteps coming my way, but gradually sensed that the maintenance crew were actually leaving the ship. It was nearing midday now so, perhaps, it was their meal-break. Whatever, it gave me the hope of continued evasion, but one due to be crushed when I heard the thud of rubber soles coming up the aluminium rungs of the ladder.

There was no doubt they were heading for my walkway and my one route of escape. I needed somewhere to hide and fast and the immediate solution seemed to be the aluminium framework of which the airship was comprised. Abandoning the walkway, I stepped tentatively out along the open girders and tubular fabrication, gripping hold of wire bracing for upper support and glancing down to see only the frail fabric of the Zeppelin's belly a good fifty feet below. Knowing I wouldn't stop if I ever dropped onto that, I clung on to my bracing wire with even greater determination, glad only that I was out of clear sight of the gangway, but just able to glimpse two crewmen in flight gear hauling what looked like ammo boxes along it. They must have heaved them up from ground level, judging by their heavy breathing and vocal curses that joined my unspoken ones when they stopped just feet from my precarious perch. Squatting down on the boxes for a breather, they chatted like all soldiers do, while I mentally translated, only with vague interest until I realized the subject was me.

"Ist er dann entkommen? – So, he got away?"

"Ja und er macht sich bestimmt auf den Weg zur niederländlischen Grenze. Aber unsere Patrouillen sind auf der Suche..also wird er sicher nicht weit kommen. – Yes, and probably heading for the Dutch border. But our patrols are out looking, so he surely won't get far."

"Ja und dann wird er sicherlich vom Exekutionskommando erschossen. – And then it'll be the firing squad for sure."

"Aber erst, nachdem sie soviele Informationen wie möglich von ihm erhalten haben. – But only after they've got as much information from him as they can."

I felt some smugness in knowing I'd thrown them a complete curve, but less so in the sureness of my fate if I was ever caught. And that seemed an imminent possibility with my grip on the wire weakening by the second. Then came a blessed shout from below that had my chatting soldiers instantly jumping up to start uncoiling belts of high calibre ammo from the boxes they'd just been sitting on. With the belts now lying on the walkway, one of them then climbed up through the hatch to those upper gun positions while his mate started feeding them up to him. It was certainly an easier way than hauling up the boxes, but of little comfort to me with that bracing wire now starting to cut into my hands as I again glanced down into the open guts of the ship and wondered how much longer I could hold on.

Just long enough, as it turned out, before the tail end of the last ammo belt snaked away, to be immediately followed up the ladder by its feeder. Realising they weren't coming down again anytime soon, I gratefully edged back onto the walkway and massaged life back into my wire-scarred fingers.

I was momentarily safe again, but the very fact that this zep was being armed seemed to indicate she was destined for a mission sometime soon. If so, I needed to be out of there and fast, and quickly beat a retreat along the gangway to the next ladder down.

Cautiously descending to the keel walkway, I soon realized that disembarkation wasn't going to be that easy with two crewmen already making their way out onto the adjacent engine gondola. Worse still, one of them paused, saw me, and shouted an order.

"Zum Dienst melden, Kamerad! Wir sind auf dem Weg. – Duty stations, comrade. We're on our way."

Realising that, in my flight suit and helmet, he'd simply mistaken me for just another member of the crew, I breathed again and waved acknowledgment before being immediately startled by the rasping blare of a Klaxon and a sudden increase of light inside the hangar. Close by me was a gun port. I leaned out, saw the hangar doors were now fully open, that hundreds of uniformed men were gathering around the ship and hauling on long lines and that, further for'ard, an officer holding a megaphone was leaning out of the control gondola. 'Luftschiff Ma-a-a- a-rch,' came the order, the lines hardened and, slowly but surely, we began backing out of the hangar.

It was a still day, bright and cold, as they guided this evil monstrosity out into the open. Would they just be mooring her outside and giving me some chance yet of making a getaway? I looked out onto this, my first daylight view of Bickendorf Air Station, desperately searching for just one airplane that might provide my magic carpet to freedom, and seeing none.

I was just absorbing this setback when there came the increasing roar of the airship's mighty Maybach engines thundering one by one into life. Then another order from the control car and the handling troops let go their lines which were just as promptly hauled up into the ship.

With dismay, I watched the ground smoothly dropping away beneath while, over the noise of the engines, I could hear telegraph bells jangling and see those big props starting to turn. Bickendorf air station was starting to slide beneath and, very soon, even its boundary fence was disappearing fast astern.

We were off and that ammo loading I'd seen earlier meant this was no local hop. I slunk back into a nearby concealed compartment, trying to come to terms with the appalling realization that this zep was heading for England on a raid and I was going with it.

*   *   *

And now Tara and I were airborne over North Carolina and heading for another equally dubious destination with consequences yet to be determined.

Thirty hours earlier and just before our takeoff from Governors, Harry Ludlow had put a cross on my map to mark the location of Miller's Savannah River base. We were heading straight for that now, or just a little west of it, using the old trick of deliberate error. It wouldn't be difficult to locate the 300 mile long waterway itself, but if we didn't spot our objective first go, at least this way we'd know which way to turn for the search. As it was, Harry's cross was pretty accurate and, even as the half-mile wide river came into view, I could see the scar of some tree-clearance running parallel to its northern bank.

Coming overhead showed it to be an unpaved airstrip, about six hundred yards long, running beside an extensive quay where a couple of barges lay moored. One of these had a large wingless airplane secured to its flat deck, presumably one of the Stouts awaiting onward transportation downriver to Savannah Port. The other barge sported a squarish form of superstructure and a gangway running down onto the dock.

On the other side of the airstrip were some wooden huts and a moderately-sized hangar, in front of which sat another of the 2-ATs, this one with its mono wing still attached and, presumably, the aircraft I'd soon be checking out on. Time then to get on the ground and start that particular ball rolling.

A lazily fluttering sock close to the runway showed only a slight crosswind and, after a close circuit, I throttled back, glided in, and was soon running our wheels on the hard earth strip. Turning at the end, I taxied straight for the apron and parked alongside the 2-AT whose size now seemed to dwarf our humble Jenny. The hangar doors were open and, inside, I could see another of those big aircraft with half a dozen mechanics busy removing its wings.

Glad at least for the stillness and silence, Tara and I climbed stiffly out and down and, as we did so, a figure emerged from one of the adjacent huts and came striding towards us.

Stockily built and with the fresh looks of someone who hasn't spent all his life indoors, he came straight up with a smile as broad as his shoulders.

"You must be Kingsley." He held out a large hand. "Wensum – Joe Wensum – Chief Pilot for Stout Airplanes."

I returned his handshake. "Good to meet you, Joe, and this is my friend, Tara Magee." I nodded towards the Stout sitting alongside. "I guess you'll be checking me out on that big ship later?"

"Sure will." He glanced up at the clear blue sky. "I know you've already been flying a bunch of hours getting here but, with this kind weather, it'd be good to get you started straightaway. How about we make your first flight in about an hour?"

"Fine by me." I glanced towards my co-pilot on this long trip here and knew what she was thinking. "Will it be okay to have Tara along for the ride?"

"We don't normally allow passengers on training flights," he glanced towards Tara and caught the almost pleading look on her oil-stained face, " but why not, as long as you don't mind a few stalls and steep turns."

"No problem. And the steeper the better."

"Okay, you're on, but I reckon you could both probably do with a freshen up first." He nodded towards the barge with the superstructure. "So, let's get you both quartered and have ourselves some coffee."

"Sounds good." With kit slung over our shoulders we followed him to what was the floating accommodation for the base. "How about Miller personnel, Chuck? Any of them here?"

"Oh yeah," he answered leading us up the gangway. "The mechanics in the hangar are all Miller men who'll be going overseas with you when the last Stout's dismantled and stowed."

"Overseas to where, exactly?"

"Haven't they told you?"

"Not yet."

"Ah." He seemed in a bit of a quandary. "Then I guess I can't either until I have the nod from the higher-ups here."

"Who are?"

"The Project Manager, Mr Smith, and the Operations Director, Carl Miller."

We were making our way along a narrow side-deck and the owner of that last name was the very man I'd come all this way to find. "Are they here right now?"

He shook his head. "No, both of them are down in Savannah Port checking details with the shipping people." He ushered us through a varnished wooden doorway into what was obviously the barge's messroom. "I'll show you your cabins later, but first let's get you that coffee."

We sat down at a long formica-topped table and were soon sipping welcome mugs of percolated Columbian brought from the other side of the galley counter and, possibly, a lot further before that. That was just one of the points to be cleared later, but right now I had another more pertinent. "This Mr Smith ... who is he, exactly, and who does he work for?"

Wensum shrugged. "Good question, and I try not to get too involved in that side of the business. But the way I see it, it's more the other way round with Miller working for him." He seemed to sense he'd given away too much, "But you'll get to figure that out for yourself soon enough, because he's heading back here now to talk to you."

"What, flying?"

"Speedboat."

"How does he even know we're here?"

"We've got contact through our own radio room here. I sent a signal just as soon as I saw you in the circuit."

Clearly not much was going to happen in this operation that wasn't controlled, but I had another even more immediate concern on my mind. "How about, Carl Miller? Will he be coming too?"

"Not with Smith. He has lots to sort with the freighter, but should be back later."

"Good. I look forward to meeting him again."

"Again?" He'd caught my last injudicious word. "You knew him before?"

"I think so," I hedged, "but I'll know for sure when I see him."

"Well, that won't be until tomorrow," said Wensum. "He's not reckoning to be here before midnight, so it'll be breakfast before you renew your old friendship." He nodded towards my empty mug. "If you're all set, I'll show you to your quarters and then we'll go get some hands-on time in the 2-AT."

*   *   *

After flying delightful little fighters like the Nieuport and Spad, the lines of the Stout were about as unappealing as its maker's name, but what it lacked in looks, it certainly made up for in size. Certainly, it was the biggest airplane I'd ever yet flown, a realization emphasised early on when Wensum walked me around the aircraft for a standard external check and I found even the main landing wheels coming well above my waist.

As Tara settled into one of the few passenger seats in what was basically the aircraft's cargo space, Wensum led me into the all-enclosed cockpit. "Don't be put off by the size," he reassured, clearly reading my thoughts as he ushered me into one of the two side-by-side pilot seats. "You'll find her a bit heavier on control after your fighters, but she still flies like any other."

I still wasn't so sure, and even less so as I looked down at ground seemingly further away than scud-running back in France. Added to these doubts were whether I would ever keep this thing in balance without the wind on my cheek to sense slip or yaw. This was the first time I'd ever flown in anything other than an open-cockpit and I voiced that concern to Wensum.

"Just keep that ball in the centre." He was pointing to an instrument on the dash something like an upward-curving spirit level. "Whichever way it's off means you need a bit of rudder that way."

I was glad to see the pedals I'd need for that were just as I was used to, but less happy about the wheel replacing the iconic joystick that had been the means of control since my first days of flying. I tried a few inputs into the one on my side which looked like it might have come straight off a Model T; not an impossibility, seeing as Ford Motors had now taken control of the Stout Company. Whatever, forward and backward movement of it produced the same elevator response as a stick, though I found it needed a full half turn either way to get the ailerons out on the wing deflecting the way they should. Clearly, handling this big bird was going to need muscle as well as technique.

The same went for the single engine powering this all-metal ship. I looked ahead along the squarish nose to where a single Liberty V12 sat ready to turn a big two-bladed prop. Big as it was, it hardly seemed adequate for the six thousand pounds gross weight it would be pulling. "Does four hundred horsepower hack it for this bird, Joe?"

"Just about. Can't say she's overpowered, but the three engine Tin Goose will be rolling out later this year and she'll be a winner." He nodded towards two coveralled mechanics now making their way towards us. "Anyway, let's get things burning and turning so you can see for yourself."

The Liberty might well have been a small powerplant for this aircraft, but its twelve cylinders still took some getting going, especially as the 2-AT's high nose meant the mechanics had to jump to catch hold of a blade tip for sucking in fuel. Then, after Wensum had set the throttle and called 'contact', one mechanic took hold of the lower blade while his buddy grabbed his other hand, and together they swung away. With each swing the mechanics changed roles while I made a mental note never to shut-down and need a restart away from base support. Finally, after four swings the Liberty roared into life and while it warmed, Wensum took me through a rundown of the various knobs, levers and instruments. By the time I'd got a rough grasp of it all, cylinder head temp was enough to run up, check the mags, and get the mechanics to pull our chocks. With me sitting back and watching how he did it, Wensum trundled us to the downwind end of the strip, went through take-off checks, got a thumbs-up from Tara in the back and then lined us up. "Right, I'll do this one and you follow through." I put my hands and feet lightly on the controls while he opened the throttle fully to send us roaring down the strip, tail up, lifting off half-way down and climbing away a hundred yards before the end.

We continued climbing, following the course of the Savannah River and with Wensum handing me control soon after he'd reduced power. "Okay, you've got her."

As predicted, after the Jenny she was heavy on control to the point of being laborious and even more so compared to some of those sensitive fighters I'd poled in my old combat days. We climbed to three thousand feet before Wensum told me to try some turns and slow-speed handling and, eventually, a stall. I turned and gave Tara a signal to check her lapstrap, throttled right back, brought the nose up and felt the aircraft wallowing before the airflow finally broke away from the wing's upper surface and the engine-heavy nose dropped way below the horizon. Control wheel forward, full power and she came out without a problem.

Wensum seemed happy. "Good, now try one off a climbing turn with power on."

This time, at a much higher nose attitude but with the thrust of the prop, the 2-AT dropped her nose more sharply and one wing, pretty viciously, into an incipient spin. I stopped that with instant rudder and she recovered with no problem, although I did glance behind to check Tara was still okay with all these hairy maneuvers. True to form, her smile showed she'd actually enjoyed it!

Joe Wensum too seemed content with the way things had gone. "Okay, let's head back now for some good old circuits and bumps." He let me stay on the controls, fished out two cigarettes from his flight jacket, lit both and handed one across. "Here, enjoy something else you'll have never done in those old windbags you flew before." He smiled as I took a welcome drag, banked us round for the airstrip and throttled back slightly for the descent. "You seem to have got the feel of this bad boy pretty good. If the landings go okay and you're happy, tomorrow you can go get yourself a few hours of consolidation."

I was certainly happy with that plan, which was more than I could have said back in 1917 as that Boche Zeppelin climbed me away from its Bickendorf base *en route* to some target and God-knows what outcome. With a flaming death over England or a firing squad back in Germany as the most likely, I could have been forgiven for my less-than positive approach to *that* new experience. As I brought the 2-AT down and back for our circuit training, I couldn't help recalling departure from that other base four and a half thousand miles east and ten years before.

*   *   *

Back there and then in that mighty airship, gradually gaining height over the Westphalian countryside, I quickly sought somewhere offering more concealment than by this open gunport. Settling into what must surely be a twelve hour mission, crewmen were already moving about their duties and I needed to be anywhere they weren't. I headed back to my vertical ladder and the working walkway above.

Up there I found a secluded section of structural framework in which to lie low. Dressed like the other crewmembers in my thick flying garb, I could possibly bluff my way out of any encounter, but avoiding contact in the first place was still the best way.

The other hazard already preying on my mind was the reception we'd meet over England. The Brits hadn't been slow in sorting their defences and, back in September, Lieutenant William Leefe Robinson had turned army Schutte-Lanz SL11 into a cascading fireball, giving all those on board an appalling death and the Londoners below, finally something to cheer about. To counter that, the Boche were turning out higher-flying zeps, and the purpose of my mission had been to gain intelligence on just that. It would be ironic now if I finally met my end in the very instrument of war we'd been trying to combat.

That was something to contemplate in the next hours as we droned ever nearer to our objective, along with wracking my brains for some way to avoid it. Back in France there'd been talk of the Germans developing parachutes for use by their pilots. Perhaps they'd already been issued to Zeppelin crews. If so, that might be one way of escape. Admittedly, it was a plan facing pretty long odds, but at least something to take my mind off blazing airships and a ghastly death as I endured those interminable *en route* hours.

As it was, it wasn't excess heat that was becoming my problem as the flight progressed, but just the opposite. I had no idea of what altitude we were climbing to, but the way insidious cold was starting to eat into my bones and my own breathing becoming ever more laboured, told me it had to be way above ten thousand.

Neither had I any idea at what speed we were crossing what I now supposed to be the North Sea. Sixty knots, I seemed to remember, was a figure associated with airships and, if so, the something-like three hundred miles I was mentally calculating as the distance from Cologne to the English coast would have us there just an hour after early winter sunset. Already, through the airship's fabric hull, daylight was fading and an hour later we were in complete darkness. Better for my concealment, but not long now and we'd be over Merry Olde England with the Brits all set to add one more zep to their score.

Although I could see nothing outside, I sensed the airship's course and, eventually, was sure we were turning to port. If so, we had probably made landfall at a coastal checkpoint and were now heading straight for the target area. That surely had to be London, and all the ground and airborne defenses the Brits had brought to bear there.

One consolation was that if we really were now over 'enemy' territory, this crew would have more to occupy them than noticing just another member going about some duty. Now seemed the best time to go looking for a parachute, and I cautiously eased once more down that vertical ladder to the keel deck. One thing I did notice was that I was breathing a little easier, which suggested we'd descended to a lower altitude.

Down there on that lower gangway, what few crew I could see in the darkness were intent on their duties. Any furtiveness on my part would only have aroused their suspicion, and so I tried to appear just one of them by going to an open port and starting my own scan of the dark night sky. Although, supposedly, looking for 'enemy fighters', in reality I was ensuring we were over land and not still the cold dark waters of the North Sea.

In the event, it was impossible to tell as we were now cruising above a dense carpet of solid stratus, stretching on all sides, a moonlit ocean of white precipitation. The clear heavens above still carried the risk of aerial interception, but I could imagine the navigator and bomb aimer cursing this cloud barrier to navigation and target identification. Up there in the heavens I could make out Polaris, the north star, which told me we were heading approximately sou-sou-west, which fitted in with my theory that we'd crossed the English coast somewhere north, were now heading for London, and navigating purely by deduced-reckoning.

That was good enough for me to start following through on my scheme to find a brolly and head down to friendlier territory. Where though, if any, did they keep their parachutes? I set off to search further for'ard, and just beyond the midships engine gondolas, found a compartment storing personal equipment. Hanging there were a few of the standard issue flight suits and helmets, no parachutes, but some almost equally welcome knapsacks of food. I tore straight into one with ravenous glee and was so intent on devouring the rye bread and cold sausage that I failed to hear above the steady roar of the engines, the approach of soft-booted footsteps or see the appearance of a figure in the compartment doorway.

"Was machen Sie denn da?"

I spun around to face the man who was demanding to know what I was doing. He was tall and about my own build, wearing the peaked field cap and good quality knee-length leather flying coat I'd seen before on shot-down pilots of the *Luftstreitkrafte*. His voice too carried all the unmistakable arrogance of the Prussian Officer. But, whatever his rank and lineage, the fact was he'd caught me completely by surprise and my shocked look must have immediately triggered his suspicion as I saw his hand instinctively go to the small leather holster on his hip.

Another millisecond would surely have him drawing the weapon he'd got there, but that was time enough for me to grab a fire extinguisher off its nearby clamp and crack it straight into his close-cropped head. He went down like a sack of potatoes without even a groan, but leaving me with the immediate problem of what to do next. Zeppelins weren't the place to be hiding bodies and all I could do was shove his lifeless form under some stored kitbags and head straight out in the ever-more urgent quest to find a chute. Too urgent and too desperate, as it turned out, because outside the compartment I ran full-tilt into another crewman coming in.

"Entschuldigen Sie, Herr Leutnant ..ich habe Sie nicht gesehen..aber wir sind bereit. – Excuse, Herr Leutnant ... I didn't see you ... but we are ready."

For what? I had no idea, but going along with this mis-identification would at least buy me some time. I didn't reply, but simply gave an intolerant nod and followed the *heine* back along the walkway to whatever it was that was 'ready'.

To my alarm, it turned out to be that infernal *cloud car*, hooked up above the screaming slipstream of the now-open hatch and all set for lowering. That *leutnant* I'd clobbered back there must have been the observer coming for his flight-kit, and all set for a ride on the end of that flying toy. Whether to check position or even direct the actual bomb run, I had no way of knowing. Only that being mistaken for him left me no option but to take his place. Filled with foreboding, I allowed a crewmen to help me into the small open cockpit while another plugged a wire from my helmet into what was obviously some sort of telephone connection back to the control gondola. Then, with offers of "Viel Glück", the winch was set in motion and, after a few alarming lurches, I was being steadily and smoothly lowered away.

With a sixty knot freezing blast now rushing past and the *cloud car*'s small fin and planes gradually stabilizing its initial swing and yaw, I went lowering down, the cable playing out with me feeling like the bait on the end of a fisherman's line. Above me, the Zeppelin rumbled on, but was only in sight for a brief moment before my bomb-like steed entered the clammy murk of the underlying stratus and I could see nothing at all. But it was what lay beneath this cloud layer that I'd been sent to report and almost immediately there came demanding words into my headphones.

"Was sehen Sie da unten?"

The question asking what I could see, came with that edge of authority that was surely the ship's commander, and even as he spoke the car broke out of the cloud and, even in the darkness, I could see we were passing over open country fields at something like fifteen hundred feet.

Whatever the height or outcome, for me this mad flight could only end in oblivion, but there was still at least one way I might help the allied cause and save a few civilian lives. I pulled the horn-shaped speaking tube closer and said in my best German, "We are over London."

I'd hoped that the crackling line between me and the control gondola had been bad enough to disguise my accent, but there was hesitancy and, perhaps, some suspicion in his response.

" Wo in London? Sind Sie sicher."

"Yes, I am sure, and there are docks ahead. Drop your bombs ... *now!*"

Would they be hoodwinked or would I be immediately winched back up to the mothership? The answer came in the form of bombs instantly plunging out of the murk just ahead of me to fall and explode harmlessly in the open farmland below. At least now I'd wasted the enemy their trip and tons of bombs, and saved a few lives.

I'd have allowed myself just a smile of satisfaction if I hadn't then, over the phone, heard the urgent call of other voices in the control gondola. Then, from above the overcast, there came the roar of engine noises very different to the zep's Maybachs, followed immediately by the unmistakable chatter of quick-firing machine guns. Something was happening up there and it had to be an attack by British fighters who'd spotted the zep cruising just above the stratus. There was more firing, either their's or the Brits, I couldn't tell, but probably both. Then an antiquated BE2c biplane came flashing out of the cloud just ahead, before pulling up and disappearing back into the murk for what I hoped was another pass.

Or did I really hope that, seeing as the zep's destruction would also surely mean mine? I consoled myself with the thought that at least it was a better way to go than the one I'd earlier contemplated. Then I heard yet more firing as the fighter came in for another attack. After that exchange of fire I noticed the farmland below getting ever closer. We were descending and I could imagine that zep commander above losing height as fast as he could for the cover of that stratus cloud bank. Or could it be that the fighter had managed to put holes in the gas bags and the loss of hydrogen was bringing the ship down anyway. Either way, if that height loss continued, I'd soon be striking mother earth fast enough for me to be the first casualty of this night's encounter. Then something else happened that brought that eventuality ever closer.

Suddenly, up there in the stratus, there came the *whoosh* of an explosion, an instant flash and then a sudden surge of heat felt even in my perch hundreds of feet below, as two million cubic feet of igniting hydrogen suddenly transformed

Germany's latest wonder-weapon into a gigantic falling fireball.

I kept my gaze upwards, fully expecting to find my own funeral pyre coming down over my ears, only to see the airship sinking slowly stern-first out of the overcast and with the fire in her innards spreading remorselessly along its whole length. Already, men were jumping to certain instant death rather than an agonising one up there with their ship.

Would this burning monster come right down on top of me? Certainly it was slowing and I was swinging more and more directly beneath it. The ground too was rising up faster and faster and, by the light of the roaring mass above me, I could see we were coming down into a small field bordered by trees and a couple of small cottages. In the last seconds, with my forward speed almost zero, I struck the ground with such force as to feel my eyes had popped from their sockets. They focussed again just long enough for me to see the zep come to its own crumpling and flaming rest just a few hundred yards further on.

It was a horrific vision that lasted only seconds before my own lights were mercifully extinguished, to be replaced by the total blackness of what could only be the other side of eternity.

*   *   *

Had the ten minutes it had taken for me to descend back to the Savannah River circuit really been enough for that whole nightmare of a recollection? I shook myself back to the task in hand, stubbed my smoke and prepared for my first landing in a 2-AT.

Joining the circuit downwind, Wensum started talking me

through the drill. "Right, power back to 1700 and speed to seventy – give yourself a good long downwind for a decent approach – base leg here, power back some more, speed to sixty – okay, final approach, keep the speed to sixty, I'll do this first one and you follow through."

We came low over the threshold, Wensum closing the throttle completely and me noting the higher flare height and the nose attitude as airspeed bled off and more and more back elevator was used to hold her off until the wheels touched and we kissed the ground in a perfect three-pointer.

With my I.P. working the pedals like a demented organist to keep straight, I could see that a tail-wheel instead of a skid on a hard surface meant lots of rudder work on the landing roll.

That was something I'd now be finding out for myself as Wensum swung around and fast-taxied us back for takeoff. "Okay, now you try one."

*   *   *

Another hour has us taxiing back to the hangar and shutting down. In spite of the state's winter temps, I wiped away the sweat generated by half a dozen take-offs and landings in a far-from nimble aircraft. But, by the end I was pulling off workmanlike landings without breaking anything, Joe Wensum seemed happy I wasn't going to kill myself or lose Miller an airplane and, in the back, Tara appeared reasonably unshaken by it all. With the mechanics already refuelling, we made our way to one of the huts to complete the paperwork.

The flight office turned out to be much like any other I'd experienced, with its scattered armchairs, aroma of burnt to-bacco, walls covered by numerous posters and model aircraft dangling from the ceiling. Most of the floor space between was taken up by a large map table and, while Joe filled in the flight log, I took the opportunity to examine the chart lying atop it.

It was a quarter-million scale covering most of South Carolina and Georgia. With my finger I traced the Savannah River up from the salt marshes of the coastal belt, past our base and another fifty miles to the fall line where it then rose up through central Piedmont to the rolling hills and valleys nudging the continental ridge of the Appalachians. It was a chart that had had much previous use, with several pencilled tracks drawn and then erased. I was particularly intrigued by one that led to an inked cross a good two hundred and fifty miles north in the foothills of the Brown Mountains. I pointed it out to Joe Wensum. "Is this another airstrip?"

He shook his head. "If it is, I've never been there."

"Okay, it's not important." I brought my finger back to the somewhat featureless terrain of our own location. "But why did the Millers chose here, way out in the boonies, to set up this base? The nearest habitation must be a good fifty miles away."

Wensum nodded agreement. "Yeah, pretty remote, isn't it. What I do know is that they set it up way back, just before the turn of the century, when they were well into early aeronautical research. Probably just a case of wanting to keep what they were doing very much to themselves and clear of prying eyes."

"Any idea what that research entailed?"

"No, and even now, no-one seems to want to talk about it. Anyway, back to the present." He nodded outside to where the mechanics were just completing post-flight checks on the 2-AT. "How did you find the old bus?"

"A bit heavy after what I've been used to, but a lot more comfortable and I think I've got the measure of it."

"Good." He flipped shut the flight log. "So, tomorrow, both of you go get yourself some practice."

"Both of us?"

"Sure. While you're getting used to the machine you'll find it useful to have a spare pair of hands in the other seat."

I caught Tara's enthusiastic smile and said, "Thanks, we'll enjoy that."

"Okay." He threw some paperwork onto his desk. "I need to get on with that, so you two enjoy some time together and be ready to fly first thing tomorrow."

We willingly did as ordered and, as we made our way to the barge, Tara said, "They all seem friendly enough so far."

I nodded. "Flying types usually are, but don't forget some others have as good as eliminated us back home. We certainly need an explanation for that from the mysterious Mr Smith."

"If we ever get to see him."

"We will, and sooner than you think." I nodded to a sleek speedboat nuzzling the jetty. "Because I'm guessing that little beauty has just whisked him back from Savannah Port."

We boarded the barge and my guess was right because, as we entered the mess-room, the man himself stood up to meet us.

*   *   *

CHAPTER ELEVEN

"Captain Kingsley ... good to see you here."

Since our last meeting on Governors Island, Mr Smith had swapped his pin-stripe suit for what looked like green military fatigues, and pretty filthy ones at that. He was quick to excuse himself when I introduced Tara. "Apologies for the grime, but I've been down in Savannah Port sorting some last minute hitches with the shipping line."

"Shipping to where, exactly?" I parked myself on the seat opposite. "So far you haven't actually said where this operation I'll be running is going to be based."

"Haven't I?" He ushered Tara down into the seat beside me and poured some coffee from a pot on the table. "All in good time, Kingsley, but for now let's just say a country in South America."

I sat back and lit a cigarette. "So, you'll tell us our exact destination 'all in good time'! At least we've got plenty to spare since you eliminated our old lives back in the Bronx."

"How did you know that?" In an instant, the *bon homie* had gone the way of his smile.

"Never mind 'how'. The fact is you're making it impossible for us to return to New York, and I'd like to know why."

He shrugged. "Simply, that things where you're going are happening faster than we thought, meaning we've had to expedite the time frame we initially gave you." Quickly swapping his exasperation for the sort of ingenuous smile people give when they've been caught wrong-footed, he spread his hands like a magician showing he'd nothing to hide. "Just think of it as our way of helping you transition to a more lucrative job doing what you love."

"Thanks for nothing. In other words, you want us to ship straight out from here to wherever it is this whole shooting match is going."

"I'm afraid so. The freighter leaves Savannah Port just as soon as the last aircraft's loaded and we plan for you to be sailing with it."

"Whether we like it or not."

Once again, that forced smile. "It's what's best for you both, but as an ex-military man, you'll surely know all about obeying orders." He eased his voice just a smidgen. "Think about it. A new career and a good life for you both ... together."

He'd found my weak spot and knew it but, if only for Tara's sake, I had to fight my corner. "How about the promise you and Wilson Miller gave me, that I'd be back to act as Lee Vennington's lawyer?"

"Forget Vennington." That too seemed more like an order than advice. "Believe me, Kingsley, the man's not worth it."

"But justice is." I stubbed out my smoke and leaned closer. "I agreed to defend that man, and still aim to do just that, no matter what little tricks this organisation of yours tries to play."

There was still a semblance of a smile, but those piercing eyes of his had fixed mine like pincers. "And just what 'organisation' do you think I belong to, Kingsley?"

"One with plenty of clout, that's for sure. What puzzles me more, though, is the interest it's taken in some down-and-out hobo whose nerves were left tattered by the war he fought on its behalf."

"Perhaps the explanation for that comes in just the one word you yourself used, Kingsley. Justice." He could see I was feeling for another smoke and whipped out a gold engraved case with an eagle motif engraved on its side. "Here, have one of mine."

"Thanks." I took one and saw that they were the new expensive *Old Gold* brand. "First time I've tried one of these."

"Then get used to them, because they, and a lot more, are something you could afford if you just went along with what we're offering you." He took one himself and lit us both from the case's integral lighter before sitting back and blowing a perfect ring up to the barge's deckhead.

I watched it rise, thinking it probably had about as much substance as his promises. "Will that also get me a gold cigarette case engraved with a State Department crest?"

"Only if your other skills are as good as your observational ones." His eyes had narrowed as he took another long drag and I knew he was thinking just how much he needed to tell me. Finally, he stubbed out his *Old Gold* and became serious. "Okay, I guess you – both of you - need to know what it really is you're getting into."

"That would certainly help."

"Right. Well, you're probably aware that our country has long had a natural interest in maintaining an influence in Central and South America."

"The Banana Wars?"

He smiled. "Well that's what Randolph Hurst chose to call them as he pushed public opinion towards imperial expansion as a way of keeping an eye on our neighbours. But then along came a World War in Europe, after which the American public's enthusiasm for international adventure somewhat waned."

"Not unreasonably, after losing over thirty-five thousand of their men-folk over there."

"Quite, but the way things have gone since has shown that an isolationist policy isn't necessarily what's best either. Consequently, our administration has decided to exert influence overseas by offering direct assistance to those countries where we can help friends and hinder enemies."

"And, presumably, some of this 'assistance' might include an air service?"

"Amongst other assets, yes." Smith glanced around the mess-room to check there were no staff eaves-dropping before lowering his voice to a conspiratorial tone. "The fact is, less-developed countries invariably cover large tracts of remote territory where transport and communication is difficult, if not impossible. Aviation is the answer, but those countries simply don't have the technical expertise or finance to provide it themselves. But we do, with the help of men like yourself."

"Working for which company, exactly?"

"In your case, Miller Air Services."

"Which, in turn, will be working for the same people as you, Mr Smith," I lowered my own voice, "who, I'm guessing, are more than familiar with the dark art of subversion."

Smith shrugged. "It's a devious world we're living in, Kingsley, where the side with the dirtiest tricks is going to be the winner. You're an intelligent man with experience who can surely see the advantages of being able to move men into, out of, or around a country at will. At the same time they can keep tabs on what's actually happening there and, if things start getting nasty, are in a position to offer immediate practical help to that government."

"If you like them, that is. If you don't, you help to replace them with one you do."

"That's how world politics are going to work from now on, Kingsley, whether we like it or not."

"By using phoney aid packages as a cover for clandestine operations."

"We prefer to see it as helping friends."

"Well, I guess looking at it that way at least helps you sleep at night." I stubbed his *Old Gold* and lit up one of my own *Camels*. "Let's see if it'll work for me as I spend mine mulling all this over."

He stood up. "Just don't mull too long. I'll need your decision in the morning, but just remember that you now know things we'd prefer went no further than this base."

"I get your drift, Mr Smith." I stood up too, glad I at least had an inch of height over his. "One more question though, before you go."

"Which is ...?"

"When will I get to meet Carl Miller again?"

"Why so keen?" Immediately there was suspicion in his cold eyes.

"Oh, you know, old comrades-in-arms and all that."

"Hmm." He still had that dubious look. "Carl is busy down in Savannah Port right now with the shipping people. I doubt if he'll be back here before midnight."

I gave a smile as insincere as the one he'd been giving me during our frank exchange. "Something else to look forward to tomorrow then."

*   *   *

Tara and I headed straight for our cabins, or at least mine, to discuss all we'd learned. She flopped onto my bunk, hand under her chin with a look of concerned perplexity.

"Did I hear that right, or was that some sort of threat he gave at the end?"

I squeezed my way onto the other end so I was facing the girl I'd stupidly brought on this foolhardy mission. "That's the way I got it too. Go with us or ..."

244

"… you don't go anywhere," she completed , dismally.

"Yeah, but no way I'm going to let it get that far."

"So, what's your plan?"

"The same as it always was. The truth from son Carl, get him back to New York and have him indicted."

"And how do you plan to do that, seeing as we're right here in the enemy camp?"

"By continuing to play along with the idea that I'm their man. Tomorrow we're going to take the Stout for some consolidation flying. One way or another, I aim to get Carl on board, head back to New York and be well clear of here before they even know we've gone."

She gave a little scoff. "There's no way he'll willingly get hijacked like that."

"No, so probably it'll be very *un*willingly."

"You mean using force?"

"If I have to."

"While everyone else around here stands back and lets you?"

It was time to admit my planning hadn't gone that far. "It's going to be a case of taking it as it comes, Tara. I've been in fixes before, remember, and managed to find a way out."

"Ah, yes, being stuck in that enemy Zeppelin base. You promised to relate how that one worked out." She glanced at the clock on the cabin bulkhead. "The night's still young, so go ahead and tell me more."

I might have suggested a more agreeable way of wiling away the evening hours, but I had promised and recalling that adventure might yet give me some ideas of how to deal with this latest one. And so I continued my account to the point when I'd hit England's 'green and pleasant land' an almighty bang in the zep's *cloud car*.

"My God, it's a wonder you weren't killed."

"I thought I had been at first. I'd avoided incineration

in the zep like the rest of its crew, but that wallop I'd met the ground with, certainly knocked me into my own black oblivion."

"So, were you badly hurt?"

Would I even live, had been my more immediate concern, as I slipped in and out of consciousness before finally descending into a deep and bewildering darkness.

*   *   *

"Nurse! He's awake."

The voice was that of an armed soldier intruding into the soft murmur of voices and hushed activity going on around me. If this were heaven, then it was blessed with pretty girls, especially the one close by my bed examining a clipboard hanging from its end. She came closer and gave me a quick examination. "Good. I'll get the doctor."

As she scuttled off, the realization started to dawn that my introduction to Saint Peter was still some time off and that this was just a very earthbound hospital. I tried a tentative movement of my limbs and was relieved to feel everything functioning. I went to sit up and found myself pressed down again by a strong hand.

"Do you speak English?"

I was conscious enough to realise the tall older figure in a white coat standing over me asking obvious questions had to be the doctor the nurse had gone to fetch. "Of course I can speak, English. Where am I?"

"You're in the Royal Free Hospital. How do you feel?"

"Okay, apart from a pretty sore head."

He nodded unsmilingly. "Not surprising. You've suffered mild concussion, but another day will have you up and about."

Surprisingly, it was the young soldier, still standing close by, who spoke next. "Sir, the major said he wanted to speak to this man as soon as he was conscious."

The doctor nodded and turned back to me. "Are you feeling up to a few questions?"

"I guess so."

"Good."

He disappeared down the ward, soon to be replaced by a smart military type with moustache, Sam Browne belt, immaculate breeches and highly polished riding boots. I guessed that the crowns on his tunic cuffs made him 'the major' spoken of by the soldier now coming to smart attention and being told just as quickly to 'fall out and disappear'. "I'm told you speak English." He had that plummy accent of the upper class Brits.

Again, that same statement. "Why wouldn't I?"

"Because you arrived in this country as the only survivor from last night's shot down Zeppelin. Except you weren't really one of the crew, were you?"

"No, I wasn't."

Just when I was thinking he was well informed, his next statement showed they'd jumped to entirely the wrong conclusion. "You are actually a spy sent here on a secret mission."

"I'm what?" I tried to sit up before the red-hot pain coursing through my head had me sinking back onto my pillow, both confused and angry. "You've completely got the wrong idea there, buddy."

"Then why are you wearing a French uniform beneath your German flying suit and carrying the identity discs of 'Sergent Mark Kingsley'?"

"Because that's who I am, a fighter pilot with Escadrille SPA66 of the *Aeronautique Militaire*."

"You don't sound very French."

"No. I'm American serving with the Lafayette Flying Corps, for Christ's sake."

"Who just happens to be in an enemy airship attacking London."

I shook my head wearily. "Yeah, I know it looks bad but, believe me, I was on the run from an op of my own and ended up stowing away. If you don't believe me, go check with the French or U.S. Embassy."

"We will indeed, but, in the meantime, and as you don't seem in immediate danger of dying, I'm going to have you moved."

"You mean I'm going to be stuck in a POW camp?"

"No, somewhere far more secure. You're the first to escape alive from a raiding Zeppelin over this country so, believe me, we have a lot more questions we need to ask you."

"You mean I'm still a prisoner?"

"Very much so and, believe me, it's for your own good. Your lot have caused the deaths of hundreds of women and children here. You were lucky our army chaps got to you first. With feelings running so high, I wouldn't have wanted to be in your shoes if the population had got their hands on you." He stood up and put on his cap. "So, we'll put you somewhere they can't. In the meantime, I suggest you use whatever time you've got left to contemplate the penalty we dish out to spies in this country."

And with that happy thought, he stomped out.

*   *   *

"My goodness, out of the frying pan and into the fire."

"Yep, and the 'fire' turned out to be one place I never ever expected to be."

"Which was?"

But Tara never got an answer to that question, with my recollections being suddenly cut short by the roar of a boat's

248

powerful engine surging past and making even the barge's considerable bulk heave slightly in its wash. "That has to be Carl arriving back from Savannah." I dashed to the porthole, but it was dark outside and the boat just a white trail of prop wash heading to the jetty where I could hear it throttling down to come alongside. I pulled Tara off the bunk. "Come on, let's go and have a look at our prime suspect."

We made our way up gangways to the open upper deck in time to see a stocky figure jump ashore. In the moonlight it wasn't difficult to recognise the man I'd last seen nine years before, leading those enemy troops at the Bickendorf r/v. "Meunier!"

Tara was peering through the darkness, close to my shoulder. "You mean Carl Miller?"

"The very one."

"So, are you going to confront him?"

I shook my head. "No point right now. With no ground crew to get us flying, we'd be stuck here and he'd be forewarned."

"So, we wait until morning?"

"That's all we can do."

My reasons were true and valid, but that warm bunk and a night in Tara's arms was a far more enticing one. "Come on, let's hit the sack. The pursuit of justice can surely wait another few hours."

We headed back down to my cabin, filled with the promise of imminent passion and completely unaware of just how wrong I could be.

*   *   *

We woke early to the sound of another roaring engine, the sun outside barely peeping above the far horizon and the cabin still in semi-darkness. I dashed to the porthole again to check whichever boat was under way, only to see the Savannah River flowing placidly by with a heron on the opposite Georgia bank lifting gracefully over a small alligator lumbering its way back to his watery lair.

Tara was now sitting up, bleary-eyed, shielding her nakedness with the blanket and running a hand through tousled hair. "What's happening?"

"Someone going somewhere, and I can guess who." I nodded outside. "No boat moving out there, so it has to have been an aircraft taking off." I grabbed some clothes and headed for the door. "Stay here while I go check."

I was back in minutes. "It was an aircraft all right. The Jenny's gone."

"Gone? Gone where?"

I slumped back onto the bunk. "Who knows, but apart from me and Joe Wensum, the only other pilot here is Carl Miller, so it looks as though our suspect has flown the nest before I even got to nail him."

"But he surely can't be going that far. Didn't you tell me the Jenny's range was only a hundred and seventy-five miles?"

"That's right, but there'll be a hundred landing places in that radius where he can hide himself and the aircraft for as long as he wants."

"Okay, but if we knew the direction he climbed away, we might have a clue as to where he was heading."

I had to admit she was thinking more logically than me. "You're right. I'll go talk to the mechanic who got him started."

"I'll come with you."

She was dressed in a minute and five more had us down at the hangar finding a mechanic about to check over the Stout.

"Did you prop-swing the Jenny?"

"Yep."

"Who was the pilot?"

"Mr Miller."

"Carl Miller?"

"That's right."

"Which way did he head out after takeoff?"

He pointed north-west along the Savannah River. "Right up there."

"Did he have a full tank?"

"Sure did, plus a five gallon can."

I told him to make sure the Stout was ready in ten minutes and led Tara over to the flight office. In there I studied the chart on top of the map table and pointed out the cross I'd seen earlier. "That has to be some sort of bolt-hole and my hunch is that's where he's heading."

She studied the location more closely. "That's not far from the town of Morganton, which was the setting for Jules Verne's ..."

"... *Master of the World* , which you reckon told of mystery lights seen near the Brown Mountain, and an airship built by some mad scientist in his lair near Table Rock." Suddenly this whole crazy jigsaw seemed to be coming together. I glanced back at the chart and made a quick calculation. "That's about two-hundred miles north of here. He could just about do it on one tank with a quick top-up from his can." I gave my lovely girl a heartfelt hug. "Tara, that's it. He's heading for the place I'm sure the Wilsons housed their own mystery airship."

She frowned. "But that story was only that, Mark ... just a story."

"But one probably based on facts Jules Verne had probably read himself. He hardly ever left his studio in Amien, but he did know a lot about the world." I tapped the cross on the chart. "That could be a non-stop flight for us in the Stout."

"You mean you aim to head up there to try and find him?"

"Why not? I'm scheduled to fly the thing anyway, so let's use it."

"And what will you do if you do find him there?"

"I'll decide that when the time comes. Are you game to join me?"

"Of course."

"Then grab your flight kit and let's go."

*　　　*　　　*

"You only flew this thing for the first time yesterday, Mark. Are you sure you're up to landing somewhere you've never been before?"

"We'll see when we get there."

Perhaps not the most professional of approaches, but things were happening fast and my blood was up as I opened the throttle to send us weaving only slightly down that narrow strip to lift off and climb away. Another five minutes had us levelling at fifteen hundred feet north-westwards following the gentle curves of the Savannah River.

"So far, so good." Sitting next to me in the co-pilot's seat, Tara was happily fingering our way along the map and, before long, pointing ahead to a largish town just coming up to the nose. "That must be Augusta and the fall line where the river drops away to the coastal plain."

It certainly marked a change in topography as we flew on with the landscape becoming progressively more rolling and hilly. "How far to Anderson and the fork in the river?"

"About eighty miles."

"Good. When we get there, we'll fly a straight-line compass course for the last hundred miles to Morganton."

"And then look for that cross on the map ... whatever and wherever it is."

I could understand her doubts, but I had a plan. "I'm hoping our speed advantage over the Jenny, and his fuel stop, might have us catching and following him the last few miles."

And so we flew on, the cultivated farmland gradually surrendering to rolling hills and valleys, but becoming increasingly rocky after Anderson as we started climbing into the foothills of the Appalachians. Now, I flew a constant heading just a tad east of north as Tara followed the trackline she'd mentally drawn on the chart.

Between glances at the compass, I was constantly scouting ahead for any sight of the Jenny. Back in France I'd prided myself in always being the first to spot the enemy, but today, as morning turned to forenoon, I saw not a glimpse of our quarry and began to wonder if I'd completely misjudged his intentions. That is until suddenly a sparkle of sunlight breaking through the increasing overcast reflected off something moving at our level and twenty miles ahead. "There Tara. That has to be Carl. We've caught him."

Gradually, the distance between us narrowed as we increased throttle just a tad and lowered the nose to follow him down. For he was definitely losing height and, as we got ever closer to the edge of the Smokey Mountains, I could see he was heading for an open, reasonably level, area bordered on all four sides by tall pine forestry.

By the time we neared the field ourselves, he was already bringing the Jenny round in a tight continuous descending turn to what I could now see was a grassed landing area with a large hangar on one side close to the treeline. I was hoping he was too intent on landing to notice our own approach as, seconds later, he rolled the wings level just over the threshold and touched down short enough to turn straight off for the hangar.

Mentally acknowledging his piloting skills being on a par with his cunning, I continued our own descent while watching him stop and straightway leap from the cockpit. I'd throttled right back now, but in that still morning air and with his engine stopped, it was inevitable that the throaty roar of our own would catch his attention. As he sprinted for the hangar, I was sure I saw him glance briefly upwards.

"He's surely seen us." Tara too had been watching our quarry's progress. "If you land there now he's going to be warned and waiting."

"You're probably right," I stuck down the nose of our own heavy old bus for quicker height loss and higher airspeed and headed straight for landing, "so no point in hanging about."

As we came barrelling in, it did occur to me that this was my first unsupervised landing in a 2-AT, and into a very confined field at that. I turned to Tara. "Make sure that seatbelt of yours is tight, because this landing might not be my usual greaser."

And it wasn't, with me touching down probably a bit too fast and certainly too heavily, with those big wheels thumping the uneven grass surface, bouncing once, and then thumping again. Finesse in technique wasn't my first priority right then, but only to get us stopped and out before Carl got his welcoming act together. Full rudder and a burst of throttle did manage to swing us towards the hangar before our prop met the trees at the far end, and by the time we were alongside the Jenny I'd already shut down the engine unbuckled my straps and was half-out of my seat. With Tara right behind me, another second had us out and down on the grass. "Right, you wait here."

She shook her head. "No way. We're in this together, remember."

"Okay." It was no place and with no time for argument. "Come on, but keep your head down."

Running the remaining few yards to the hangar with her close by me, I fully expected the man we'd come so far to find, all set to make sure we didn't get any further.

As it was, when we reached its long wooden side and edged towards the small personnel door set half way down, there was only silence except for Tara's whispered voice. "This is one big building."

I nodded. "And I'm pretty sure I know what it was built for." As furtively as I could, I raised the door's latch and eased it open a crack. "You ready?"

She nodded nervously back. "As much as I'll ever be."

"Right, let's go."

I pulled the door fully open, relieved not to meet a hail of gunfire from the hangar's innards, but still stunned by what we saw.

*   *   *

CHAPTER TWELVE

Entering that wooden cavern of a building, I stopped, frozen dead in my tracks as I stared up, open-mouthed, at the thing hanging there from the hangar roof.

It completely filled the building, a deflated sausage, grey with dust and giving every appearance of some reptilian creature that had come here to die. Tara edged closer to me and grabbed my arm. "Is that what I think it is?"

"Yep, an airship, and perhaps the first one ever built and flown in this country." In size, it was a fraction of the one I'd last flown in, but infinitely more intriguing. "Right there, Tara, must be Jules Verne's inspiration for the legend of the Brown Mountain lights."

I scanned the ship's near two-hundred foot length, its external keel with a single propeller at the aft end and an open working area for the crew. So absorbed was I that it was only then that I saw a man seated at what must be the pilot station. On his face was that same cruel, humorless smile that I'd seen before, so long ago. Even more disconcertingly, in his hand and levelled right at us, was a 7.63mm broom-handled Mauser.

"Well, well, Captain Kingsley. Fancy seeing you again."

Carl Miller climbed down from the airship with that Mauser never wavering a degree from my torso. To me, he was still Meunier, the Legion bully from that other life of years back, with that bull neck, stocky frame and the livid scar I'd given him ten years before in those Flanders trenches. I managed to force a smile of my own. "Thanks for the promotion but, unlike you, I only ever made *sergent* in one country's army."

He chose not to rise to that and instead, for just a milli-second, waved the pistol back in the direction of the tired ship behind him. "So, what do you think of our little creation?"

"Very impressive ... or it must have been back in 1910 when you were test-flying it over the Brown Mountain."

He gave a little chuckle. "Oh, way before that, Kingsley. How about the end of the last century?"

He'd just confirmed my original suspicion. "You mean this was the mystery ship seen over Sacramento and San Francisco back in '96?"

"The very one, flown by my father and with me as his little helper." There was a hint of pride in his voice now. "But go back fifty years before that to my grandfather, old Johann Mueller. He was a man fascinated by the possibilities of lighter-than-air transport and who'd been conducting his own experiments."

That last bit was a revelation, but his own experience was something I wanted to hear more about. "You can't have been very old when you embarked on those early flights with your father?"

He nodded. "Only ten, but old enough to be entranced by the adventure of it all."

"And then, after California, you flew this contraption into other states?"

"You mean the later sightings in Nebraska, Illonois, Minnesota and Texas?" He gave another little chuckle. "Yep, that was us, even landing sometimes and scaring the locals."

"But then you ended up here. Why?"

"Technical issues." He shook his head. "Father had planned our final destination to be New York, where our dramatic arrival would have shown the world what airships were capable of. But our flights by then had shown the limitations of our electric motor and its heavy batteries. He could see that the future lay in the rapidly developing gasoline engines, and so we brought our wonder-ship here to this remote location to continue our research and test-fly the results. To maintain the secrecy, and like all the previous ones, these were done under cover of darkness."

"And so triggered the legend of the Brown Mountain Lights. But what prevented you taking it any further?"

"The problem of marrying hot gasoline engines with highly flammable hydrogen." He nodded upwards to the deflated bag hanging above his head. "My dad realised a less-volatile alternative had to be found, and so we began experimenting with non-explosive helium."

"From Miller Industry's own chemical works."

"Correct, Kingsley. You're well informed."

I smiled. "As were the Germans when they realized you had the means to stop their own wonder-weapons going down in flames. I bet they were prepared to pay big money for that secret, and Miller Industries was doubtless happy to ring the cash register." I folded my arms and met his gaze. "So, whose idea was it for you to go the route of the traitor? You or your father's?"

But, before he could even answer that question, Tara stepped forward with one much closer to her own heart. "What I need to know is why you murdered my brother?"

Carl Miller gave another of those innocent smiles, edged closer and sat down on a nearby packing crate. "That's a long story, Miss Magee, and, doubtless, a lot different to the one you're imagining."

"And one you can save for the authorities back in New

York." There were a whole lot of questions I would have liked answers to right there, but I didn't intend him ever being able to plead that they'd been obtained under duress. "Because that's where you're going back with us now, Miller."

"Oh, really." He frowned mock puzzlement. "And why would I do that?"

"Perhaps to save at least some of your family's reputation." I took the chance of stepping forward just that bit closer. "Lee going to trial is going to expose a whole plethora of skeletons from that shady cupboard of yours. At least my way will allow you and your politically-ambitious father to give your side of the whole sorry tale."

Strangely, my answer seemed to give him pause for thought, though his response was predictably defiant. "Except that won't happen, Kingsley, because, by the time it does go to court, you won't be around to defend him." He waved the muzzle of the Mauser between the two of us. "Neither you or your girlfriend here."

Seeing that weapon briefly aimed at Tara sent an ice-cold dread through my heart, but also the motivation, split second of time and the chance I'd been waiting for. It was now or never as I dived faster and harder than my last football tackle at Harvard, sending him flying one way and the Mauser the other.

But his years in the military hadn't been wasted as he rolled away from my grip, leaped up to grab a rusty monkey-wrench off a nearby workbench and throw it with sufficient accuracy to catch me a glancing blow on the skull. Then he was on to me, those gorilla hands around my throat with enough grip to prevent even a smidgen of air finding its way to my starving lungs. I felt my strength ebbing as a dark veil rapidly clouded my consciousness and what sounded like a hundred African drums beat their own retreat inside my head.

Then I heard a vicious crack, the pressure ceased and he

rolled off me like a hammered bullock with blood pouring from a gash just behind his right ear. I struggled upright to see the divine image of Tara Magee, blooded Mauser in hand, covering the semi-conscious figure beside me. With some air returning, I managed to gasp, "Thanks lover. You saved my life."

"Probably not for the last time." She rolled those lovely eyes before handing across the Mauser. "What now?"

I nodded to Miller, struggling to sit up while rubbing his head. "We fly him to New York."

"A long trip with a man who doesn't want to go."

"True." I levelled the Mauser at our quarry, shaking consciousness back into his blooded head. "So, which way will it be, Carl? Quietly and easy, or rough and hard?"

"Why the desperation?" He was also upright now, obviously still groggy but back into coherence. "Why make a fool of yourself, getting yourself involved in something you obviously know nothing about?"

"Perhaps I know a whole lot more than you think."

"Take it from me, you don't." He paused just long enough to finger that livid scar running down the side of his battered face, and I could imagine the bitterness still burning as fiercely as that knife-cut must have felt when I gave it to him that night in the mud-filled foxhole. "Didn't you ever wonder, Kingsley, why, back then in 1915, I didn't kill you when I had the chance?"

So he remembered it was me and Lee who'd been there that night of his defection. Even so, his last words had set me thinking.

"Reticence? Indecisiveness? Perhaps even a deep-buried sense of compassion."

He smiled. "Or perhaps, simply, that we were two men fighting on the same side." He caught my look of skepticism "There's a lot to this whole strange business that you don't understand, Kingsley, so perhaps I'd better enlighten you."

Legal procedures or not, this was something I'd just flown nigh on a thousand miles to find out, and I wasn't about to miss the chance. I sat down on a nearby crate with the Mauser still covering his every move. "Okay, I'm in no rush, so let's hear what you've got to say."

*   *   *

CHAPTER THIRTEEN

"This is one hell of a diversion from normal police procedure, Kingsley."

I was back in Pat Nolan's Bronx Precinct office, Tara by my side and facing the Chief of Detectives across a desk almost hidden beneath a pall of cigarette smoke and mounds of untouched paperwork. The latter hadn't been eased by the extra burden I'd placed on him in the three days since our arrival back in New York. With Carl Miller 'helping with enquiries' and his father demanding to know what the hell was going on, I'd thankfully managed to keep my head down while Nolan dealt with government agencies.

"But a necessary one, Pat."

He grunted, sat back and loosened his tie. "Must be, seeing how authorisation has come right from the top." He nodded across to Tara. "You sure you want to sit through this meeting, Miss Magee? Could be pretty unsettling, hearing things you'd rather not."

She fanned away the results of the chief's third *Lucky Strike*. "If it gets us the truth of what happened to Richard, it'll be worth it."

Further discussion on that point was interrupted by the arrival of District Attorney Gary Shreeve, blustering his way in, completely ignoring me and clearly not happy with this unusual turn of events. "What the hell's going on, Nolan? This is way out of line."

"Not if it's been authorised by the Attorney General, it isn't. And, anyway, you ought to be glad to hear any new evidence."

Mention of the AG had our DA instantly backing off and seemingly noticing Tara for the first time. "Okay, but what's she doing here?"

If Shreeve thought the victim's sister was easy fodder to his egotism, he was soon put straight by the girl herself. "Finding out who murdered my brother." Tara's tone made clear she was managing to resist our DA's dubious charm. "Isn't that what you want as well?"

"What I want is the man I *know* did it, paying the price, Miss Magee. What I *don't* want are useless pre-trial hearings such as this."

"We'll soon see what's useless around here, Attorney," said Nolan with a meaningful look before glancing at the clock on his office wall. He stubbed his smoke and stood up. "Okay, follow me and let's go hear what others have to say for themselves."

As Nolan led us out and along to our meeting room, I thought back to what it was like defending myself against false charges and how helpless I'd felt facing the might of a powerful state. The fact that I'd pleaded my case in a setting steeped in history hadn't helped ease the fear and uncertainty I felt at what the final outcome might be.

In just that short walk through the Precinct's corridors, my memories were taking me back to a very different place – back again to 1917 war-torn London and a mighty stronghold that had seen the ignominious end of much grander persons than Mark Kingsley.

*   *   *

The Tower of London.

Of course, I'd read about this impressive-looking London fortress with its history of heraldic greatness and harrowing accounts of mediaeval torture, imprisonment and beheadings, but never once imagined I'd ever end up there as a prisoner myself. Nor what the future held, as there was just one sentence for convicted spies, and those executions were held right here at the Tower. What was made clear very soon was the loathing the British held for Zeppelins and that, having just arrived in one, I couldn't expect too much in the way of compassion.

As it was, I was treated reasonably well by the army garrison manning the high walls overlooking the River Thames, and by the several officers from Army and Navy intelligence who, for two solid days, bombarded me with questions about enemy airships and their mode of operation.

Now all that snooping I'd done in the zep back at Bickendorf, and what I'd learned on the flight here, paid off. With London and other industrial areas suffering constant Zeppelin raids, I could understand their interest and I willingly told them all I knew, including details of my own abortive mission. I hoped it would all show where my loyalties truly lay, but at times still wasn't sure whether I was being questioned as an ally or an enemy. I guess it had to be the latter until they checked my credentials, during which time they remained frustratingly tight-lipped as to their conclusions.

That came to an end on the morning of the third day when I was taken from my cell and marched out to the flag-stoned courtyard. For all I knew, this was *it* and my dawn appointment was with the firing squad.

Instead I was thankfully ushered into a waiting car whose

uniformed driver soon whisked me out over the ancient drawbridge and on through the streets of London. It was a journey I would have enjoyed more if I hadn't been imagining suspicious glances from the citizens and recalling the major's words about their possible rough justice. I knew better than to even ask my military escort where we were going or for what reason, but the drive was a short one and soon we were passing between high ornamental gates before drawing up in front of an imposing red-brick building, several storeys high and with conical turreted towers on its corners.

In through the main entrance, we paused only momentarily to check in with what appeared to be London Bobbies, before then heading up a grand staircase to an upper floor where the spacious landing was softened by pile carpet and the smell of newly polished walnut. Here I was handed over to a dapper civilian in dark jacket and pinstripes who looked with disdain at my worn and oil-stained rough-serge tunic, dismissed the escort, and bade me follow to an inner office. On its wide varnished door, the brass nameplate read ASSISTANT COMMISSIONER – CRIME and, in its opulent interior, presumably, the man himself in high winged collar, impressive moustache and searching eyes appraising me from beneath hooded lids. He was sitting at a very large desk amidst an enveloping cloud of pipe-smoke, but stood up as we entered, not offering his hand but, at least, giving some semblance of a smile.

"Sergeant Kingsley. I'm Sir Basil Thompson. Welcome to Scotland Yard." He gestured to a nearby padded chair. "Take a seat."

This whole transition from suspected agent to a meeting with a titled British high-up was seeming a bit unreal, and even more so when he asked, "Tea?"

"Er ... coffee , if that's okay."

He didn't say, but gave a meaningful nod to his lacky, who

departed silently in pursuit of the requested beverages. While I sat wondering just where all this was leading, Sir Basil sat examining a file before him. Then he looked up and said, "Well, Kingsley, you certainly seem to have had an exciting war."

"It's had its moments. I've survived so far, thank God, which many haven't."

"Indeed." He glanced again at the file and tapped the page in front of him. "Anyway, you'll be glad to know that the French army have confirmed you as being who you say you are."

I tried not to show the relief I felt, helped by the arrival of a servant-type bearing a silver tray of steaming cups. After days of sweetened English tea, that coffee certainly tasted good and mellowed me enough to ask a question of my own. "That brass plate on your door, Sir Basil. Where does 'crime' come into all this?"

He took a sip of what smelled like Earl Grey tea from his fine china cup, and smiled. "The intelligence services of this country do a good job hunting down spies and traitors, but they don't have the power of arrest or prosecution. That's left to me as head of Criminal Investigation."

"And are you investigating me?"

"Oh, yes."

I felt some of that relief swiftly dissipating. "But you've just told me the French have confirmed my background. Surely I'm now free to return to my unit?"

"Not quite." He took another sip of his tea. "First, I'd like to hear just how you came to be flying over this country in an enemy airship."

"I've already explained that many times to the intelligence boys."

"I know, but tell me."

I once again went through the whole mission from ambush

to waking up in an English field, and realising, as I related it, just how far-fetched this true account must sound.

When I'd finished, Sir Basil stayed silent for another minute, eyeing me again through those hooded lids of his, as though assessing the plausibility of it all. "Quite a story, Kingsley. And you're sure this trap you flew into, and which cost the life of one of our agents, was a pre-planned affair?"

"Very much so."

"And have you any theory as to how the enemy got wind of the mission?"

"I know *who* was behind it." I told him of Meunier, of his treachery and how I'd recognised him back there at the r/v."

Sir Basil nodded sagely. "Yes, we do know of this Meunier, but the enemy were acting on information passed to them before you even took off." Thompson's piercing eyes became even narrower. "Someone talked, Kingsley, and now both us and the French want to know who."

"And you suspect me?"

"You or others. Did you discuss the flight with anyone outside of your escadrille commander or the pilot first assigned to the mission?"

"Absolutely not. And who would there be to talk to anyway?"

"We have our theories," Thompson tapped his pipe into a bowl on his desk and laid it down beside, "which we'll be following up."

I could see where this might be going. "Does that mean I can't go back to flying?"

"Not exactly, but with what we *do* know, the allies have decided they don't want you back in France." Thompson opened a leather document case beside him, took out some official-looking papers and slid them across. "These are your movement orders and warrants. Tonight you'll be heading down to Southampton to join a troopship bound to your next theatre of operations."

"Which is ..?"

"Salonika."

"Salonika!" I banged my cup down so hard that coffee splashed over his beautifully polished desk. "You're telling me I'm off to the Macedonian front where we're not only fighting the Germans and Austrians, but also the Bulgarians?"

"... in attempting to maintain Serbia's independence." Thompson sat back and placed his finger tips together. "You could have done worse, Kingsley." He smiled that cunning smile. "It's certainly warmer there than winter on the Western Front."

"And a long way from where you think I might have indulged in some mythical espionage."

"Not knowingly, but possibly through being too close to the wrong person. So, to make sure that doesn't happen again, you've been posted to Escadrille N507." He stood up and offered his hand. "Good luck. There's a car waiting to take you straight to Southampton."

As if bidden, the lackey reappeared to usher me from the office and guide me back downstairs, unescorted this time, to the main door. I made my way down the ornate staircase, trying to grasp the new direction my life had taken in the last few minutes.

On the next landing I paused to let it all sink in. Thankfully, I was still a free man, but left with the bitter taste that I was being virtually exiled for supposedly, and perhaps innocently, betraying the country I'd given the last two years of my life. And in Salonika, there was a good chance I'd be giving all of it that I had left. Ah well, I'd first come to Europe seeking travel and now I was going to experience more of it. And, at least, I'd still be flying, and once again in the good old Nieuport.

Even as I reassured myself with those crumbs of comfort, a door leading off the landing swung open to reveal a private waiting area. In there, a police constable was standing beside the seated figure of a woman. In the same second, she caught sight of me and her calm expression was instantly replaced by one of frightened recognition.

I recognised her too. She was someone I'd seen only the week before. It was Margreet MacLeod.

*   *   *

I brought myself back from memories of the most famous police station in the world to the reality of the present mundane enclaves of the 48th Precinct, where Nolan was leading us into a good-sized room. It was furnished with a long table, around which were seated Carl Miller, his father Wilson Miller and, beside them and looking far from comfortable, Father Huber, the now priest-in-charge of Saint Winfred's Church.

It was Miller senior who stood up abruptly as we entered, casting a soul-freezing look to me, but directing his venom towards the unfortunate DA. "Is this your doing, Shreeve?"

"Absolutely not." Our DA was always at his most grovelling when facing authority. "I'm sorry, Mr Miller, but you can blame Kingsley."

"Don't worry, I'll deal with *him* later, but if *you'd* done the job you're paid for, it wouldn't have even come to this." With the intolerance of a man not used to doing anything he didn't want, our nominee senator slammed back into his seat. "Damn waste of time. I've got better things to do than sit listening to excuses, so let's get on with it."

"We will when we're *all* here," said Nolan, signalling through the still-open door to a uniformed policeman on the other side. "Bring him in."

I don't think anyone expected it to be Lee who now came shuffling in between two police guards. Wearing an ill-fitting suit, he still had the unkempt look of a felon, though his drawn face brightened when he saw me, and recognised Carl Miller sitting close by. I could imagine his relief at seeing I'd fulfilled my promise to bring in our old nemesis, but all I could do right then was return his smile and nod him to a seat.

As the guards retired to the back of the room, Shreeve jumped to his feet. "This really is beyond the acceptable. No way should a man on a capital charge like Vennington here, be having this sort of hearing prior to trial."

"However, even *you* are going to learn some facts of which you are blissfully unaware, Attorney," said Nolan, making an effort to stay judiciously composed. "So, I suggest you sit down, get off your high horse, and *hear* them." He turned to me. "Starting with what Kingsley here has to tell us. That way we might get to really know who murdered Father Richard Magee and why."

*   *   *

I stood up, but before I could even begin my oratory, Wilson Miller showed he wasn't finished yet, especially with a man he'd only just hired. "We already *know* who the murderer is, Kingsley, and anything you've got to say is a waste of our time and yours."

"The truth – the whole truth – is never a waste of time, Mr Miller, especially when a man's life depends on it."

"Yeah, well Father Magee had a life too."

"He did indeed." I gestured around the room and the intent faces fixed on mine. "In fact, *several* of you here had motives for ending it." I met the hard, characterless eyes of the thin, dog-collared man sitting piously just a couple of chairs away. "Even you, Father Huber."

Those eyes suddenly widened with indignation. "Me! Have you the temerity to suggest that I would commit such a sinful act?"

"Why not? I suspect you were more than happy to fill Father Magee's shoes at Saint Winifred's when he went off to serve his country, and somewhat resented it when he returned, especially when some of your church funds went to setting up his veterans' shelter. *Winifred's Welfare* was clearly a contentious issue with you and when you got the chance to take it over you grasped it with, I'm sure, the firm intention of closing it down at the first opportunity."

I could see the truth of that last statement in Huber's face, but it was Wilson Miller who came to his defense. "That's a ridiculous accusation, Kingsley." He gave the cleric a dismissive glance. "Okay, for a man of the cloth, he leaves a lot to be desired, and I for one will ensure that *Winifred's Welfare* stays open, but Huber hasn't the will or the guts to commit murder."

I had no hesitation in agreeing with my erstwhile employer. "No, he hasn't, Mr Miller, but *you* do."

Seeing the chance of saving some face, Gary Shreeve was back on his feet. "Now you really are going *too* far, Kingsley. If you think you're helping your client by accusing respected citizens ..."

But I stopped him right there. "No, that's *your* job, Shreeve, but until you choose to do it, sit down and shut up."

Surprisingly, Wilson Miller chose to agree. "Yes, keep quiet, Attorney. I'll fight my own corner without your incompetent help." As the DA shrank down, Miller turned back to me. I could see his expression now was one, not of anger, but of tolerant curiosity. "You really think I would commit murder, Kingsley?"

"Yes, or at least someone connected to you would if it eliminated a threat to your political ambitions." I lowered my voice to what I hoped sounded something like advocacy. "You're a rich man, Mr Miller, who inherited a prosperous business empire, but your desire for even more power led you to seek election to the senate. Some charitable endeavour to support that goal probably seemed a good move, and so you embarked on a crusade to help disadvantaged veterans."

"So, what's wrong with that?"

"Nothing, except you made the mistake of enlisting Lee Vennington to your cause and being photographed with him. Father Magee saw that photo in the *Tribune* feature and realized the hypocrisy of the whole thing."

"What hypocrisy?" Unused to being faced up to, he was clearly making an effort to control his anger. "What are you talking about, Kingsley?"

"I'm talking about treachery, Mr Miller, the word Father Magee used in his dying breath. But let me offer a scenario by going back three decades to the unexplained night-time appearance of some mystery airship over Sacramento and San Francisco."

Wilson Miller made a brave show of inconsequence. "What's that got to do with anything?"

"It's got *everything* to do with what came later, because it was *you* flying that contraption." He went to protest, but I cut him short. "Before you deny it, you should know that Carl here has told me everything, and I've seen the actual ship."

"You ... what?" The withering glance Miller senior shot his son told me he was genuinely unaware of all that had been disclosed.

Carl's expression in return was a mixture of acquiescence and contrition. "There was no point denying it, Dad."

"Or anything to be ashamed of," I injected, to ease the atmosphere. "What you achieved back then was something to be applauded, and even more so when you later made other flights over the mid-west before ending up at your Savannah River base. That's where you investigated the possibilities of using helium as an infinitely safer lifting agent than hydrogen. Then, when the Great War erupted in Europe and Count Zeppelin was desperately seeking a solution to that problem, you saw a fortune to be made by offering him your own hard-earned expertise."

"How would I do that?"

"Not easily without exposing yourself to accusations back here and suspicion from the enemy. So, let me paint a scenario of how it might have been done. Let's say you sent your son Carl into the *Legion Etrangere* to eventually fake capture in the front line. I'm sure you didn't envisage two other Yanks being there when he changed sides for what we thought was simple sympathy for his original German ancestry. Whatever, later in the war, when Lee had transferred to the USAS, he related that whole business to his new friend, Father Magee. And then, just weeks ago, Magee saw a photo in the *Tribune*, recognised your likeness to the traitor Lee had known in the trenches as your son, Meunier, and straightway contacted you to demand you withdraw your senatorial candidacy. You couldn't let that happen and so sent Carl to eliminate the problem, which he did. Fate then threw you another lucky roll by Lee also going to see the good Father that night, being spotted by Carl, and so becoming the perfect fall-guy."

Wilson Miller smiled condescendingly and shook his head. "A good story, Kingsley, but your hypothesis is so wrong from the start. Firstly, there was no way we could ever have supplied helium to Germany, seeing as it's only found here in the U.S. and impossible to transport."

"I did say it was only 'a scenario', Mr Miller." It was time to admit the real truth to him and everyone else around that table. "In fact, you and I know that there is an even stranger, but far more honourable, explanation for all those events enacted back there in war-torn France. They've remained a secret to this day, but they did ultimately lead to the murder of Father Richard Magee."

*   *   *

"This was never meant to be disclosed," admitted Wilson Miller with an air of acceptance, "but perhaps it's time that at least the few of you know that there was some deeper meaning to all that treachery business."

"And that Carl here was really a hero of the Great War rather than a traitor," I completed for him while gaining some satisfaction from the shocked expressions on the faces of the others around that table.

Especially from Lee. "What are you talking about, Mark? Are you forgetting that we saw Meunier's ruthlessness ourselves back in the Legion. How he damn-near had us killed that night he went over."

I nodded. "Yes, he had us all fooled, but what no-one knew at the time was that the whole business of him joining the Legion and then deserting to the enemy was a deception jointly contrived between our government and the French." I turned back to Carl. "And knowing that makes sense of so many things I couldn't understand at the time. Like that night back in Toulouse, when I caught you having a clandestine meeting with Colonel Lepayre."

"You saw that?"

"I did."

"But never reported it."

"Who to? Things were obviously happening at a higher level than a mere legionnaire such as myself. I thought it best to simply keep quiet, especially as I'd also witnessed your spat with that Serbian Pavlovic and his threat to disclose something he knew about you."

"Knew what?" persisted Lee. "What was the big secret?"

"The real reason he was there in the Legion."

"Which was?"

"Airships, Lee. Both our government and the French were anxious to know of Germany's Zeppelin operations and Mr Miller senior here had come up with scheme for finding out."

"But the U.S. wasn't even in the war at that time," broke in Tara.

"No, but that didn't mean we weren't keen to know all we could of airship development," answered Wilson Miller, "and the allies were just as anxious for us to share it with them."

"Father predicted that Zeppelins were going to play a significant role in the war," continued Carl, "and that the sooner we got hold of their secrets and found a way to combat them, the better. So he came up with that plan to plant me in there as a *supposed* traitor selling our knowledge but, in reality, finding out all I could about theirs."

"Only with official backing and his own enthusiasm for the idea," added Wilson. He gave an admiring glance towards his son. "Carl had inherited my own taste for thrills and was only too keen for a spot of adventure of his own."

"You were still taking a hell of a risk."

"Oh, sure, but one that was worth it. I had contacts in the government who eventually gave the scheme their support together with the co-operation of the French."

"Who were only too happy to help in a spot of valuable espionage," continued Carl. "So, they arranged my enlistment into the Legion with the plan that I'd later be infiltrated into the German lines."

"An ingenious scheme." I conceded," but how come that Serbian, Pavlovic, got to learn of it?"

"Carelessness on our part," admitted Carl. "Back at Si-di-bel-Abbés, it had been his duty day for collecting the mail. Little hustler that he was, he'd already me put me down for a rich kid, saw my latest letter was from my father, figured it might hold some handy greenbacks and pocketed it for himself.

"Only to find it contained information even more valuable."

"Exactly. When that letter didn't arrive, I suspected him of stealing it and told my superiors. By the time I was trans-ferred to Toulouse, French Intelligence had checked Pavlov-ic's antecedents and found he had German sympathies. The Colonel met me that night to warn me but, when I related the earlier drunken outburst in the canteen, agreed it was time to eliminate that threat once and for all."

"And so next day you got promoted and Pavlovic ended up dead."

Carl shrugged. "That was war, Kingsley, with no room for sentiment when the greater good was at stake. So the scheme went ahead with me leading those night patrols into No-Mans-Land and passing on information enough to convince the enemy I really did want to change sides."

"All pretty cold-blooded, nonetheless, seeing as many of our own comrades never came back from those patrols."

"No, but taken prisoner rather than killed," Carl was quick to explain. "The way the war went, I probably *saved* their lives, and that was how it could have been for you if you hadn't gone and sussed me. Ironically, that night you followed me and did this," he touched his scar, "finally convinced the Boche I really was a turncoat. What with my German ancestry, airship expertise and flying experience, they soon accepted me into their ranks, commissioned me into the *Luftstreitkrafte*, and assigned me to Bickendorf to work on their latest Zeppelins. Eventually, though, I started to fall under suspicion, things got too hot and our people decided to pull me out and infiltrate another agent."

"A job which eventually fell to me," I disclosed for the first time.

"*You*?" Another factor he was obviously unaware of. "It was *you* flying in that exchange agent that night?"

"It sure was, but little knowing I was flying straight into a well-laid ambush. When I saw you at the head of those German troops, I simply assumed you were leading them, when in fact ..."

"... I was escaping from them." Carl Miller allowed himself a cynical smile. "It would have been good to see your face if you'd found out it was me you'd been sent to pick up."

"I doubt if the agent I was bringing would have seen the joke. It cost him his life."

"Yes, I know, but that was due to lax security at your end rather than carelessness at mine." He gave me a look somewhere between pity and admiration. "At least *you* got away."

"Just." I thought back to that time stowed away on the enemy zep, listening to the exchange between those two Germans saying how men were out searching for someone on the run, assuming they meant me, and now realising it was him. "You must have had an exciting time of your own avoiding capture."

"*Too*, exciting." For a second, his face showed all the grimness that memory carried. "But I finally made it to neutral Holland, determined, if nothing else, to get whoever betrayed that mission."

I could see those last words and what they might imply, had struck home with Tara. "You're surely not saying it was my brother Richard who betrayed it and that that was why you murdered him?"

But Carl shook his head. "No, this was way before your brother even came to France, Miss Magee. But he did eventually pay with his life for what happened that night, and the man who took it is right here in this room."

*   *   *

Tara turned to me, desperate for some sense to this whole business.

"So, if Richard was blameless and Carl here wasn't a traitor, who was?"

I had to force myself to answer that, turning towards the man himself as I did so. "It was Lee."

My client shook himself out of what must have seemed an enveloping nightmare. "Have you gone mad, Mark? What are you saying?"

"I'm saying it was *you*, Lee, who betrayed the Bickendorf operation to the Germans – you and your girlfriend, Margreet MacLeod. She was probably the one who got word to the enemy, but it was you who helped her get the details from that French pilot."

"But I would never have risked the life of my best friend."

"You didn't know you were when you took off for the Oroville secondment that morning. It was just an accident of fate that had me flying the mission, and one which damn near cost me my life."

"But why would I do it anyway?"

"The oldest reason in the world, Lee – love. You were totally besotted with Margreet and would have done anything to keep her affection, even if it meant betraying the country you'd chosen to serve."

I could see my words were hitting home and that he was struggling with ones of his own. When they finally came they were as painful to hear as they must have been for him to say.

"You're right, Mark, and it's a sin I've lived with ever since."

"But then you went and met Father Richard Magee's in the AEF and, like a good Catholic, felt the need to confess." I tried not to sound unduly judgemental. "And there was more than one transgression troubling your conscience, wasn't there, Lee? Shooting down a French aircraft must have been weighing heavily on top of everything else. '*Perhaps, dear God, I killed a mother, when I killed a mother's son.*' No wonder you quoted that old doggerel with such feeling, but it wasn't the enemy you were remembering, but the life of that French pilot."

He raised pleading eyes. "I didn't intend that, Mark, even though my heart was in turmoil. I was coming back alone from an evening mission, brooding about the cruelty of war and my personal loss and not scanning like I should have. I guess that crazy Frenchman intended teaching me a lesson by making a phoney pass. Before I knew what I'd done, instinct had taken over, he was in my sights, my finger on the trigger and he was going down in flames."

"But, before that, you'd sent the Belgium agent to a sure death, and damn near had me killed as well."

"For which I'm truly sorry."

"Are you?" It was Wilson Miller back in the fray. "Then how come you went and murdered Father Magee in cold blood... the one man who offered you salvation?"

"And the one man I truly trusted." Lee hesitated, as though realising that what he would say in the next few minutes would seal his fate forever. "Richard Magee was my padre in the old 42nd Division and, yes, I confessed to him some unforgiveable mistakes I'd made in my past. I was desperate for absolution and knew I could confide in him and that it would remain our secret."

"Until he saw that photo in the *Tribune*, and was torn between confessional confidences or saving a respected statesman facing potential scandal." I was still Lee's defense lawyer, but guiding this old friend to the truth seemed the best help I could give him right now. "In the end, he decided public honesty was the greater good."

"... and contacted me direct," added Wilson Miller. "He told me there were issues with Lee Vennington's war record I should know about, but only if it remained strictly confidential. I agreed to that and we decided the best way was for my son Carl to go to Saint Winfred's and personally hear what he had to say."

"Which should have sorted things right there," I continued, "except the good Father, honest man that he was, decided it was only fair to tell you, Lee, face to face, what he intended to do."

"With lethal consequences," chipped in Gary Shreeve, clearly re-energized at hearing his own take on the case finally panning out. "It's like I surmised from the start. Just after Carl here had left, Vennington arrived, full of anger, and murdered Father Magee in cold blood, only to be caught red-handed by Father Huber. But Carl had heard Father Magee's cry and swiftly reported it to the patrolman."

I turned to Lee. "Is that the way it happened?"

He shook his head. "Not quite. I wasn't angry at all when I went to see Richard. In fact, I was full of hope." My client seemed strangely calm, as though relieved to finally relate the truth. "I'd just teamed up with Mr Miller here to help struggling vets, was elated at finally doing something worthwhile again and felt my luck had finally changed. Then I got a message at the shelter from Richard saying there was something he urgently needed to discuss. I knew he would have seen the *Tribune* photo of me with Wilson Miller, and so I went, assuming he wanted to talk about supporting a cause so dear to his own heart."

"Only to find that he was going to rain all over your parade."

"More like drown it completely. As soon as I got there I could tell he was really upset, and found out why when he told me what was happening. He said he'd prayed hard and searched his own conscience, but finally come to the conclusion that Wilson Miller should know the truth about the veteran he was working with. I begged him not to give me away and reminded that confessions were sacrosanct. But, despite our years of friendship, and much as he regretted it, he said his mind was made up, even though he knew how hurt I must feel. He even related some lines from Shakespeare to show he understood how I felt."

"'*Ingratitude, more strong than traitors' arms.*' I wondered about the significance of the quotation Father Huber found in Richard's hand. But you'd already seen Carl Miller when you arrived at the church, so you must have realised the secret was already out and that further pleading was useless?"

He shook his head. "Not at all. I didn't even know *why* he was there, but I was incensed at the thought of a man I still regarded as a traitor, seemingly untouchable as the son of a rich statesman, while a derelict like me was simply being hung out to dry. I told Richard how I felt, pulled out my bayonet and said there was more than one way to stop a man talking."

"You resorted to violence?"

"Only the threat of it. I never meant to harm him. But he said he'd seen enough of man's inhumanity in wartime to not fear death. I guess he then tried to shake some sense into me by saying I'd brought all my misfortune on to myself by associating with a loose woman."

"Margreet?"

"Of course, but that was one subject guaranteed to boil my anger. I told him of my genuine love for her, and he countered by saying that, in that case, I should have had the guts to die with her."

"A dagger to your heart."

He nodded. "Enough for me to plunge mine straight in his."

"And so the deed was done?"

"I'm afraid so."

Carl Miller leaned forward. "But you still tried to shift the blame to me."

Lee turned and faced the man who'd been such a thorn in both our sides since those first days in the Legion. "Only after I realised it must have been you who reported me to the cop. Then I thought I might turn the tables and put you in the frame as one way of at least bringing some meaning and poetic justice to the whole sorry business."

It was time for me to admit my own failings. "Which I, so naively, took on board."

He nodded. "Yes, I'm sorry I had to deceive you, of all people, Mark."

"A nice story." It was Pat Nolan with his own view of things. "Except you must have gone prepared for violence, Vennington, tooled up as you were with that German bayonet."

Lee gave a little humourless chuckle. "You really have no idea of what it's like to live on the streets, do you, Inspector? Believe me, there are plenty out there prepared to take out a vagrant just for the fun of it. So, that saw-toothed keepsake was always close to hand and more than once had them changing their minds." He shook his head. "But how I wish I hadn't had it on me that night at Saint Winifred's."

"Not as much as Father Magee must have wished it," said Shreeve, standing up. "So, that's it then, case closed. I'll see you in court, Kingsley, to complete the inevitable."

As our DA slammed his way out, Lee was clearly thinking of that same outcome "I'd like a private word with my attorney?"

Pat Nolan gave the nod to one of his officers, and we were straightway shown into an adjacent small office. I expected Lee to vent his bitterness, but he seemed strangely calm.

"I guess the truth had to come out, like it always does, Mark. I'm glad it has. I've already spent too much of my life living with lies, though I guess this life isn't going to last a whole lot longer now, is it?"

"No, Lee." I handed him a cigarette together with some brutal honesty. "We've no option now but to plead guilty. What I *can* do though is to make sure the judge and jury know of your previous honorable war record and ask them to realise that it was only fate that finally took you down the wrong road."

He took my light and a long draw of his smoke. "And you think that'll keep me from the Death House?"

"No, I don't. Back then, with the country celebrating victory, our people chose to keep your collaboration under wraps. No-one likes a traitor, and they let it ride until you gave them the chance to settle the score by murdering Richard. This time the forfeit will be claimed, Lee, but I'll make sure they know they're not sending a coward to the chair."

"And I promise they won't think any different on the night." He stubbed his smoke. "Sorry I even tried to hood-wink *you*, Mark, but I need to ask a couple more favors yet?"

"Which are ...?"

"That you be there for me on the night. It would be good to know I'd got my old buddy still on my wingtip when I make that last trip."

I inwardly gulped. "If that's what you want, Lee ... if it will help you face it."

"It will. Do you remember what the Legion told us when we first signed up? That we may not have lived well, but at least they'd help us die well." He shrugged. "I guess now I'm finally going to prove them right."

"You don't have to prove anything to me, Lee, but what's your other ask?"

He told me and I agreed to that also. Then the officer returned and told him it was time to go. One quick embrace and then he was gone and I returned to the rest of the group next door.

*   *   *

Along with Gary Shreeve, Father Huber had also left. I had little doubt that words passed to his bishop would soon see our hard-nosed Jesuit looking for another parish. That left just Tara in the room along with the two Millers. I was surprised to find Wilson looking almost sad.

"A tough call, Kingsley, but it had to be." He frowned. "When did you first suspect the truth?"

"En route to the Savannah River to join your outfit." I sighed. "I guess, in the back of my mind, I'd always suspected Lee of being somehow involved in that Bickendorf debacle, but just never wanted to admit it."

"Better you finally have." Wilson frowned. "But why go through all this tonight? Why not just let the trial take its course and leave a jury to decide?"

I nodded. "Good question, but there was no way I wanted to defend a man on false pretenses, no matter how much I valued his old friendship. I needed to know the truth and, when it came to it, how we were going to honestly plead. This way, none of that old dirt need ever come out, the American public will never know one of their own was a traitor and Lee will just go out as an ex-hero who fell on bad times."

"Leaving my political reputation unsullied and Carl's secret service forever a secret." Wilson Miller gave a nod of acknowledgement. "You did the right thing, Kingsley, and I appreciate that."

"It's what you planned anyway, wasn't it? First giving me a job overseas with Tara, and then shutting up shop for us both so there was no coming back?"

He gave a slightly-mortified nod. "It seemed the kindliest way to avoid you fighting a false, but embarrassing, battle in court."

"Well, that's not going to happen now, which probably means I hold the record for shortest ever employment with Miller Air Services."

"I wouldn't say that." He allowed himself just a slight smile. "I like a man who's not afraid to make tough decisions, Kingsley. If you still want it, the job's yours."

I nodded. "Thanks, Mr Miller but, even with a guilty plea, I still have a client to represent at trial and ..."

"... see it through to its end," he completed, as though guessing the obligation I'd made to Lee. "That's okay. South America and what I'm setting up there for the government will still be around when the other business is over."

"By which time I'll be only too glad to get as far from here as possible." I shook his hand. "Okay, count me in."

*   *   *

CHAPTER FOURTEEN

A month later, a dark and rainy Thursday midnight in Ossining village, and me leaving Sing Sing Prison with feelings as dismal as the weather.

In a way, I was almost glad of the persistent rain, as though it was cleansing me of the sordidness of what I'd just witnessed. Helping more than anything, though, was the sight of Tara standing there waiting, as she'd promised.

She came towards me with a comforting hug and kiss. "How was it?"

"Not something I'll ever forget."

Just two hours earlier I'd been entering that great limestone edifice on the banks of the Hudson and showing them my letter from the warden.

IN ACCORDANCE WITH SECTION 507 OF THE CODE OF CRIMINAL PROCEDURE YOU ARE HEREBY INVITED TO BE PRESENT AS A WITNESS AT THE EXECUTION BY ELECTRICITY OF LEE HAROLD VENNINGTON WHICH WILL OCCUR AT THIS PRISON ON ...

After being ushered through one clanging steel door after another, I'd found myself in a room with twenty or so other reasonably-subdued men, to be briefed on the conduct demanded at the forthcoming ritual. Then we were escorted across the yard to the Death House itself to witness this final act of the justice process.

"And Lee?" Tara's voice was the perfect antidote to my emotions.

"He went quietly. I could tell he'd seen me, and that seemed to steel his nerves."

"I'm sure it did" She took my arm and led me towards the railroad station for our return to New York. "I remember you telling Wilson Miller that you first had suspicions on our flight down to the Carolinas."

"Yep, at that stop at Newport News when the refueller told me some facts about Lee's service in the USAS. But, actually, it was something you'd related earlier that first planted the seed of doubt."

"Me? What did I tell you?"

"Something Richard had said to you. Of how love can drive men to do the most uncharacteristic things."

"Yes, that remark makes sense now." She gripped my arm that much tighter. "Lee must have really loved that Margreet. What actually became of her?"

"The fate of most spies. Facing a firing squad."

"Poor girl."

"Poor Lee, for the bitterness her execution left in his heart. I can see how it broke him, especially when he learned that her last thoughts had been, not for him, but for that Russian pilot, Vadim Maslov. She'd written letters to Maslov asking him to visit, but he'd just ignored them all, so her heart was broken too. Some would say that was poetic justice, seeing as she'd made an art-form of seducing men for their secrets."

"Had she been an effective spy?"

"Not really. She'd certainly seduced several high-ranking French military and government officials, got snippets of intelligence from them and passed it on to the Germans, but nothing of any real value. I don't doubt that it was Margreet who lured the French pilot into giving away details of his mission, but that Lee was also a party to it, if only to get back at the man flirting with his lady."

"Not much of a 'lady', by the sound of it," scorned Tara, "but how was she caught in the end?"

"By being stupid enough to stop off in London after a visit to Portugal. British Intelligence already had their finger on her, interrogated her at Scotland Yard, and passed what they knew to the French. She was tried, found guilty and ended up paying the price."

"I guess she got what she deserved."

"In a way, but she'd had a pretty rotten start herself out in Java married to an alcoholic Dutch army officer. And then, back in Paris trying to make her name as a dancer."

"But still no excuse for treachery." A particularly heavy shower was passing over and we ran to the shelter of a shop doorway where she turned and faced me. "A lesson, though, in how careful you have to be in choosing the person to share your life with."

I took her hand. "I agree, and I've already decided the only girl I want to share mine."

She gave me one of those lop-sided looks. "Mark Kingsley, is that a proposal of marriage?"

Across the road, rain was sheeting down in the harsh white glare of Sing Sing's floodlit walls. "Not the best of evenings or the most romantic of settings, I grant you, but, yes, if you'll have me."

She nodded. "You're right about the time and place, but my answer is still the same. Of course I'll marry you."

The rain was heavier than ever now but, with lightness in my heart, I took her in my arms for what I knew would be a lasting union, "in this world and the next."

"Amen to that," completed Tara, "and perhaps even Lee is now with his beloved Margreet again. Whatever her faults, she clearly had something that drove men to open their hearts."

"And, unfortunately, their mouths," I added with just a smile at the irony of it all. We'd reached the station now, running the last few yards into the dryness of its ticket hall where I wiped away the raindrops running down that sweet face. "I guess I didn't want you to think that badly of Lee, so I never did tell you the name Margreet adopted when she was a dancer in Paris"

"Which was?"

"One I'm sure you've heard of before. It was Mata Hari."

*   *   *

All a lifetime ago now as I came back to 1986 with the S76 clattering its way towards the downtown New York heliport, and me mentally reliving all those blissful years Tara and I had shared together.

Back then, with Lee's trial and execution behind me, I'd thankfully left for South America and that job with Miller Air Services, but only after Tara and I had lovingly tied the knot. So, we'd headed out there together and faced a decade of challenges in a variety of operational locations. Dealing with government agencies, getting the operations up and running and then the exciting flying that followed in a life I'd always dreamed of, enhanced all the more by the loving and ever-stimulating girl by my side.

Within a year Ford Aircraft had started rolling out their new tri-motor and we'd taken delivery of our first, using them to good effect to help friends and hinder enemies along the way. Another spin-off was being able to fulfil that promise to Tara of teaching her to fly.

Ten years overseas, though, is enough to have anyone yearning for the old country and the need for a new challenge. It was time then to return to my original calling of the law and, with the healthy bank balance we'd accumulated, the funds to set up a new practice in Lower Manhattan specializing in aviation and associated cases. That too had prospered to the point where, forty years on, I could now leave the day-to-day running to my bright young lawyers and just enjoy perks like flying in this corporate helio down the East River *en route* to the Manhattan Heliport.

"Straight in, Mr Kingsley?" It was my skipper, Chuck Arnold, again, checking what he needed to call in to Air Traffic.

"Just one more short diversion, Chuck. Over the Upper Bay."

"Where, exactly?"

"Hard to describe, so I'll talk you over it."

We carried on past the heliport and out over the boat-streamed water to the south. "Just a little to the right, Chuck – steer one-nine-zero and bring her down to a few hundred – okay, right here – just circle this spot."

There was nothing below to mark this particular little area of the bay, marked now only by the spray thrown up by the downdraft of our rotor. We went around three times and then I told him to head straight for the heliport. He didn't ask why I wanted that recon and I could never have explained that it was here, sixty years before, that I'd fulfilled that other promise to Lee and scattered his ashes from an old Curtis Jenny borrowed from Governors. Long years, painful thoughts, another world.

That remembrance fulfilled, we headed straight in to our assigned spot at the heliport, flaring off speed and touching down right on our assigned H. Even as Chuck brought the engines back to ground idle I was looking towards the small terminal and the sight of a tallish lady with grey but still-thick hair waving enthusiastically. How come, after all those years of marriage, Tara Kingsley still had the power to excite me. The rotor braked to a stop, the engines whined down and I was out, walking towards her as fast as my old legs would allow and meeting as we always did with a heartfelt hug and a kiss.

I nodded down to the large, paper-wrapped parcel beside her. "I see the auction produced some results."

"Very much so." She picked it up and we made our way inside for a coffee. "It cost a bundle, Mark, but I know you'll be as thrilled as me."

"And, it's a genuine Dellschau?"

"Absolutely. I've got the certificate of verification."

I wasn't sure which of the thousands of illustrations from Dellschau's notebooks this was, and I didn't really care. All I knew was that I'd been wanting to own one ever since they started coming on the market in the mid-seventies.

Representing as they did, seemingly fantastical depictions of experimental airships, they'd come to light on a Houston garbage dump and, thankfully, been rescued by a local furniture restorer. No-one knew too much about Dellschau himself except that he claimed to have been the draftsman for a mythical group calling themselves the Sonora Aero Club, supposedly a collection of some sixty eccentric aviation enthusiasts who, in 1850s California, had been trying to somehow get themselves airborne in a variety of experimental designs. Whether that whole tale was a bunch of hooey was open to opinion, but I had my own theory.

"So, you really reckon that time and place fit in with old Johannes Mueller's early days? That he was an actual member of the Aero Club?" Tara knew why I'd been so keen to have my own example of this unique work.

"I like to think so, Tara. It would surely be one of the missing links to that whole mystery airship saga."

She smiled. "Yeah, well let's get it home so you can hang it in your study and spend idle hours just caressing the thought."

"Right."

How many years left now to do just that? Did it matter, rich as the past ones were with thrilling memories of airborne adventure and fulfilled love? I put my arm around that love of my life and led her back out to the waiting 76. Overhead some multi-jet liner went climbing away to who-knows-where. I didn't envy them and knew Tara didn't either. To use an old Irish saying for both us and Lee, 'We had known the days'.

THE END

Having cut his own aviation teeth in open-cockpit biplanes, flown helicopters overseas with an American expatriate outfit, and listened to many of his father's WW1 reminiscences, author Chris Crowther is well armed to tell a tale appealing to any reader with a taste for early aviation, high adventure, crime investigation and the mysterious world of unexplained happenings

Made in the USA
Las Vegas, NV
22 November 2023

81360374R00167